RECKLESS
Together

Gina Robinson

Gina Robinson
SEATTLE, WASHINGTON

For my college sweetheart

If I had known the truth, my life would have been different. Would it have been better? There was no way to know. In any case, I wouldn't have been here, fighting for the love of my life against increasingly mounting odds.

I hated my mother. She'd done it again. This time from across the state. Intruded on what should have been one of the most beautiful moments of my life. After swearing for my entire existence I'd never have sex with any guy I wasn't totally sure was long term, I slept with Logan Walker. Trusted him with my heart and my body. He was so sweet, thinking he could protect me from Mom. That *anybody* could. He didn't know her like I did. Didn't know how cunning she could be. How devious.

Just like I hadn't known it was possible to feel such an intricate cocktail of emotions—love, lust, ecstasy, total happiness, fear, and blinding rage. It would have been absolutely heady, except for the anger. I'd kept my fury under control while I'd been with Logan, focusing all my attention and thoughts on staying in the moment with him. The guy had literally had a heart in his hands. A balloon heart. But still, how could I resist that? And the sweet, funny way he'd stocked up on protection? And how he couldn't stay away from me, no matter how hard he tried?

But now that I was back in my dorm room, thoughts of my mother and her Snow White's Evil Queen Stepmother act popped into my mind. Or maybe she was more like *Alice in Wonderland*'s Queen of Hearts playing a giant chessboard with my life. What was her game? What was her next move? Whatever she had planned, I had to stop it.

My hands trembled as I pulled my cell phone out. I took a deep breath. She and I had been estranged since she slept with Austin, my boyfriend before Logan. And I left her and came to college to find my bio dad, Jason Front. I had a delicate new relationship with him and his wife and baby. Mom could destroy all that, too. She didn't know I'd come to the university to find him. She didn't know he was here at all.

I hesitated on the verge of battle. I had to risk it. I'd chance anything to keep her away from Logan and me. I stared at the phone another second as I gathered up my courage. We hadn't spoken since before Christmas. It was nearly March now. She'd take my call. I knew she would. In fact, I was certain she was waiting for it. I hit the button that dialed her and braced myself.

"Ellie!" She picked up before it even rang. That was how confident she'd been that I'd call. That was how expectant she was.

Which put me even more on edge—what did she want? Melissa Ann Sawyer always wanted something. She never gave anything away and she never played for free.

"Leave Logan alone! Stay the hell away from him!"

It was the wrong way to lead. I'd let my anger get in the way of my scheming and common sense. I'd forgotten my own chess metaphor.

She laughed. "So you finally slept with him." Her voice was amused and as nubby as raw silk, not quite her usual polished self. But as grating as ever in its confidence. "I was wondering how long you'd hold out. He's a handsome boy. Now you can finally stop blaming me for ruining your life. You've turned out just like me."

"Not just like you," I said. "I'm not pregnant."

"That you know about. Be extra careful, Ellie. We're fertile girls when we're young and careless!" She laughed again.

Mom had a laugh for everything, like life always amused her, even when it was tragic. Even when there was absolutely nothing funny about it. This time it felt like she was laughing at herself as much as at me.

"I didn't say I slept with him." And I hadn't said I hadn't. Semantics were everything when playing with Mom's fire.

"Of course you have. That's why you're so protective and possessive of him now. He finally felt close enough to you, confident enough to tell you that he and I have been talking. And so you rushed to protect him from big, bad me. It all adds up. And I can tell from your voice you've lost your virginity."

"You cannot."

She'd used that "I can hear it in your voice" tactic on me since I was little. I'd outgrown my belief in her magical abilities to read voices and see out of the back of her head.

"I hear it in your denial."

"Just stay away from him!" I pulled the phone away from my ear, ready to hang up.

"Or what?" Devoid of laughter and completely serious, she was the ice queen, full of menace.

I froze, unsure how to deal with a serious her.

"Stopped you short, didn't I?" Her voice was the very essence of smugness. "You were going to hang up on your sweet mommy. You haven't answered my question—what are you going to do if I don't stop talking to him? Cut me off?"

"What do you want from me?" I said. "Isn't it enough that you slept with my last boyfriend? When are you going to stop competing with me for everything?"

She made a sigh of exasperation. "Austin! You have to let that go, Ellie. For your own good. Hanging on to it will just make you bitter.

"I'd undo it if I could. Not for Doug's sake, but for yours and Austin's. I'm really sorry. I was vulnerable and made a mistake. Even so, it turned out my mistake was for your own good. How true was he to you? How much in love with you if I could snatch him away in a moment of weakness? If he could be tempted to cheat so easily?"

"He wasn't tempted. He was tricked. You trapped him."

"Is that what he told you? Is that what you call it? I didn't drug him. I offered something he wanted and he took it happily enough. I did you a favor, Ellie."

"Well, then, stop doing me favors. I don't want your help."

"But *I* want something—a relationship with my one and only child."

I snorted. "Right. You have a funny way of showing it."

She ignored me. "Mom's Weekend is coming up. I'm coming. And I expect you to hang out with me and give me the full Mom's Weekend treatment—the activities, the concert, the entire college deal. After all, it's your fault I never got to go to college." She laughed again, like she was teasing about the last part.

I was in no mood for her jokes. "No! No way. When are you going to stop blaming me for everything that's gone wrong in your life? For every mistake you made? Don't come. I won't see you."

"You can't stop me. I can pop up unexpected any time. And you know me. That's exactly what I'll do. Isn't it better to plan for me? One weekend, Ellie. That's all I'm asking for."

My heart galloped unevenly, pounding with rage and fear. I knew her. She wasn't joking now. She'd come and wreak her havoc when I least expected it. She was right—it was better to plan for her. I could warn my dad Jason to stay out of sight. I could keep Mom away from Logan. Contain her. I had no choice. I had to. But I wasn't going to concede without getting something from her. "If I agree, you have to promise to stay away from Logan. No flirting with him. No traps. No tricks."

She sighed, and there was pity in her voice—pity that I was so naïve. "Haven't you learned anything from me? I can promise you *anything*. But that doesn't mean I'll keep it. Never trust another woman around your guy." She laughed again, like she was laughing at herself.

I shuddered. "Promise or the deal's off."

"Honey, I don't want your *boy*."

"You wanted the last one." The thought of Mom turned loose onto a happy hunting ground full of horny young men during one of the biggest cougar-fests of the year made me almost physically sick.

"Maybe I'm more sensitive to your feelings now," my mother said. "You're obviously really into this one. Austin was a passing phase."

"There's no place to stay here," I said, still fighting when I knew resistance was futile. "The hotels have all been booked a year in advance."

"I'll stay with you. Isn't that what most moms do?" Her voice was too sweet and happy to be genuine, and sharpened with a warning edge.

"I have a roommate and she has a mom, too. It will be crowded."

"Too many excuses, Ellie. I'm coming. Get over it." Her tone had become firm.

"Okay," I said. "But I reserve the right to kick you out. Once glance at Logan and you're sleeping in your car."

She ignored my terms. "Excellent! Plan something fun." She laughed a little too brightly. "Plan lots of fun things! Don't they have a whole host of things for moms to do? A mother/daughter mani and pedi would be great. My treat. And I want to meet all your friends. And their moms. I'll be in touch." She hung up.

I stared at the phone, stunned and wondering how she'd gotten what she wanted so easily. My mind raced with tasks. There was so much to do—warn Logan and Jason. And hope Jason didn't fight me when I asked him to hold off on telling Mom about him until I was sure of her motives. Which meant, like, never telling him, because you could never trust her. I had to give my roommate Bre the bad news that Mom was coming to town. Make plans to keep Mom busy and out of trouble...

I took a deep breath, wondering if there was a way to get Mom out of my life for good. Something short of murder. As long as I had a hot guy in my life, Mom was going to be a clear and present danger.

A knock on my dorm door startled me. The door burst open before I could answer it. My two good friends Nicole and Taylor rushed in, jovially arguing with each other.

"She's back!" Tay turned to Nic. "I told you she was. I thought I'd seen her come in." She plopped onto Bre's bed across from me.

Bre was out, probably with her boyfriend Dan.

"No, you said you saw a car that looked a lot like Logan's pull away. Not the same thing."

I was happily invisible until Nic swung her gaze to me. "How come you didn't come find us?" Nic had an accusing tone in her voice. "You knew we'd be dying of curiosity! After that totally adorable way Logan was waiting for you at Up All Night with his balloon heart in his hand, how could anyone resist him?

"You're just lucky you got to him before someone else stole him away. You owe us for not letting you chicken out and run away." She plunked next to Tay on the bed and fixed her interested, yet accusing, stare on me.

"I told you Falcon26 was going to be awesome!" Tay beamed and wore her smug expression.

Falcon26 was Logan's screen name when he played *League of Legends*. It was a long story, but basically while Logan and I had been broken up, I'd played LoL with Falcon26, not knowing Falcon26 was Logan. Falcon26 flirted with me all the time. I thought he was a lonely geek.

"You drew him as a beak-nosed, winged nerd," I said.

Tay shrugged. "Artistic license. I was just teasing you. What I told you is that you should meet him because he was so sweet and he could be the one. Thank me later." She made a bowing gesture, like she deserved tons of applause and even more eternal gratitude.

Nic interrupted. "Enough!" She pointed at me. "Dish."

Tay studied me and frowned. "Why aren't you glowing?" She glanced at Nic. "She should be glowing. What's gone wrong *now*?"

"No, she should be walking like a cowboy." Nic winked. "Bowlegged and sore in the saddle." She laughed until she saw my face. "What the hell *is* wrong? Don't tell me Logan is impotent."

"Or a totally sucky, selfish lover," Tay added, and sighed. "No, I can't believe that." She glanced at Nic. "That goes against every rumor we've ever heard about him."

"What rumors?" I said.

Nic shrugged and doggedly hit her point again. "Why aren't you grinning from ear to ear? You should be flying."

"Maybe they had a fight." Tay shuddered. "Don't tell me you blew it. No more secrets, right? He knows about your dad. You know about him and the chem prof. It's all out there now."

I sighed. "What makes you think I slept with him?"

"Oh, come on! You did." Nic pinned me with a look. "If you didn't, I'm going to have to kill you."

"Get thee to a nunnery!" Tay was reading *Hamlet* for her English class.

"Why wouldst thou have me be a breeder of sinners?" I shot back, hoping I wasn't breeding anything.

Getting accidentally pregnant was one of my biggest fears.

"You modified the quote," Tay said.

"Good. You get an A in English Lit." I sighed. Thinking about Logan, happiness bubbled up inside me. I couldn't hold down my smile.

Nic's smile returned. "She slept with him."

Tay's eyes lit up. "So? How was it?"

"The rumors are true." I glanced at the heart-shaped Mylar Logan had given me. It floated in the corner and made my heart swell just looking at it. I grinned. "That's all I'm going to say."

"You're no fun." Tay made a pouty face.

Nic was undeterred. "We'll get it out of her eventually." Her eyes were a dark, deep brown and usually sparkled with fun. But they turned serious. "Seriously, though, what's bothering you?"

I sighed heavily and bit my lip. "Logan has met my mom."

Nic and Tay made a collective gasp and their mouths popped open.

"Crap," Nic whispered. "Met? Like in person?" She was way too tentative. Nic rarely danced delicately around any issue.

She and Tay knew about Mom sleeping with Austin.

"He'd been talking to her while we were apart," I said. "Trying to keep her away from me so I could get to know Jason without her interference."

"Whoa!" Tay put her hands beneath her thighs and stared at me as if she was measuring how I was holding up.

"So, yeah," I said. "He hasn't pulled an Austin."

"Then why are you upset? It sounds like he's been playing hero. Don't you believe him?" Nic studied me. "There's a reason I didn't come right to see you—Mom called just as I got back to my room. She's coming for Mom's Weekend. There's no way to stop her." Nic whistled and winced. "Ouch."

I nodded. They both knew our sordid history.

"What are you going to do?" Tay said. "Are you going to tell her about your dad?"

I shook my head. "No! No, no, no, no. And ruin everything? Including his life? Are you kidding?"

Nic tried to take a pragmatic approach. "Didn't you say Jason was just a friend to your mom, a one-night stand with a brainiac guy she thought was beneath her? Why would she even care about him now?"

"That's what Jason said," I replied. "He may even be right. But you give Mom way too much credit if you think she's going to happily let bygones be bygones. I ruined her life. And I'm here because of Jason. You don't think she'd like to take her revenge?"

Tay shook her head. "You're being melodramatic. She never told him about you. There must be a reason. Maybe she won't want to see him. Besides, he's happily married with a baby and another on the way—what can she possibly do to him?"

I wagged my finger at them. "You are so naïve! Mom never lets a man get away. *Never*. It's a matter of pride with her. She likes to think all her ex-men are still longing for her tragically. She'll do something. I *know* she will.

"With Lyssa pregnant and emotionally vulnerable, the last thing she needs is to be ambushed by my mom. No, I won't let it happen."

"What are you going to do?" Tay asked.

"Ask Jason to stay out of the way and keep Mom as far away from him and Logan as possible."

"We'll help," Nic said. "My mom is coming and she can badass with the best of them. She'll keep your mom out of trouble, or in trouble, if that's what you want."

"My mom can't make it. Too much to do at work." Tay's face fell. Her mom put work above her too often. "I'll have to be your wingman."

"The sorority has a tons of functions for the moms I'm obligated to attend, but I'll break away when I can." Nic had gone through informal rush at semester. "We'll plan every minute of her stay. No downtime. No time for trouble. She'll be so busy, she won't have enough energy to cause trouble. We'll tag-team her if necessary." Nic nodded like she approved of her own scheme.

"Sounds good to me," Tay said. "Could be fun."

I rolled my eyes. "Fun? Hardly. Mom says she wants the full college experience." I snorted. "I'm assuming without the studies and test pressure. Which are the only parts I really want to give her."

"I'm guessing she probably wants the men," Nic added.

"Shut up."

"Oh, I think we could find her someone to keep her distracted." Nic had a wicked grin.

I rolled my eyes and ignored her suggestion.

"Forget guys," Tay said. "If she wants the full experience, the first thing you need is matching sweatshirts. There's a Facebook group where Geeds can order matchy-matchy sweatshirts online and pick them up at a house just off campus a few days before Mom's Weekend."

"Dress her up in a bulky sweatshirt! I like the way you think, Tay." I grabbed my laptop, prepared to order Mom a size too large.

"Okay, order your sweatshirts," Nic said. "But you're not getting out of giving us the details of your first time with Logan."

After Tay and Nic left, Dex called. Something was up. He usually texted.

"Why the fuck didn't you tell me Falcon26 is Logan? If this is your idea of a sick joke at my expense—"

"Whoa! Hold on. First—how did you find out? And second, I only learned the truth last night when I went to the SUB to meet Falcon. He asked me out and I let Tay and Nic talk me into going. I was fully expecting him to be a geek."

"How did I find out?" Dex sounded slightly mollified. "Tay tweeted it."

I mumbled something about killing Taylor.

"You really didn't know Logan was Falcon26?" Dex didn't sound fully convinced.

I spent the next five minutes assuring him I didn't and relating the whole story to him.

"Well, that explains why Falcon is so good and why he favored you and helped you all the time. Damn," Dex said. "I suppose you've gone over to the dark side now—his side?"

I laughed. "Yeah."

"I won't be able to use you as my secret weapon anymore."

"Nope. But cheer up. He's graduating this semester." *And leaving,* I thought with a desperate sense of hopelessness. I didn't want him to go.

Dex hesitated. He wasn't a touchy-feely-talky guy. "You and him back together—you're okay? He's not going to break your heart again, is he? The odds of me finding another guy like Falcon for you are pretty slim."

Dex didn't often show soft emotion, but the protective tone was there in his voice. He was sweet, not wanting me to get hurt again.

"There are no guarantees in life," I said. "But I hope not."

"He's okay with Jason being your dad?"

"Yes. We're good."

"Good." Dex sighed. "At least one thing is looking up. This has been a shitty day already."

"Why? What else happened?"

"My mom called. She's coming to Mom's Weekend."

I pictured him making a face.

"I thought you and your mom got along great. What's the problem?"

"She babies me. And acts all girly. She wanted a daughter instead of me and sometimes she still doesn't act any different. Did I tell you that she didn't cut my hair until I was nearly three? I had curly ringlets. Everyone thought I was girl until Dad finally took matters into his own hands and sheared me like a sheep." Dex's tone was full of affection for his dad. "Do you know what Mom's done now?"

"No, astound me," I said.

"She ordered us matching Mom's Weekend sweatshirts. She actually expects me to pick them up here and wear mine. Like a real man dresses like his mom. How she found that damn website..."

I cracked up. "You're going to look so cute, you and mommy dressed alike."

"Shut up, Ellie, before I have to kill you."

I took a deep breath and forced myself to hold in my laughter until my eyes watered. I didn't want to get on Dex's bad side. The guy could prank me into extinction. "There must be something in the air. I got a call from my mom this morning. She's coming, too."

"Shit." Dex knew the whole story. "I'm sorry, Ellie. I feel like a douchebag for complaining about my mom now. Matching sweatshirts pale in comparison to sharing a boyfriend. What are you going to do?"

"The only thing I can do—I ordered matching sweatshirts and now I'm scheming like crazy to keep her away from Logan and Jason." I couldn't resist teasing Dex. "Hey, any chance you'd take one for the team and sleep with Mom to keep her away from Logan? It would prove your manhood."

Dex laughed. "Gladly. But from what you've said, I'm not her type. I'd need about a thousand hours at the gym before she'd even look at me. I don't have time for that shit."

"And your mom would kill you."

"Seriously, Ellie. Anything I can do to help short of banging your mom. I'm here for you."

CHAPTER TWO

I had a ton of homework to do that afternoon, but I couldn't keep my mind on it. I kept worrying about Logan and Mom. Just how much had they been talking? What ideas had Mom filled his head with?

Mom was a charmer, a seductress, a siren. *A liar.* She'd done something to Austin to take him from me. I'd been so furious at Austin and hurt by the whole affair that I had pushed him from my mind, refusing to think anything good about him at all for a long time. But now I forced myself to go back and revisit our failed relationship from the beginning and examine the good times.

At first, Austin had seemed totally into me, the way I was into him. I couldn't believe my luck to find a guy like him—hot and sweet. Willing to wait until I was ready. Sympathetic about why I couldn't go all the way with him. Everything was a go and we seemed so right for each other. We were both from around Seattle and lived on campus at a university in the city. It was easy for either of us to pop home whenever we wanted. I rarely went home, except to do laundry and pick up my mail.

I wasn't thrilled with my then-stepdad Doug, although he was the best of the three I'd had. Don't even get me started about Mom. She and I have always been best apart. I loved living my life separate from hers. I kept Austin a secret from her until she noticed how happy I was and pried the news out of me. Even then, I didn't want her to know I was falling in love with him. I didn't change my Facebook status to "in a relationship." I didn't post pictures of him on my page. I didn't tweet about him. I never mentioned him to her. *Ever.*

But eventually she pried the fact that I had a boyfriend out of me and wanted to meet him. After fending her off as long as I could, I agreed to a double date with Mom and Doug. They took us to Teatro ZinZanni, which was part dinner theater, part circus, and a lot of fun. There wasn't much time for talking, which was good.

Mom and Doug picked up the tab. She behaved herself, acting like a normal mom. Not like she usually did, flirting with my boyfriends and guy friends. That should have been my first clue she was up to something. Austin was by far the hottest of the guys I'd dated. I should have recognized her indifference for what it really was—out-and-out jealousy.

I let my guard down. That was my fatal mistake. I wasn't making it again.

Looking back, I wondered how I could have missed the signs. And now I had to know. Austin was the only one who could tell me what tricks Mom had used to woo him from me. How she'd kept it secret.

I'd never wanted the details before. Had gone so far as to push them from my mind. But I couldn't be an ostrich now. This time I was going to be prepared.

I grabbed my cell phone and punched his name before I chickened out. I didn't have any idea if he'd talk to me, or be straight with me. But I had to give it a shot.

"Ellie?" He sounded totally shocked. "Did you just butt-dial me?"

"No, this is purely intentional."

"You called me on purpose? Are you drunk?"

I laughed nervously. "Do I sound drunk?"

"You sound good. It's great to hear from you."

I felt guilty. He sounded too hopeful. Last time I'd seen him was Halloweekend. He'd come to campus to party with his friend Schwartz and made a point of looking me up and apologizing. Which I respected. It took a lot of guts for him to do.

I'd let Austin know we were through. We both understood that. He was over me, too, but hoped we could be friends, and I still couldn't see that happening. Not after everything.

"What's up?" he said.

"I need to talk to you...about my mom."

"Shit, Ellie! Are you sure you want to go there?" There was a bunch of noise in the background, the sounds of guys laughing and joking. Austin lived in a frat. Maybe that was where he was. "Hang on. Let me get somewhere private."

I heard the sound of him breathing and walking. Then a door slammed shut. The background noise grew muffled. "Are you still there?"

"I'm here," I said. "Thanks for not hanging up on me."

"I'd never hang up on you, but this is out of the blue," he said. "Are you in some kind of program? Family counseling? Or did my talk with you about how I think your mom is sorry finally sink in?"

"None of the above," I said, making a split-second decision to be straight up and honest with him. "I need your help."

I paused and bit my lip. I trod on delicate ground here, uncertain how to proceed.

"My help?" He sounded truly stunned and a little wary.

I couldn't blame him. "I've been thinking about us and you. I was so mad for so long that I couldn't think straight. I blamed both you and Mom equally for what happened. But with some distance, I've realized that while you weren't without fault, you were at least hapless. She made an effort to catch you. That makes her worse."

"Yeah?" he said.

I crossed my fingers, hoping he wouldn't hang up. "Yeah. I want to know how she did it—how did she reel you in?"

"Serious?"

"Yeah," I said.

"Why?"

"Because I don't think yours was an isolated incident. Mom will strike again."

"Is this about your new boyfriend? Logan, right? The one who decked Schwartz at the football pregame party."

"You heard about that?" I said, deflecting.

"Come on, Ellie. Was there any doubt Schwartz would tell me? He was epically pissed. If I were you, I'd stay the hell out of his way."

"Like you have to tell me!" I shook my head. "I don't know why you hang with him. Schwartz is an ass. That wasn't his finest hour."

Austin laughed. "We've been friends forever. But Schwartz can be a real douchebag."

"I won't argue with that. But he's loyal to you. I'll give him that."

"You're afraid Melissa is going to go after Logan," Austin said. "And you don't trust him."

"I don't trust *her*."

Neither of us spoke for a moment.

"That's probably smart of you."

"Look, Austin, you're a decent guy. We were good together. What did she do? How did she get to you?"

"I don't like to talk about it, Ellie." He sounded really uncomfortable.

I hated to push him, but I had to. "I know. I wouldn't ask, except it's important."

He sighed. "I owe you, I guess. Otherwise, I wouldn't say shit." He sighed. "I still have a criminal assault case against Doug. And my parents filed a civil suit against him for damages and hospital expenses that we're in the middle of settling. This is completely off the record."

"I understand," I said. "This is for my ears only. Hey, the police took my statement. I shouldn't be talking to you, either."

"As long as we're clear."

"I'm clear."

He paused. "I don't know where to start."

"The beginning's always good."

"Yeah, but where's that?" He snorted then took a deep breath. "It all started with you. She messaged me, saying she was worried about you, and asked for my help. She said she wanted the best for you and was worried because you were so naïve and vulnerable.

"You mom has a sympathetic, charming way of finding common ground and building from there. She made me feel like the hero in your life, and then I became the hero in hers."

I bit my tongue to keep from swearing. *Hero.* Logan wanted to be my hero. Unless I missed my guess, Mom had homed in on that desire. By keeping Mom away from me, Logan thought he was protecting me. But I worried he had wandered haplessly into her trap. I went suddenly cold. My mom was a genius when it came to manipulating men. I swallowed hard and white-knuckled the phone to keep it from trembling in my hand. I didn't want to hear more, but morbid curiosity and desperation kept me hanging on.

"I can't even tell you when the switch happened. She listened to my problems and sympathized."

"How?" I asked. "You talked to her? In person? On the phone?"

"It started with direct messages. Then texts. It progressed to phone calls." He hesitated. "She showed up on campus once. Ambushed me between classes. We had coffee. And talked about you and school and shit. She was lonely."

"She had Doug." I closed my eyes, picturing Mom coming on to Austin. "You never mentioned talking to her."

"She asked me not to. She shared her crap, like how she and Doug were having problems and things were falling apart for her."

"Falling apart?" Why didn't I know about that? "She was making that up. She had to be."

I could almost hear him shrug.

"I don't think she was. She was pretty emotional and upset by it."

"Did she come on to you then, when she was sharing her problems?" I was thinking of Mom ambushing Logan at the airport. The cold I'd felt before became arctic ice.

"I don't know, Ellie. It was hard to tell. Your mom is hot. She makes guys nervous. She made me nervous."

I frowned. "That's all?"

"She stroked my ego and made me laugh. I was in love with you. But attracted to her at the same time." He paused. "Sorry, Ellie."

I swallowed hard. "No, I get it. That day..." I said, unable to finish my sentence. But he knew what day I meant and it wasn't the day they met for coffee.

He hesitated and took a deep breath. "She called me over to talk about you. I knew right from the beginning that I shouldn't go. On some level, I realized I was asking for trouble. But I couldn't stay away. I couldn't refuse her. When she came onto me, I went with the flow.

"She was like an older, experienced you. I'm not blaming you. I'm just saying, she gave me what you couldn't. And made me feel good about it. Until you and your stepdad walked in on us.

"And I realized what deep shit I was in. And how she'd seduced me. And ruined things. I've regretted it since. Live and learn. I'm sorry, Ellie. I wish I could take it back and start over with you."

I'd heard those words before—from Mom. I swallowed hard. "Yeah. Some things are unrecoverable."

"No shit," Austin said. "My parents would have my head if they heard I'm talking to you. It's nothing personal. It's because of her."

"Guilt by association," I finished for him. I couldn't blame them.

"Does that help?" he said.

"Yeah," I said. But it scared me to my core at the same time. "Thanks."

"Anytime," he said. "Hey, Ellie, I'm trying to keep you out of this court shit against Doug. My parents are insisting your testimony is vital to the case. I told them to keep you out of it. This is your mom we're talking about. It's shitty. It's all shitty. I'll do what I can."

He paused and his voice broke. "Ellie, I *miss* you. I really wish we could be friends again."

CHAPTER THREE

Logan

Logan Walker sprawled on his bed. He was supposed to be writing a paper on the ethical issues of computers and technology as they pertained to technological advancements enabling computer crime for his four-hundred-level class Computers and Society. Despite the dry title, the subject matter fascinated him. Damn, though, he hated writing. With a passion. Anything English scared the shit out of him. The thought of writing a forty-page paper that his final grade and graduation hinged on gave him waking nightmares.

Right now, though, his hatred of writing wasn't the problem. No matter how much he tried to concentrate on his essay, his thoughts drifted back to El naked in his bed. To making love with her for the first time last

night and the heady feeling of her being his. He grew
hard at the memory and ached with palpable, pounding
need to touch her again.

El told him early on that if she ever gave herself to
him, she'd never be able to stop making love with him.
He hoped that was true. If it were up to him, she'd never leave his bed. Initially, her innocence had appealed
to him. Now he wanted to make a real, experienced
woman out of her.

He had a fantasy of shower sex. El naked and glis-
tening with water droplets. Hot and wet in the steam.
Ready for him.

He had to stop thinking these thoughts.

El wasn't like any girl he'd ever dated or casually
screwed. She was gorgeous and totally unaware of her
power over guys. Sweet and seductive without trying.
Vulnerable and strong at the same time. A study in op-
posites. He loved her. He wanted to protect her. And
damn it, he would. Especially from her first-class bitch
of a mother. Bitch in constant heat. Melissa Sawyer was
a piece of work. But she didn't know whom she was up
against.

His cell phone rang. He answered without looking at
the number, hoping it was El.

"Logan! The phone barely rang. Were you waiting
for my call?"

Logan's heart stopped for the instant it took him to
recognize the voice. "Melissa."

She sounded so much like El it was unnerving, right
down to her tinkling laugh. Only hers was edged with

manipulation and confidence, while El's was always genuine and pure.

"I just got off the phone with Ellie," Melissa said. "Congratulations on finally screwing my daughter. You have succeeded where other fine, horny young men have failed. My hat's off to you."

"What the fuck are you talking about?" El wouldn't have told her mother.

"Exactly! You're so cute denying it. Go ahead and brag. I'm not your typical mother. I'm actually proud. Glad to know my daughter's no longer a prude."

"El didn't tell you anything."

"She didn't have to. I heard it in the glow in her voice and the fierce way she protected you and told me to stay away from you. She's crazy for you, Logan. You should be thrilled."

Logan swallowed hard, fighting a tic in his jaw.

"A word of friendly warning from her mama bear— don't hurt my kid, Logan Walker. Treat her nicely. She's glommed onto you. I expect you to stick with her, at least for a while. I hope you're not the kind who puts a notch on his bedpost and moves on."

"What do you want?" he said.

"Diversionary tactics—nice. I knew there's a reason we get along so well. I'm actually calling to tell you I took your advice and now I'm coming to Mom's Weekend. Isn't that wonderful?"

Logan scowled, wary. "What advice?"

She laughed. "You must be in a study fog. Your sage advice about waiting and giving Ellie time to cool off and come to her senses so she could see that she needs her mother."

"She invited you?" he asked, stunned. He couldn't believe El would. How had Melissa twisted her arm?

"No, of course not! I invited myself. But she didn't refuse me." She laughed again like she'd scored a great triumph. "So we'll be seeing each other soon. I'm looking forward to meeting your family. Your mom *is* coming?"

Logan cursed beneath his breath, recognizing a grandmaster manipulating him. The gentle flirt in her voice put him on guard. She could be charming, even when she was being diabolical. She toyed with emotions and lives as if it came naturally to her.

She'd claimed all along that she wanted a relationship with El and nothing more. He didn't believe her. He recognized another damaged person when he saw one. She wanted something more. If he had to guess, her motives were purely selfish. She wanted to feel good. She wanted to be adored. She wanted to be young again and live through her daughter. Melissa's problem was that she wasn't content to live through El. She wanted to *be* El.

"I have no idea," he said. He hoped not.

"What are you waiting for? Call and invite her!"

"Why?"

"Why not? Now that her boy is sleeping with my baby, we should all meet each other, don't you think?"

"Not a good idea. You won't like my mom."

"You mean she won't like me!" Melissa laughed again, almost manically bright. "No answer? You're not going to rush to reassure me that's not the case? That she'll absolutely love me?

"Don't worry. Save yourself the trouble. Very few women like me. It doesn't bother me. I've learned to live with it. But I'd like to meet the woman who raised the man my daughter is crazy for."

Logan wondered where Melissa was getting her information. El would never have talked to Melissa about him. If she was trying to flatter him, she had failed in the attempt.

Melissa changed the direction of the conversation abruptly. "Has the court set a date for your testimony? It has to be coming up."

"My lawyer called Friday. I'm set to testify against *Her* the week after Mom's Weekend."

Her was Dr. Rhonda Rogers, his former chemistry professor and rapist. Despite attempts to get Dr. Rogers to plead guilty to multiple counts of rape and save her victims the embarrassment and agony, she had insisted on going to trial. She was crazy. Certifiable. Logan had to stop her. His dad was furious at him for insisting on going to court to testify. The old man could go to hell. Logan needed this. This and his work with Kelsie at CAPSA, the Campus Alliance to Prevent Sexual Assault, kept him sane.

"Oh, baby. That's *rough*." Melissa's tone changed to genuine sympathy. He liked her better when he caught a glimpse of the real Melissa, not the troubled woman. The Melissa who reminded him of El.

Every time she came out, he vowed to protect El so that she never became her mother—permanently damaged.

"I don't know what to tell you. It's going to be excruciating. Embarrassing. Infuriating. She'll be there right in front of you, staring you down, trying to intimidate you and daring you to defy her..."

She sighed, sounding almost faraway and lost in old, tormenting thoughts. "The courtroom will be small, so much smaller and more intimate than they look on TV. That's part of the reason—" She cut herself off.

He heard her take a deep breath.

"It's why I chickened out in the end and didn't come forward as one of his victims." She paused again, like she needed to screw up her courage to talk about it. "I went to the courthouse and sat in on a different rape trial just after it happened. When the victim testified against the bastard who raped her, he stared her down, full of rage, looking like she was trash, not him.

"He was an animal. A filthy, disgusting piece of what could barely be called humanity. His lawyers weren't much better, bringing up her love life, how many sex partners she'd had..."

All these years later her voice wavered with fear and there was a shade of frightened girl in it just beneath the surface. "I couldn't face it. But I paid the price in other ways. Such a great price."

Her voice became hard again. The girl disappeared. "Never mind. It was a long time ago. You'll survive it. Like I did. You either survive or die. What other choice do you have? If you die, even on the inside, they've won.

Don't give her that power. *Never* give her *anything* but justice."

He hoped he survived it a hell of a lot better than Melissa had. But he was no different from her, really, and that scared the shit out of him.

"There are two main ways victims cope after a rape," Melissa said. "Remind the jury of that if the lawyers drag up your sex life. You either retreat into yourself and are afraid of sex. Or you become super sexually active to prove that sex doesn't defeat or own you. Each reaction is completely normal.

"I liked sex. I wouldn't let it beat me. So I became the local slut. If anyone had known I'd been raped, they would have believed I deserved it. Don't you ever believe you deserved it. Do you hear me, Logan?"

"Yeah."

After his rape, Logan had gone crazy. Hypersexual, his counselor called it. He'd slept with so many girls he'd lost count. He didn't remember half of them. Being a guy had its advantages—he gained a reputation as a great lover. No one but him and his counselor knew his real motivation.

"How is your work with the Campus Alliance for the Prevention of Sexual Assault going? What do you call it, CAPSA?"

"They've been supportive, even though their mission is geared ninety-nine percent toward women. Working with them has been healing. After that reporter outed me as one of the victims, I didn't have much choice. I could hide or fight back and protect others."

"Logan, the good superhero," Melissa said without being condescending or belittling in any way. "At least you have a group to talk to. And you're still one of the security escorts for women walking alone?"

"I help out as often as I can."

"Does Ellie know what you do?"

"Only if she's read the campus news during the time we were apart. I haven't specifically told her."

"You should. Tell her about the nasty emails, too. She'll understand. My kid is sympathetic and has a good head. She'll help you deal with them. Have you received any lately?"

Logan snorted. "Only like every day. I'm not sharing that vile shit with El. It's the last thing she needs."

"Logan—"

"I know what I'm doing."

"Yeah, I'm sure you do. We all think we do, anyway. Just think about it, Logan. Take it from me—it's way too easy to make a mistake right now. Let Ellie in."

In keeping with her mercurial mood changes, Melissa laughed again. But it was definitely forced and bitter this time. "Maybe you'll get lucky at trial. They sure as hell can't accuse you of wearing tight skirts and low-cut blouses that enticed the attack."

She paused. "You're a *hot* young man, Logan. Let's hope there's a double standard still in existence and they won't use your sex appeal against you, like I'm sure they would have against me."

She wielded their common experience expertly, using it to get close to him. He saw through her, but felt a bond with her all the same. She was one of the few people he could talk frankly to without embarrassment. Unlike his father, she never judged.

"There is a double standard. A much worse one— women can't rape men, remember? I'm not a rape victim at all, just a horny guy who likes older women."

Every time he thought of *Her*, which was the only way he could think about Dr. Rogers—she was his she-who-shall-not-be-named—his palms went cold and clammy, bile rose in his throat, and he felt like vomiting. Now was no different. He felt broken and didn't bother hiding it from Melissa.

"Oh, Logan, sweet boy. Don't talk like that. *Ever.*" Her voice cracked with sympathy but her tone was fierce. "It was too bad you weren't underage when it happened. That bitch was smart, preying on college guys. They've put many female teachers away for statutory. But there *were* drugs involved. That takes away consent. The court will *have* to find her guilty. You'll have to make them."

Her voice grew hard and determined. "With any luck, they'll lock her up for life and throw away the key. If you ever need to talk, I'm here. Anytime."

Against his better judgment, Logan had sympathized with Melissa from the beginning. No matter what her other faults were, it was good to talk with her because she understood.

"Are you ever going to tell El about your past?" He wondered why she hadn't.

"Maybe. Someday."

"She'd be more sympathetic toward you."

Melissa laughed again. "I don't wear sympathy well. I've had way too much of it already. I certainly don't want any from my baby girl."

Logan understood her position all too well. He was damned tired of sympathy.

"There are some things a parent protects a child from. This is one of them." Melissa sounded almost vulnerable again. "You *promised* you wouldn't tell her."

"I haven't." Though he wanted to. Desperately. But he understood being a victim and couldn't violate Melissa's privacy and trust. "I won't."

"Have you told Ellie the date you're set to testify? Do you want her there?"

"Not yet. I haven't had the chance," he said.

Melissa hadn't known he and El had been apart these last months. She thought they'd been happily together. That was part of the deception, part of how he'd kept her away from El while El got to know Jason, her father.

"Make up your mind soon about whether you do or don't. The sooner, the better. Whatever you decide, be honest with her. If she loves you like I think she does, she'll respect your decision."

El would insist on being there. He wasn't sure he could handle her seeing his vulnerability on the stand, and he sure as hell didn't want the details of that night lodged in her mind. He hoped Melissa was right and wondered how she could swing back and forth so easily between empathy and sage advice and cruel, self-serving behavior.

Neither spoke. Melissa broke the silence. "I have to go. I'll be in touch to talk about Mom's Weekend plans!" She laughed again. "Take care, Logan." The line went dead.

Logan's cell rang in his hand before he could set it down. He looked at the caller ID and frowned. His mother was calling. He picked up. "Hey, Ma."

"Logan." She sounded upset and worried. "I just found out the date for your court appearance. Why didn't you tell me?"

"Mom, *I* just found out." It was a partial lie. He'd known long enough to tell her.

Fortunately, she ignored his excuse. "I'm coming for it. Don't try to talk me out of it. Your dad will be there for the annual advisory board meeting and business plan competition. He has a room. We won't be any trouble. I'll come for Mom's Weekend with him and we'll stay straight through your testimony."

Logan cursed beneath his breath. He'd been bracing for his father's visit. Harlan was on the advisory board for the College of Business. Their meeting and the business plan competition they judged every year always coincided with Mom's Weekend.

Harlan had been to Mom's Weekend every year. Logan's mom had never come. It wasn't her thing. Harlan usually took Logan out for a meal while he was in town, and that was enough bonding for both of them. Logan had been anticipating—and dreading—his father's visit. He feared his dad would make a final bid to keep Logan from testifying.

His mom spoke before Logan could react. "Caleb's coming, too."

Fuck. The last thing Logan wanted or needed was his mom *and* his brother hearing the gory, humiliating details of his ordeal.

"Doesn't Caleb have to play ball?"

"His team has a bye that week. And he pulled a hamstring yesterday and is out of action for a few weeks. He's made arrangements to do his physical therapy at the university while we're there."

Shit. There'd been a time when he and Caleb were so close he would have been the first to know about Caleb's injury and not had to find out about it from their mom.

"Ma, there's no need for any of you to come. This is going to be ugly—"

"Don't try to talk me out of it, Twenty-six. We're coming and that's it. We support you. We're going to be there for you."

A message popped up on his laptop.

When are u gonna stop screwing old profs and claiming you dont like it, dickhead? Guys like u make me sick. You werent raped. Your a playor. Everyone knows it. Stop acting like your a real victim.

CHAPTER FOUR

Ellie

I was picking up my phone to call Logan when Bre stormed in.

"Douchebag! Asshole." She glanced at my heart balloon floating in the corner of our room and scowled.

Last night she'd been totally supportive when she came with me to meet Falcon26, who turned out to be Logan. I had expected her to want all the news, just like Tay and Nic had.

Something had obviously gone wrong between her and her boyfriend Dan. "What did Dan do now?"

She took off her coat, threw her purse on her desk, and plopped onto her bed. Her eyes were puffy and rimmed with red, like she'd been crying. "He's been sexting another girl. Some bitch from high school."

Oh no. We were in for a crash. Bre was psycho where Dan was concerned. The anger in her eyes masked a deep, vengeful hurt. She and Dan had been dating since the first week of school. I'd always thought she was more into him than he was to her. I'd guessed it was only a matter of time until he broke things off, but I'd been dreading the day and selfishly hoping it happened after the school year ended so I wouldn't have to deal with it. Now the timing was impeccably bad. My happiness was only going to shine the spotlight on her *un*happiness.

"You're sure?" I asked.

She glared at me. "I saw the texts. And the naked pictures of her."

Ouch. Not good. "How?"

Like I really wanted to know. Just like morbid curiosity can cause you to gape at a gory scene you know you shouldn't look at because it will give you nightmares, sometimes you can't help asking a morbid question. Because it seems like what a friend would do.

She looked at me like *I* was crazy. "I read them on his phone."

"You spied on his phone?" So, so not good.

"He was in the bathroom. His phone was just lying there on his bed. It rang. A text popped up. What was I supposed to do? Ignore it?" She practically screamed at me. She was on the ragged verge of hysteria.

I pictured a scene from that old movie Mom used to watch, *Fatal Attraction,* about a woman who gets revenge on her married lover after a one-night stand. I always thought vengeance ran too deeply in Mom's blood. On reflection, maybe she'd pictured herself as the married lover and was looking for ways to protect herself from the inevitable psycho. Whatever. Bre had that vengeful look now, and it wasn't pretty.

"Don't look at me like I committed a felony when *he* was the one fooling around behind *my* back." She pulled his phone out of her pocket and shook it. It must have been his phone. It sure wasn't hers. "Want to see?"

I swore beneath my breath. Bre had lost it. There was no way to reason with her. I should have shut up, but my mouth had a mind of its own. "You need to give that back to him. Don't make things worse."

"Worse! How can things get any worse?" She jumped off the bed and went to the window like she was going to throw his phone out of it.

"No!" I jumped up and grabbed her arm to stop her. "Bre! Don't go crazy on me. Don't do something you'll regret."

She glared at me and backed away from the window. "You're right. Throwing this away is stupid."

I took a breath, relieved but still wary. "Did you break up with him?"

She narrowed her eyes. "No! We're not broken up. He's not breaking up with me. I'll show him." Her eyes snapped. She lifted her shirt, unhooked her bra, and snapped a picture of her naked breasts.

My mouth fell open as she typed something and texted the picture to someone. "Showing him what he's missing?"

Her eyes glistened with hatred. "You think way too small, Ellie. That's always been your problem. I just texted the bitch like I'm Dan. I told her, 'My girlfriend's tits are better than yours.' That will show her. And him. She'll dump him any second." She stared at the phone and grinned expectantly, like she couldn't wait for the returning teary text.

"Oh, Bre."

"Shut up! Just shut up and leave me alone. I know what I'm doing. I'm not afraid to protect my territory."

In that second she reminded me way too much of my mom. I suppressed a shudder and shut up.

My silence only infuriated her. "Wipe that stupid 'I'm so happy,' smug look off your face. You think you have the world's best guy just because he showed up with a balloon? After he fooled you all those months by pretending to be someone else? After you moaned and moped because of Kelsie and Amber. He's a player. You're the dupe, Ellie. Not me."

I knew she was hurt and angry. But that didn't give her the right to attack me. I grabbed my jacket. "Don't lash out at me because you're unhappy." I slung my backpack over my shoulder.

"Coward! Where are you going?"

"Out until you calm down. You need some space. Maybe you'll get some perspective."

"Get out! Get out and leave me alone."

"Gladly."

Dan's cell phone buzzed in Bre's hand. While she was distracted by it, I made my escape. I refused to be party to her games. I paused at the door and looked back at her. Bre was smiling as she read the text.

"If he's cheating on you, dump him." I slid out before she could respond. The door shuddered behind me. I jumped as I heard the tinkling of broken glass. What had she thrown? I had visions of my best perfume biting it. I took a deep breath, hoping it wasn't something of mine but betting it had to be.

Outside, the sun was shining and the crocuses were coming up. As I walked toward The College Grind, the joy of being with Logan bubbled up, egged on by the sunshine and flowers and dreams of spring. Suddenly, I was smiling and walking with a bounce in my step that should have been there all along. This was powerful stuff—not even my mother or my roommate's tantrums could kill it.

I was grinning as I pulled my phone from my pocket and called Logan.

"Hey. I was just about to call you," he said in that low, sultry way he had. The sound of his voice was like the sunshine outside. It made me hot all over.

"Beat you to it." I put the heat I felt in my voice.

"Can I see you? I miss you already," he said. "*And* I have news." A cloud momentarily masked the husky sunshine of his voice. Like the news wasn't happy.

Happy news was all I wanted. Happy news and him. I hesitated. "I do, too."

"Good! We can share our news. I've been trying to study, but my head's not in it. I keep thinking of you." He lowered his voice. "And last night."

Okay, that really did curl my toes. I clenched my fingers and suppressed a sigh. I wanted him again. I smiled even larger, like I was a different person today than yesterday. I'd been thinking of last night, too. I couldn't keep it out of my mind.

"I'm on my way to The College Grind to study. Meet me there," I said.

"Not your room?" His voice was laced with innuendo and promise of more, too.

"Definitely not there. Bre kicked me out."

"Bitch. Is that your news? On the outs with the psycho roommate again. What now?"

"Man troubles. Or maybe I should say *Dan* troubles and sexting outside the relationship."

"Shit." Logan laughed. "Down with douchebag guys. Come crash at my place."

"Love to. But first I need coffee."

"I have coffee."

"With frothed milk and dark chocolate syrup."

"Shit, El. You know how to string a guy along. I'll meet you there and buy your damn coffee. And then you can come back to my place."

Fifteen minutes later, I was sitting at The College Grind sipping my mocha when Logan walked in. Like I would let him pay. He spotted me and flashed that smile that made my insides turn to mush and my knees go weak. When he reached my table, I jumped up and threw my arms around him like it had been way too long since I'd last touched him.

It was warm outside for almost April. He wore jeans and a T-shirt that showed off his fabulously toned arms. How had I scored a jock like him? As I smiled back at him, I traced one bicep with the tip of my fingernail, daring him to shiver beneath my touch.

He grinned back and wrapped his arms around my waist. "Tease." He tipped my chin up until our mouths met and the heat we felt went into our kiss.

The barista interrupted, calling out my name.

When Logan finally pulled away, I was dizzy with the taste of him, leaning on him for support. Breathless.

"Right on time," I said. I had ordered a mocha, trying to time it so it would greet him. "That's yours."

"I thought I was buying."

I grinned and walked with him, my arm around his waist, his around mine, as he picked up his coffee and took a sip. "Hot. Just the way I like it." The way he looked at me, he didn't just mean the coffee.

He led me to a nearby booth with a window that overlooked the sidewalk. We slid in side by side. I couldn't keep my gaze off him as he settled in with his coffee and spread his books in front of us.

"Now we can claim we're studying." He slid one arm around me and wrapped his other hand around his coffee, resting it on the table.

I was ecstatic to be with him again. Everything about him, even the simple squareness of his hand, thrilled me.

He looked at me over his cup as he took a sip. "What's your news?"

"Jumping right in?" I said.

"I have the feeling this isn't good news. Let's get it over with and get on to the good stuff."

I didn't want to ruin the mood. Silently cursing my mother, I spilled it. "My mom is coming to Mom's Weekend." I watched his reaction closely.

He shrugged. "That's funny—that's my news."

"That my mom is coming for Mom's Weekend?" I teased, knowing he meant his.

A guilty look crossed his face. "Yeah—that, too."

"Wait a minute—too? You know about my mom already?" My heart started racing and I went cold.

He nodded slowly and stared at his cup before meeting my eyes. "She called and told me earlier today. Right after she talked to you. I didn't want to tell you over the phone."

I took a deep breath and shook my head, dumbfounded and furious with her. "She told you before *I* could?"

"Don't look like that, El." He let go of his coffee and grabbed my thigh, squeezing it like he wouldn't let me go. "It's good she trusts me. Between the two of us, we can stop her from making any trouble."

I shook my head. "I don't like this, Logan." I rushed on. "I would have called you immediately after she did, but Bre walked in. That's another story."

"Don't freak, El. I'm not like Austin."

No, he wasn't like Austin. He was much hotter. Much more honest. And so much more vulnerable. "What did Mom say?"

"That she'd done an end-around on me and somehow got to you. I'm sorry, El. What happened?"

I told him about our conversation.

He shook his head. "Evil."

"You're telling me." I paused, studying him, feeling like he knew more than he was sharing and hating myself for the thought. "I'm going to keep her so busy she'll have no time to get into trouble or bother you and your mom."

"She wants to meet Mom," he said. "And Caleb and Dad are coming, too."

"Caleb *and* your dad? Why?"

Logan sighed. "Dad is always here for the first part of Mom's Weekend. He's on the College of Business advisory board. They always meet that weekend and judge the business plan competition. I guess so the business majors can show off for their moms."

"And Caleb?"

"Pulled a hamstring and wants to join in the family fun."

He stared at me, but he couldn't mask the guilt and pain in his eyes. "There's something else—the court set a date for my testimony. Tuesday, the week after Mom's Weekend."

My eyes went wide. "Oh, Logan." I stroked his cheek, resting my hand against it, unable to pull away. I wanted to take all his hurt away, but I didn't know how to help him. I knew the trial was starting the week after Mom's Weekend. It was all over the campus news. But I hadn't known what day Logan was scheduled.

I got it now—his mom was coming to support him. His dad Harlan was probably coming to town to talk Logan out of testifying at the last minute. I had no idea

why Caleb was coming, except to show off and score
with college girls.

"I'll be there." I didn't mean to sound so fierce.
"Nothing will keep me away. And if Harlan tries to pull
any of his usual crap, I'll—"

Logan grinned and touched my lips with his finger,
cutting me off. "I love it when you go all protective on
me. But I can handle my dad."

Could he? I kissed his finger and pulled it away,
leaning up to kiss him and let him know that nothing
would scare me away.

"Ellie? Logan?"

CHAPTER FIVE

I jumped, startled, and pulled away from Logan. My dad stood at the edge of our table, peering down on us with a puzzled, worried look. I'd been so absorbed I hadn't heard him come in. He loved The College Grind. I hadn't been thinking. I should have picked someplace safer and kept things between Logan and me quiet until I could tell Jason we were back together. But I really hadn't thought Jason would be on campus on the weekend.

Jason. I still had a hard time calling him Dad. He liked Logan. But he was my dad through and through. He didn't like guys breaking his little girl's heart. And he knew Logan's past, which would give any decent dad a reason for concern.

My cheeks flamed, as much from guilt as anything. I crossed my fingers, hoping Jason wasn't as sharp as Mom and couldn't read my recent loss of virginity on my face or in the tone of my voice like she could. I was an adult and had waited way longer than anyone I knew to have sex. But dads were dads. They were supposed to chase guys away.

"Dad!" I tried to gauge Jason's reaction to seeing Logan and me together.

Jason had been the one who helped Logan put his life back together after Logan's baseball career-ending injury and rape by Dr. Rogers.

Logan thought of Jason like a second big brother and mentor. Or he had until I came on the scene and put a wedge between them. Unintentionally. Jason had been boss to both of us until my secret that I was his daughter was revealed. Then I had to transfer to another department because the university had a policy against family working for family. Logan quit the IT job he loved working for Jason, feeling betrayed by both of us.

Jason and his wife—my stepmom, Lyssa—had spent the months since Christmas trying to get me out of my funk and mold the lump of hurting jelly that had been me back into some semblance of a person. And now here were we. Worry etched his face. Jason was easy to read—he knew how much I loved Logan. He hoped this was good, but he feared the worst, that I was back on the rollercoaster again.

Jason didn't wait for an invitation. He slid into the bench seat across from us. "This is new." His tone was neutral and firm and a complete statement of fact.

"Very," I said, trying to match Jason's calm as I beamed at Logan. "We just got back together last night." I squeezed Logan's hand.

Jason arched a brow and stared at Logan. "You know what I do to guys who break my daughter's heart? I make their cyber life miserable. Just saying."

Logan broke into a grin.

Jason shook his head. "You think I'm joking. Treat her right, Walker. Be the man I know you can be."

"Yes, sir."

Jason grinned. It was hard to tell if he had accepted the situation so easily. Or if he was simply resigned to the fact that Logan and I being together was inevitable. I knew he liked Logan. And I knew he had reservations about Logan as the guy for me. I decided to tread carefully.

"I haven't seen you around," Jason said to Logan, which was the understatement of the century. He hadn't seen Logan at all since Logan resigned from the IT department that Jason headed. Even though Jason had made an effort. "I hope I'll be seeing more of you now." It was almost a command. Jason leaned back in his chair. "We're short staffed. I know it's only for a few months, but I could use you."

Jason was offering the proverbial olive branch. Or maybe he was looking for a way to keep an eye on Logan and exert some control.

Next to me, Logan stiffened. "Really?"

"You're the best IT tech we've ever had. So yeah, really."

Logan had loved that job. He turned to me for confirmation—should he take it? I shrugged, letting him know it was his decision, but I was okay with it.

"Then yeah." Logan broke into a grin.

"Good. Then things can go back to normal. *Finally*," Jason said. "Come in tomorrow. We need you right away."

Logan nodded and relaxed. "Anything you say, boss."

I relaxed, too, and felt the weight of coming between them ease off my shoulders. Everything was working out. Everything would be okay.

Jason and Logan had been so close. Now that Logan was heading into the trial, he needed Jason's support. Maybe that was what Jason was thinking, too. My dad was great that way.

"Brad Lang from graduate school admissions contacted me the other day about your application," Jason said. "He had a few questions about the recommendation I gave you last fall and the work you've done for me. I reinforced my glowing praise." Jason paused. "Brad said he's still waiting for you to schedule your interview. They'll be making their offers soon."

My heart pounded. I turned to Logan, wide-eyed. "You never mentioned—"

Logan shook his head to warn me off, then looked down at his coffee as he spoke. "I haven't made a decision. Other things on my mind. Other appointments to worry about."

He meant the trial. We all knew he did. I was stunned and didn't know whether to be ecstatic and hopeful that he'd go to graduate school and be here for my senior year. That our relationship might really have a chance to grow. Or if I should be totally depressed that I'd been out of the loop with him. That he hadn't confided in me. That he'd struggled alone all this time. His roommates Collin and Zave had never mentioned anything other than Logan applying for jobs out of state. The thought of a long-distance relationship made me nauseated. I couldn't think of one that had worked out in the end. I'd been trying to push the thought from my mind.

"Whatever you decide," Jason said, easily, "I'm here for you and ready to help in any way I can."

Logan nodded and lapsed into silence.

Jason became conversational. "Is your mom coming for Mom's Weekend?" he asked Logan.

Logan sighed. "Yeah."

Jason laughed. "Don't sound so excited."

Logan rolled his eyes. "I've told you about Mom. She can be a handful."

"Afraid she'll beat you at beer pong?" Jason laughed again, but his eyes were serious as he turned his gaze on me.

I gave him a look that said, "Don't go there." Jason was the consummate forgiver. Mom had treated him horribly. She hadn't even told him I existed. He knew she'd slept with Austin. He knew all the gruesome details. That didn't change his mind. Somehow he saw something redeemable in Melissa Sawyer, something no one else saw. But he'd known a different her. A young, soft Melissa that didn't exist anymore. I was sure of it.

In the months since Christmas, he'd been trying to convince me to reconcile with her. And I'd been resisting. Jason didn't seem to understand that some people were toxic and any relationship with them was polluted.

Logan nudged me like I should confess to Jason that Mom had invited herself for the weekend. I would. Eventually. But here wasn't the place and now wasn't the time.

"You haven't ordered your coffee yet. I'll get you one." I made a move to slide out of the booth.

Jason stopped me. "No. Thanks. I'll get one myself and be off. Lyssa will be expecting me. Tomorrow, Logan. No backing out on me."

After Jason got his coffee and left, Logan turned to me. "You have to tell him she's coming, El. You have to."

"I will."

"You sound like you don't want to. What if he accidentally runs into her? Do you want him blindsided?"

Logan was right, and I didn't want to argue with him, but I hesitated.

"He has his own issues with her. He'll want to see her. She'll cause trouble for him. I know she will.

"He thinks he knows her, but he doesn't. He remembers a young Melissa. Someone different than what she's become. He thinks he can handle her. But he's completely wrong. She'll ruin his life. And enjoy doing it."

Logan frowned, looking thoughtful. "El, secrets are dangerous."

I sighed. "You're right. I'm just worried she'll ruin his life. And mine."

"He's an adult. He can handle it."

Logan's confidence worried me. He underestimated Mom, too. The thing was, even if Jason could handle Mom—and I had huge doubts—could Lyssa? I loved my new family—Jason, Lyssa, Mia, and the baby Lyssa was expecting. I was determined to protect all of them.

"Let's think about something else. Something much more pleasant." I wrapped my arms around Logan's neck to distract him, smiled into his eyes, and kissed him like we were the only two in the place, melting into the returning, urgent pressure on my lips.

When he pulled away, his eyes were bright and his pupils large, even in the sunlight streaming through the windows. "I hope you aren't going to just tease me." His voice was ragged and lusty.

I gave him an innocent look.

He grabbed my hand and pulled me out of the booth into his arms.

"Where are we going?" I whispered like a conspirator.

"Where do you think? My place."

I leaned over and whispered in his ear, "Is sex all you have on your mind?"

"Yeah. Disappointed?"

I grinned back at him.

At his apartment, Logan let us in and dragged me by the hand to his bedroom, right past Zave, who was sprawled on the couch watching TV.

Zave popped up to acknowledge us over the back of the couch. "Logan. Ellie, back so soon? You haven't had enough of this douchebag yet? Logan's conquests don't usually come back for seconds."

"Can it, Zave."

Zave shrugged and laughed. "Just keep it down in there, will you? I'm trying to watch TV out here with a pounding hangover. My head can't take any more thumping and screaming."

Logan tossed a pillow at Zave and pulled me into his room, shutting the door behind us before Zave could retaliate. I wore a short cotton skirt, ballet flats, and a light cotton top. Logan dropped his backpack on the floor and stripped his shirt off.

Logan had the perfect male triangle build—broad shoulders, toned arms, hard chest, narrow waist. If I had my way, he'd never wear a shirt at all and I'd just stare at him all day. I barely had time to enjoy a split second of the view before he was next to me with his hot, talented hands working their way beneath my top. With his fingers clasping my waist, stroking my abs, and playing with my bellybutton ring, I couldn't think at all.

"I've been wanting you again since the minute you left." He put his hot lips on my neck as he unbuttoned my blouse and slid it off my shoulders. He sucked my neck. Hard. With so much urgency, I gasped as the heat of his mouth on my neck radiated out, coursing through my body. I didn't care if he branded me as his. I wanted him to. I wanted *him.*

As I arched my neck, he unfastened my bra like he knew sleight of hand. One minute it was there. The next it fell away, disappearing onto the floor. When he caught my tightly budded breast in his mouth, I sighed. The heat between my legs flamed. And I was lost. I laced my fingers around his head and held his hot, hungry mouth to my breast. His window was open a crack. A spring breeze blew in, rustling the mini-blinds and flowing over my skin like one of Logan's caresses.

"I need to feel you against me, El. Naked against me." His words brushed against my skin. He tugged my skirt off, then my lace thong panties, and stood back to stare at me. "You're so fucking gorgeous, I could almost come right now just looking at you."

When he slid his jean and briefs off he was erect and ready and totally unselfconscious as I stared blatantly at him. He grinned. "Like what you see?"

I smiled back at him. "Put that thing where it belongs."

The returning look in his eyes was a challenge. His eyes were dark and his nipples erect. He bent at the knees to even our heights. Then he pulled me against him and slid between my legs, not entering me, but teasing from the outside, stroking me until I was wetter than I'd ever been and trembling with desire.

"Logan," I whispered, and teased him by pulling on his nipples until he moaned.

His lips came down on mine and he kissed me with such fervor that I lost myself as he gyrated his hips, grinding into me, stroking me with his dick until I moaned, too.

He hovered at my opening, pushing into me like he was going to enter me. His dick was hot and hard and thrilling against me. And the feel of his skin so much more erotic and enticing than condom rubber. If I let him, he'd plunge in without one.

I wanted him to. But I was afraid. "Logan."

"Yeah. I know." He grabbed my butt and kept me pressed tightly against him, still between my legs as he walked us toward the bed and pulled a condom from somewhere. He slid it on and fell on top of me on the bed.

I opened my legs for him and stared up into his eyes. "What are you waiting for?"

"You to be ready." He reached between my legs to stroke me.

I pulled his hand away and guided his dick in. "I'm ready now." I arched up into him.

No longer a scared virgin, I was wet for him. He slid in as I gasped again and wrapped my legs around his waist and rocked into his rhythm again and again.

"Harder," I whispered in his ear, and ran my tongue around the rim and thrust it in his ear.

"Fuck, El. You make me lose all control."

"That's the point. Lose it, Logan. Lose it with me." I clasped him to me.

He thrust harder and deeper. Deeper and deeper until I lost track of everything but the heat of his body and the pleasure building between my legs. Just when I was so tightly wound I thought I would snap, someone gasped and moaned. I realized it was me. Wave after wave of pleasure radiated through me. "Oh, oh, *oh. Logan*!"

He clutched me to him. "*El!*"

I lay beneath him, totally content. We were both breathing hard when we pulled apart and he rolled off of me. I lay on my back with my breasts budding and pointing at the ceiling, my arms outstretched.

Next to me, Logan leaned on one elbow, his free hand tracing the valley between my breasts as he studied me. "That was amazing."

"Amazing." I smiled. "Do you think we added to Zave's hangover headache?"

"I damn well hope so. He's probably in his room jacking off now."

"Shut up."

"Sorry. That was crude. Who wouldn't get turned on hearing my name on your lips and the way you cried out?"

I studied him. "Like, anyone else but you. You're terrible."

He laughed and bent to kiss my breasts. "El, you know what I want more than anything in the world?"

"Hmmmm, let me think. To win the world's largest lottery?"

"Close, but no." He leaned in and whispered in my ear. "I want to slide into you someday, just me. No condom."

My heart raced with both fear and desire. I pushed the fear aside. "You have simple wants."

"Does that mean you'll think about it?"

"Maybe." I smiled coyly.

"Okay. I won't push. But, you know, graduation is coming up..."

There was a thump in the living room that startled us both and saved me from having to reply. I laughed and cuddled into Logan like he should protect me from anything. The noise was followed by Zave cursing.

Zave's voice brought back something he'd said. About all the girls Logan had brought back to the apartment, but only once. I knew about Logan's past and how he'd fallen apart after being raped and went on a sort of girl binge, sleeping with just about everyone.

I should have bitten my tongue, but I didn't. "Logan? How many?"

His brow furrowed like he didn't understand. "How many what?"

"Girls." My heart threatened to pound out of my chest. I traced my fingers over his abs, refusing to look him directly in the eyes.

He frowned. "I don't know. I lost count. Shit, that sounds harsh. It's not like it mattered, and I was drunk or high most of the time. I'm not the kind of guy who puts notches on his belt or his bedpost or whatever the hell."

He tipped my face so I couldn't avoid looking him in the eyes. "I'm clean, El, if that's what you're worried about. I was tested. No STDs. Nothing. But I'll get tested again if that's what you want."

I didn't answer right away. That wasn't what I was worried about. Not really. I was terrified of running into more of them. Of an unintended consequence down the road. Something like me.

"Me too. I'm clean. You're the only one."

The way he smiled at me nearly broke my heart. "Let's keep it that way. I love you, El." He kissed me lightly. "So you *are* the kind of girl who keeps count."

"What are you talking about?"

"Don't worry. I don't mind. I'll even carve the notch on your bedpost for you."

CHAPTER SIX

Logan

El was so beautiful, especially after sex. All Logan wanted to do was El, again and again. She was naked and entwined with him, totally unselfconscious as her breasts budded and rubbed against his chest. He couldn't keep his hands off her. And it was like his dick had a mind of its own.

She was the first girl since the incident he'd been able to open up to. There was something about El that turned him on and made him want only her. He didn't want to analyze it too hard or think about it too much. He didn't want to lose her, either.

He nuzzled her neck, thinking how awesome it would be to slide back into her, when her words stopped him cold.

"Why didn't you tell me you're thinking of going to grad school?" El's tone wasn't accusing. It was not like it or the question should have set him off. But she sounded way too optimistic. And it was clear what she wanted even without looking into her eyes.

He tried to keep his heart from racing. He didn't want her to feel his fear. "When would I have told you? We just got back together last night?" He laughed like it was a joke to deflect her attention to something else.

She shrugged in his arms and her breasts rubbed against him erotically. She was trying to kill him.

"Falcon never mentioned it. Never even *hinted*. You could have said something as him and then I'd know now. I ran into Collin and Zave a couple of times while we were apart. They never breathed a word. It's like they were sworn to secrecy on penalty of a slow, tortured death. There's no other way they could keep a secret." She stroked his arm, running her fingers so softly over the hairs she brought goose bumps up.

He shrugged now, too, trying to seem casual when his heart pounded an uneven cadence. "I didn't saying anything to them and they didn't ask."

"Guys! Don't you ever talk?"

"No." He laughed. "Should we?"

She gently slapped his arm. "You haven't answered the question—were you trying to keep it a secret?"

"No. Like I told Jason, it's no big deal. I haven't made up my mind what I'm going to do."

"But you never said a word before, either," she said. "When did you decide to apply?"

"Last fall. Before...everything."

"Oh." She bit her lip. She looked so cute when she did that. "You could at least interview. Keep your options open." She pushed up to lean back on her elbows and stare at him and implore him without stating it.

He knew what she wanted, but he wasn't sure he could give it to her.

"It's not that simple, El." He swallowed hard, not wanting to think about it, not wanting to spell it out, but she deserved an answer. "I'm not sure I can stay here for another year or more...after the trial."

Her eyes went wide and round with fear and sympathy. He hated sympathy. He was fucking tired of sympathy.

"*Logan.*" His name sounded sad on her lips now, breaking the spell from earlier.

He took a deep breath to fight back the anger burbling up inside. That old familiar, terrifying rage. He hated all this shit and how the rape had changed his life. Before, no one had pitied him. He'd been the envy of everyone—athletic, from a rich family, destined to be a pro baseball player. The injury that ended his baseball career and the rape that followed had taken away more than his dreams and aspirations. They'd robbed him of his pride. Nearly three years later, he still didn't deal well with all this shit.

"I'll be there for you—after and at the trial—"

"No! Don't. I don't want you there." The words popped out almost before they were even conscious thought.

A quick look of hurt crossed her face. Her mouth quivered. Shit. He immediately wished he could stuff the words back in. He'd hurt her again.

He leaned forward and pulled her into his arms, relieved when she didn't push him away and reject him. "I'm sorry. It's not you. I don't want you anywhere near that bitch."

After all that counseling, he thought he'd taken control of his emotions and turned them into something useful. He was losing control again. "I don't want her to get to you. "

"Logan."

He must have looked as fierce as he felt. El's eyes were wide with fear and worry. He felt like crap for scaring her.

"It's okay." She stroked his chin. "You don't have to explain to me. *I* understand. I wouldn't want to sit in front of a group of strangers and lawyers and talk about the day I walked in on Austin and Mom. It's too personal and painful.

"In fact, I told Austin that right after it happened. That I wouldn't testify against Doug. That I'd be a hostile witness. I don't have your courage. And what I went through is nothing compared to what you did..."

He grabbed her hand that was stroking his cheek and squeezed it. He would not break down in front of her.

"You're incredibly brave," she whispered.

"I'm not brave. I'm scared shitless. If there was any way I could get out of it and still live with myself, I would."

The thought of facing *Her* made him break out in a nervous sweat. Deep down, he was afraid he'd get an involuntary hard-on when he saw her. The fear made it seem more likely and loom large. He'd been dealing with the guilt and disgust since the violation. *She* repulsed him. Always had. *She* wasn't the kind of woman he'd ever go for. Not even if she'd been his age. But he'd gotten aroused when she'd touched him. He hated himself for it. Despite all the counseling and reassurances that his body had merely reacted the way nature intended, he worried he was some kind of sicko. He blamed himself—he should have been able to fight through the fog of the drugs and fend her off. He should have been limp as a noodle no matter what she did to him. He should have never come.

He covered his disgust with himself by trying to sound noble, though it was the last thing he felt. "I have to make a stand for all the guys like me. Guys who've been raped but were too afraid to report it because they thought no one would believe them. Or think they started it. Or wanted it. Or whatever shit society believes because men are always supposed to be the sexual aggressors.

"I've been working for CAPSA as a security escort and helping them raise awareness about safety and sexual assaults."

El nodded. "I know. I read about it."

He nodded. "I can't let them down. But I don't want to be their poster boy forever, either." Logan kissed El's hand. "El, forgive me. But I'm not sure I'm strong enough to say what I have to say to the court with you

there, knowing you'll hear every shitty detail and wondering what you'll think of me."

"Logan you know I'd never—" She stopped herself.
"If you change your mind..."

He nodded. But he knew he wouldn't.

"Schedule that interview. *Please*. Just keep your options open."

Ellie

I spent the night with Logan. Like I could help myself when he begged me to. I was still lying in his bed,
dreading going back to my dorm room, when Logan
came in carrying a dining hall tray loaded with a bowl
of cereal, a piece of toast, and a cup of delicious-
smelling coffee.

"Get up, sleepyhead."

"Go away!" I rolled over and pulled the covers over
my head. "I'm no good in the morning."

"You're very good in the morning."

We'd made love again at three a.m.

"Was that morning? I thought it was the middle of
the night."

"Technically, it was morning." He pulled the covers
off and set the tray next to me. "We both have class and
you have to talk to Jason and tell him your mom is
coming."

I grabbed the coffee and cupped it between two
hands, blowing on it to cool it. Logan seemed back to
normal this morning. But I still worried about him.
"Don't remind me."

"El, you're going to tell him?"

"Only because you keep pointing out how dangerous secrets are." I nodded toward the tray, which looked suspiciously familiar. "Traying season is over. I thought you were going to return this?"

"It's not graduation yet, is it?" He paused and then flashed that devilish smile of his. "And I was thinking—I might still need it next winter."

My breath caught. "Really?" That came out way too excited. I tried to cover my excitement and sound casual. "Are you? What changed your mind?"

He sat on the bed next to me. "I thought about what you said about keeping options open. I'm going to schedule my graduate admission interview today."

I set the coffee down and threw my arms around him. "Logan!"

"Don't get your hopes too high, El. It's just an interview. It doesn't mean I've made up my mind."

"No, never. Absolutely not," I said. But my hopes were already floating away with me. I wanted him to stay. In the worst way. Maybe it *was* selfish of me.

"It might not work out. After four years of college, I'm sick of studying," he said.

"Who isn't?" I inched my face toward his for a kiss.

"I'm tired of my old man calling the shots. I want my own money."

The business with Amber, the horrid Double Deltsie alum. In my joy, I'd temporarily forgotten about her and the dubious dealings Logan had with her. "Perfectly understandable. Admirable, even." I hesitated before deciding to plow on. "I thought that's what that top-secret deal with Amber Ranklin was for."

Logan's eyes went cool. "I thought you were against that?"

I shrugged. "It's no secret I don't like Amber. It's nothing personal." Though it was. "I don't like any of your exes."

"I thought you liked Kelsie. She helped save your life. You at least owe her gratitude."

"Okay, maybe Kelsie. So? The deal with Amber?"

"Still in the works." Logan was way too casual and noncommittal. "It'll be wrapped up soon."

"That's all you're going to say?"

"That's all you need to know. For now. When the big money comes in, you'll know it. I'll take you out to celebrate."

"Okay, big shot. I'm counting on it." I leaned in until our lips nearly met.

"El?"

"Yeah?"

"Tell Jason about your mom's visit before my shift."

"You just want him distracted so he doesn't notice you're glowing and realize it's because you're sleeping with his daughter."

"About that—change before you see him—"

I cut him off with a kiss.

Logan dropped me off at my dorm on his way to class. As I walked up the steps to the building, I saw the curtains to my room were still closed. Bre should have been in class. Which meant one of two things, and I didn't even want to contemplate one of them.

I let myself into the building, climbed the stairs to my floor, and unlocked the door to my room with some trepidation. Inside it was dark and smelled overpoweringly of my favorite perfume. I'd been right—that was what Bre had thrown. It combined with the smell of stale beer and unwashed body to make a truly lovely stench. The kind of smell when you hole up in your room without ventilation and sweat beneath the covers, hiding from the world because even darkness seems too bright. It smelled like a bad breakup.

As my eyes adjusted to the dim light, I spotted Bre in bed. I knew I was stepping in it, but I spoke up anyway as I gingerly picked up the broken remains of my perfume bottle and dropped them in the wastebasket. "Shouldn't you be in class?"

"Shut up!" Bre's voice had that ragged, raspy edge, the sound of someone who's sobbed their eyes out all night. "It's over."

I didn't have to ask what. "I'm sorry." I sat down on my bed across from her. "What happened?"

"I don't feel like talking."

That was fine by me. I really didn't feel like hearing. "Okay, I'll just change and get out of your way."

"He broke up with me! The slut texted one of Dan's friends. He wouldn't say who. The friend relayed the message. Dan realized his phone was missing and came over, demanding it back and calling me a bitch. Can you believe it?"

I sort of could, but I wasn't stupid enough to say so. "I'm sorry."

"Yeah." She hiccoughed like a person does after a long crying binge, but her voice was hard. "He'll pay."

"Give it some time," I said. "Let your head clear." I got up and got her a bottle of water from the mini fridge and an acetaminophen from the ancient medicine cabinet above the sink. She was still burrowed when I stood over her bed to give them to her. "Take these and get some rest. I'll be back later."

This day, which had started so well, was lapsing into one joy after another. I cleaned up the rest of the perfume damage, changed, grabbed an energy drink from the fridge, and headed out to tell Jason about Mom coming to campus and left Bre to wallow in her sorrow. Sometimes, wallowing was the best thing. She'd put up with plenty of mine. She'd earned some understanding from me now. I'd probably even have to forgive her the perfume incident.

I found Jason alone in his office and knocked on his door. "Got a minute?"

He looked up and grinned. "For my oldest daughter? Always. What's up?"

I came in, dropped my backpack on the floor, and plunked into the chair across the desk from him. "Thank you for being cool with stuff and giving Logan his job back." I got emotional all of the sudden and my eyes teared up. "That was nice of you."

"Hey, it was purely self-serving. Logan is a tremendous asset to the office. He does the work of two or three techs. We need him here. We've missed him."

It was like Jason to downplay things. I nodded. "Well, if that's the only reason..." I laughed. "I'm still glad you did. He'll need your support now more than ever."

Jason knew how guilty I'd felt about coming between him and Logan. We didn't need to say more about it. He nodded. "That goes without saying. So you just came by to thank me?"

"Mostly." I was still hedging.

Jason cocked one eyebrow. "Mostly?"

"Before we get to the rest, I have more profuse thanks to offer."

"More?" He laughed. "What kind of a daughter did I raise? Wait, I didn't raise you. Someone else has instilled this extreme politeness in you."

I laughed back. "Hardly. I was raised by a she-wolf. This inconvenient polite streak has more to do with genetics, I fear. Since I have only one polite parent, you're to blame."

He grinned.

I didn't wait for him to say anything, just tumbled headlong with the news that made my heart sing. "Logan is going to schedule his graduate school admission interview today. Thanks to you."

Jason's grin froze on his face as he studied me in that intense, fatherly way. "Good. He should keep his options open." He hesitated. "Just don't get your hopes up that he's going to stay, Ellie. The trial is going to take its toll. It won't be easy on him."

"But I thought you wanted him to stay. Are you unhappy that we're back together?"

Jason took a deep breath, looking like he was trying to temper his words. "I want him to consider all of his

options. I want you to be happy. But realistic. I still
have my doubts. Logan is about to be tested in a trial
by fire, the powerful fire of words and public opinion.
After it's over, it may be best for him to escape this
place and start fresh somewhere else. Away from all
these memories.

"Only Logan can decide that. Don't pressure him to
make a decision that's not in his best interests. It will
burn you both in the end."

"Since when did you become the issuer of dire warn-
ings?" I couldn't hold back my snark.

"Since I became the parent of a college student. I
think it's part of the contract." Jason paused. "Ellie,
you know I'm on your side?"

I nodded. "Yeah, I know." Then my guilt got the
better of me. He was being so reasonable. He deserved
my honesty. I bit my lip and just blurted my secret out.
"I have something to confess—Mom has invited herself
to Mom's Weekend. Blackmailed me into it, really. I
wanted to tell you in private. Logan insisted I tell you
today. He doesn't want anything to come between you
and me."

I gave Logan all the credit, hoping to ease some of
Jason's concerns. Logan wasn't going to go crazy again.
He was tougher than that. I believed it, even if no one
else, including Logan, believed it.

At the mention of Mom, Jason paled and somehow
managed to look hopeful at the same time, an odd, ex-
tremely acrobatic emotional combo. They should probably teach it in acting school. If an actor could do a
convincing "pale hopeful," they could win an Oscar.

Jason cleared his throat. "That's great, Ellie."

"Don't get your hopes up," I said, mimicking his earlier crap about Logan. "I haven't forgiven her. I'm only telling you so I can ask you to stay out of sight during the weekend."

"Ellie—"

"No, listen to me, please." I had spent some time working on how to approach Jason about this. "This is going to be a really tough weekend for me. There's so much between Mom and me already. So much to heal and work through. I'd kind of like to keep you a secret for a while longer. At least until we see how the weekend goes.

"She never told me about you for a reason. Whatever that reason is, it's important to her. Maybe she's horribly jealous of you and insecure she'll lose me to you. This could make things worse. I mean, I do prefer you to her." I gave him a lopsided smile as I watched his inner struggle play out on his face.

"What about your vow not to keep secrets?" How could he sound so reasonable and be so unreasonable at the same time?

"It's not forever. Just for now. Until I can figure things out with Mom. I know it's a lot to ask."

He looked resigned. "You make some really good points. But at some point, she needs to know you've found me and we need to work things out so she knows she doesn't have to be jealous of me."

She'd always have to be jealous of him. I loved him more and always would. "I know. But is now the time? This is the first time I'll have spent any time with her since...you know." I looked Jason straight in the eye. "Promise me you'll stay out of the way. I have enough to deal with already—she wants to see Logan and meet his family."

"See Logan?" Jason looked puzzled.

I nodded. "I told you she blackmailed me. You have no idea how conniving she is—she found out about him and ambushed him behind my back. I don't know what she said to him, but he's sympathetic to her. She's up to something."

Jason's expression was unreadable, but I sensed he was upset. "You may be right. The timing is off. But we need to tell Melissa you've found me. Soon. She'll be upset we haven't told her already."

I shrugged. "I don't care what she thinks. I really don't."

CHAPTER SEVEN

Logan

Logan scheduled an interview for graduate school. But he felt like crap doing it. He had no intention of hanging around the university for a minute longer than he had to after graduation. It was a small mercy that his testimony was scheduled so close to the end of the year. He had to get through a few things before he was free of the trauma of the last few years. Mom's Weekend. The trial. The fruition of his joint business venture with Amber. The job offers he was expecting. Dead week. Finals. Graduation.

El was the problem—how could he live without her? She was his main addiction now. But would she want him when everything was over? Would she hang with him long distance?

She hadn't seen the personal attacks he received. Nasty anonymous notes saying he deserved what he got.

If *Her* lawyers were any good, they'd drag up his past. All the girls he'd slept with. They'd claim *She* was another conquest. They would attack his character and go into detail about what he'd done after his injury.

Logan had told El everything, just not in minute detail. He'd given it more of a glossy finish. His testimony was a week and a half away and he was already having nightmares.

In his fantasies, he got through the trial unscathed. His business venture paid off as he hoped—wildly. He got offers from at least five of the companies he'd interviewed with. Why five? He had no idea. It just sounded like a good number. All that and he was set. He could turn them all down and tell his dad to go to hell.

If he lost the money from his grandpa that he'd invested with Amber, he was sunk until he turned twenty-five and got control of his trust fund. He'd have to go to Caleb for a loan. His baby brother. Shit. The thought left him cold.

Logan's cell phone buzzed. He picked up the call. "Amber. Give me some good news."

"Logan, you crack me up." Her voice slid through the phone with a sexual overtone. "Everything's on schedule for the IPO on the Tuesday, April eighth, just like we've been talking about all along."

Logan swallowed hard. "The eighth?"

"Yes. What's wrong?"

"Nothing." He hesitated. "I've been called to testify that day."

"Logan, I'm sorry. Are you sure you want to testify? There has to be a way to get out of it."

"I'm going to do it."

"I'm sure you'll be fabulous. You're wonderful at everything you do." Her tone held just a hint of innuendo.

Logan ignored it. "Yeah."

"Harlan will be right there with you, I assume? Doing damage control."

"Yeah again. Don't give me any bad news that day, Amber. I won't be able to keep it from him."

"Logan, Logan, Logan, you worry too much. By the time you got off the stand, you'll have all of your original investment back and a handsome profit. Enough to last until you come into your trust fund. Enough to tell Harlan where to go."

"I hope so. I bet all my savings on this, Amber. It was reckless."

"No, it was passionate. Don't get cold feet on me now! You took an acceptable, calculated risk. That's all. If you want to play in the business world, you have to swim with the sharks."

Logan was lost in thought. Tuesday, April eighth was looking like his day of reckoning.

"Logan?"

"Yeah?"

"After this is over, we'll celebrate together. I mean *really* celebrate."

He should have told Amber he was back with El. But he didn't. He didn't need any more complications. He knew Amber was expecting more out of him. He wasn't vain, but it was blatantly obvious what kind of cele-brating she was talking about. She wanted to rekindle what they'd had. He couldn't tell her she'd been just one of many he'd slept with to forget. And now he wanted to forget her.

It was better to wait until the deal was done and he had his money back. He would have worried he was stringing her along, but Amber could watch out for herself.

Ellie

That evening when I got back to the dorm, Bre was still playing hermit and hating the world in my room. The atmosphere was definitely not conducive to study-ing, so I left her there alone in her misery and went in search of Nic and Tay. We joined up in the dining hall to study.

"I'm in deep trouble," I said as we sat down at a booth with our energy drinks and fries. "I can't live in my room with Bre, the hater of light."

"She hasn't come out all day?" Tay shook her head, like *What can you do with a broken heart?*

"Nope. Not that I could tell. If she did, she shouldn't have. Not in that condition. Unless she was thinking of playing zombies. With those red eyes and bed-head hair, she looks the part."

Nic made a face. "Cut her some slack. I remember someone else who refused to go to class after a bad breakup. That girl had someone click her in so her grade didn't get dinged." She gave me a pointed look.

"Guilty as charged. I didn't mean to imply I'm not sympathetic. Dan is a douchebag and has been since the beginning. If you repeat this I'll deny it, but I've felt all along he was only with Bre until he could shag someone better. His thoughts, not mine.

"She's better off without him. But will she recognize that before she spirals too deeply into self-destruct mode? I'd be willing to give her all the time in the world to pull her act together, but I'm on a deadline. She has to snap out of it before Mom's Weekend. I've been afraid to bring the subject up with Bre. I don't even know if her mom is coming. Where is my mom going to stay?"

"If she has her way? At a frat." Nic laughed.

"Shut up!" I paused. "Okay, that's actually a pretty genius idea." I was only teasing. But it would solve a lot of problems.

"Here's an idea," Tay said. "She stays in your bed and you stay in Logan's. Mom has someplace to stay and you know exactly where Logan is. Win-win."

"Wow!" I winked at her. "I hang with a couple of smart chicks."

"I know," Tay said. "We're diabolical, too."

"And excellent event planners." Nic opened her laptop. "I say we bag Econ and whatever you two are studying and schedule a little Mom's Weekend fun. I've already scoped out the Friday night frat parties. If your mom is really the cougar you say she is, there are a couple that look promising. One of the houses in particular has a reputation for trying to pick up moms."

"Eww!" Tay and I said in unison.

"Really?" I frowned. "Is that a hazing ritual or what?"

Nic laughed. "Maybe. Who knows? They throw a good party and the moms like it. That's all we care about."

I pursed my lips, thinking. "Mom likes jocks."

"Don't we all?" Nic winked. "No problem. I'm sure we can find someone. In that frat, jocks like moms."

Tay rolled her eyes. "I'm so glad we have an inside source in the Greek system to give us all the crap on the frats."

Nic laughed like she wasn't at all insulted. "I figure we take her there. Introduce her around. And problem solved, at least for Friday night."

"You're really counting on my mom's skankiness," I said.

"Hey, I'm only going on what you told me. You said your mom wants the college experience. What's more collegiate than being hit on by a bunch of drunk frat guys? It's like a rite of passage, right?"

I laughed. Thought about it a minute and shrugged. "You're right. Mom asked for it. That takes care of Friday."

"Okay, what do we have for the rest of the weekend?" As Nic brought up the event webpage, Tay and I scooted next to her.

"Hmmmmm. The ag college is having a plant sale." Nic was so absorbed in studying the schedule that she was almost mumbling to herself.

I snorted. "Maybe for your mom. My mom would be bored to tears. The only green thumb she has is that kind that's good at picking out and picking up a rich husband. That's the only green that matters to her."

"You come from such good stock," Tay said.

Nic ignored us. "Yeah, lame. Though my mom might like it." She pointed to the screen. "What looks good?"

"Mom said she wants a mother/daughter mani and pedi." I scanned the list of events. "Great, one of the local nail salons is offering them at the SUB. Sign me up."

"The craft fair looks fun," Tay said.

"I agree. Add some shopping at the craft fair," I said.

"You're going to need to throw in an athletic event for the Walkers. I figure that's where you meet up with them. Baseball game or track meet?"

I winced. "Baseball? Might be a sore point, given his history and Caleb. I'll talk to Logan."

"Okay, we'll put TBD right here in this handy online schedule planner." Nic filled it in. "That's a pretty full day. Now you just need dinner reservations. The good places are already filling up. I could squeeze you two in on ours. We're going to the Mexican place downtown."

I nodded. "That would be great."

"After dinner, we take your mom barhopping. The next morning, we round her up from wherever we find her and pack her off for home. Weekend planned! Sound good?" Nic beamed at me.

"How are we going to go barhopping? We're under-age."

"I have connections. I can scare you up a fake ID," Tay said. "You might have to dye your hair purple, though."

"No thanks."

"No problem," Nic said. "They're having a special Up All Night for the moms. Want to take her there? There will be dancing."

I hesitated.

"What's bothering you?"

"I hope Mom goes for it."

"Why wouldn't she? Up All Night is tradition. You can't go to college here without going to at least one. You're only other option is taking her to a movie or one of the plays or hang out in your dark room with Bre. Or hang with Logan and his family."

I held my hands out, palms up, acting like I was weighing something in each one. "The lesser of two evils?"

Nic laughed. "See what I mean?"

"Email me the schedule. I'll need to send one to Jason so he knows where to stay away from."

"You got it."

My cell buzzed. "It's Dex." I grabbed it. "Hey."

"You have to help me." He sounded desperate. "Mom's called me three times already asking what

we're doing for Mom's Weekend and telling me I'd better plan and sign up for things now before they're all
booked up. She's already made plans to go to the plant
sale."

I couldn't help myself. I laughed.

Tay frowned, curious, and mouthed, *What's so funny?*

I mouthed "plant sale" back to her and pointed to
the phone.

"It's not funny," Dex said. "She'd going to drag me
to the wooden boat competition at the college of engineering and the natural history exhibit."

"Your mom sounds like a real party animal," I
teased.

"Shut up, Ellie. You owe me. After all that crap,
she'll probably want to do something stupid and girlie
like drag me through the craft fair while we're wearing
our matchy-matchy sweatshirts."

I sighed and rolled my eyes. "Hang on," I told him. I
turned to the girls. "Do you mind if Dex and his mom
hang with us for a while on Mom's Weekend?"

Nic shrugged as if it didn't matter to her.

I spoke to Dex. "You can hang out with Nic and me
and our moms at the craft fair."

"Thanks, Ellie! You won't regret it. I promise. I owe
you one." Then he laughed evilly.

I recognized his prankster laugh. "What are you
planning?"

"Nothing. Just a little surprise for Mom."

"Dex—"

"Don't worry. Mom can take care of herself."

I didn't like the sound of it.

Dex changed the subject. "Will Logan and his mom be joining us?"

"With any luck, no."

Dex laughed again. "That's too bad." He seemed lost in thought. "Are Nic and Tay there? Are any of you crafty?"

"We're plenty crafty."

"I mean like in crafts crafty."

I shrugged. "We like Pinterest."

"Good enough. You wouldn't happen to know where I could get some invisible-ink fabric paint?"

CHAPTER EIGHT

Logan

Logan sat at the kitchen table with a pile of engineering books in front of him, untouched. He should have been studying. Instead, he'd been poring over the day's mail. Two substantial, exciting job offers had arrived. He'd been expecting them—hoping for them, anyway. He should have been thrilled. He was. He would have been ecstatic, except he knew they'd make El sad.

One was an offer from a high-tech firm in Silicon Valley. Another from a company in South Carolina. He'd been so damn eager to get out of this university and away from his dad, and even the torture of being so near El and not being with her, that he hadn't applied at any of the premier high-tech companies in Seattle or

Portland. Now he was regretting that decision big time.

It was way late in the game to line up a job in Seattle immediately after graduation. The best companies had started interviewing in January or earlier. It wouldn't be impossible to get a job with one eventually, not for someone with his credentials. But it would mean moving back home for as many months as it took and taking crap from his dad for everything, including turning down two good offers for no good reason. Big-time shit. Unacceptable.

Now that he and El were back together, he was rethinking his post-graduation plans. He wanted to be near her. But could he turn down these opportunities? Was it even smart to let a girl influence his plans? El was different. *But.*

Whatever he decided, El wouldn't be thrilled to see these offers. He'd have to tell her about them. But he didn't look forward to it.

Almost as if he'd conjured her up by thinking about her, El called just as an email from her came in. Logan couldn't help smiling as he answered the call and slid the offers beneath a pile of junk mail on the counter. "Hey, I was hoping you'd call."

"A real man of action! If you wanted to talk to me, you could have called. What's the matter? Are your fingers broken?" Her voice was filled with tease.

"Cramped from writing out equations and solutions."

"Poor baby." She laughed. "That's a lame excuse, by the way."

"I'll do better next time."

"You better. I've been dying to hear how your first day back on the job with my dad went."

"That's the only reason you called?"

"One of the reasons. Are you going to keep me in suspense?"

"Maybe. Maybe I'll make you drag it out of me." He put a hint of innuendo in his voice.

"Drag it out of you? That sounds promising." She laughed. "I have my ways."

"My first day back was just fine. Normal. I joked around with Jason. Karen seemed happy to see me, too. I went out on a few calls. There's not much more to tell. What's this you just sent me? Planned our weekend already? That's so girly."

"You may not have noticed, but I *am* a girl."

"Oh, I noticed." He took a deep breath, trying to hold his interest at bay. "I'm thinking about that now."

"Don't tease."

"I'm a horny guy. I never tease. Come over?"

"It's late."

"Spend the night."

"There's an enticing idea. I was hoping you'd ask. Bre is still in major depressed mode. Going into our room is like approaching Mordor. The sense of gloom is palpable."

"Sucks for her."

"Yeah, and me. She may be like this a while."

Logan made a snap decision. "Pack a bag and come stay with me until it blows over."

El paused. "Ah, that could be *quite* a while. In the state she's in it could take days just to get back up to depressed. Are you sure?"

It hit him that he'd practically asked her to move in. "Pack enough for a few days and we'll play it by ear. I promise I'll be a lot more fun to be around than Bre."

She laughed. "That shouldn't be hard. I'll hold you to it. Zave and Collin won't mind?"

"You are way too polite and considerate. They won't care. Do I have to beg you?"

"Yes, beg, boy, beg. I'd love to hear that." She sounded relieved and happy.

"You really want me to beg?"

"No, just come pick me up."

"I'll be there in ten."

He texted El as he pulled up in front of her dorm. She was waiting for him and came bounding out with a playful bounce in her step and a suitcase trailing behind her. He got out and kissed her, finally breaking away to help her hoist her luggage into his trunk.

"I scheduled my grad school interview today," he said, trying to sound casual, like it was no big deal.

Her smile made the agony of pretending to believe he could return to the university after the trial and go to grad school almost worth it. When she grabbed his head between her hands and pressed her lips to his again, caressing his mouth, he thought about skipping dinner and taking her straight back to his place.

She broke the kiss all too soon. "Do you have anything to eat at your place? I'm starving. I have RDA dollars. I can treat."

"Dining hall food? You're kidding." He was ribbing her. Some of it wasn't so bad. But after a few weeks in the dorms, the limited choices got old real fast. "I'm taking you out."

"Great. We can celebrate."

"What are we celebrating?"

"Your interview appointment and Jason taking my news that Mom is coming for Mom's Weekend so well and agreeing to stay out of sight."

Logan was happily surprised. "Yeah, I was relieved he wasn't in a bad mood on my first day back. I knew Jason would be reasonable about it." Logan generally avoided talking about Melissa much, afraid he'd give something away that he shouldn't. "So he's cool with staying away?"

El shrugged. "I don't know if he's cool. Resigned, maybe. He wants Mom and me to learn to get along, so he had no choice. It's a lost cause. I hope he'll realize that eventually."

Logan was surprisingly on Jason's side on this one. If El knew all the shit Melissa had been through, she might at least understand why Melissa was the way she was. Not that he ever expected them to be best buds or anything. Melissa had done too much bad crap to El for that.

Logan took El to Burger Country, the locally owned fave of students and alums alike. It had been in town forever, since Logan's parents' student days and before. He had a double cheeseburger, fries, and a chocolate shake. El had a kid's meal and the world's tiniest dipped ice cream cone, the baby size that came with the meal. Caramel.

"Are you ever going to grow up and eat adult-size portions?"

The sparkle in her eyes turned him on. "Take me back to your place and I'll show you how grown up I can be."

"Let's go."

He had a hard-on the entire drive home. He grunted the barest greetings to Collin and Zave as he pulled El past them to his room. He was aching with need by the time he got her into his room and shut the door.

She pulled her T-shirt off over her head, kicked off her shoes, and slid her jeans off as he matched her move for move. He was turned on and breathing hard just staring at her in that lace bra and matching thong panty.

As she reached behind her back to undo the bra, he couldn't stand still. He took over for her, kissing her neck and unhooking it. He wanted her. He needed her.

He grabbed her butt. She wrapped her legs around him. He carried her to the bed as she ran her hands through his hair and nibbled on his neck. He had her on the bed, legs sprawled, hair spilling over the pillow almost before he could think. He was so hot and ready as he pressed between her legs, he just wanted to enter her. He forced himself to slow down and stay in control. Control was everything to Logan.

She moaned as he stroked her breast and kissed her. He would take his time and slowly arouse her if it killed him.

"Don't mess around, Logan. Get a condom and let's do this." She stroked his dick with one hand and reached for a condom in the nightstand with the other.

He beat her to it, unwrapped it, and rolled it on, because he didn't know if he had enough control to hold back if she did it. She arched against him. He plunged in and lost all rational thought. When he was with El, there was nothing but her and wave after wave of pleasure. The rest of the world disappeared. He needed the escape as much as he needed her. But the total loss of control scared him, threatening to push him to the dark side.

He thrust again and again as she moaned and squeezed him.

"El, you are so damned tight. Shit."

"Let go, Logan. I'm right there with you." She grabbed the back of his head and pulled him into a kiss as she rocked with his motion and stroked the inside of his mouth with her tongue, mimicking the thrusting of his dick in her.

He was trying to hold back and wait for her. But he lost the battle and fell over the edge into waves of pleasure and a climax so strong it must have registered on the Richter scale. He gasped, breathless as he pulled El so tightly against him it was like she was part of him.

She moaned softly and gasped like the pleasure surprised her. "Logan." She relaxed beneath him.

He'd lost control. El made him lose all restraint. It unnerved and unmanned him. He wanted to make love to El again, right then, to prove he could hang on and manipulate the situation. Come only when he purposely let go and not before.

He'd slept with dozens of girls since the assault. Had a rep as a great lover. Oh yes, he knew how to please. He knew how to torment himself and keep him and his partner just on the edge of release. For as long as he wanted. He had phenomenal, legendary staying power. Because he'd learned how to control his sexuality and climax. It was like a game he'd played with himself sometimes, seeing how long he could go.

The girls said he wasn't greedy. He didn't come too early and fast like a lot of guys his age. He thought only of the girl's pleasure. He didn't care what they believed. He never bothered to correct them. But they were dead wrong. It was all about him.

He'd learned to control his body. Learned to control his sexual release. Practiced by letting girls try to drive him over the edge of pleasure and turning his full attention back on them, working to please them. By thinking thoughts that allowed him to turn himself off and slow down if he needed to. Because he'd be damned if anyone ever controlled his body again like *She* had. He refused to be a victim of his own natural responses again. Refused to let his manhood and his sexual tastes be questioned again.

He decided when he came. *He* did. He'd gotten to the point where he was sure he could go for hours and not come. That there was nothing any girl could do to him to make him come until he decided he would.

He never let his purely animal, physical instincts take over. *Never.* El *defeated* him. And it scared the shit out of him. She had power over him she didn't, in her innocence, even know. He couldn't hold out against her.

He never thought he'd be weak again. But somehow he was. He wanted to prove—and at the same time he didn't—that he was still in control when he was with her.

"Logan?" She stared at him with a worried expression. "Are you okay?"

"I am *way* more than okay, El. Way more." There was no way he could tell her how afraid he was of her. He needed her more. "I wasn't too fast?"

She smiled lazily and sighed. "You were just right." The way she caressed her words, she may as well have said she loved him.

"I love you, El." His words came out fiercer sounding than he intended.

"I love you, too." She yawned and stretched as he rolled off her and tossed the used condom in the wastebasket. "I am happily sated."

"After doing it only once?"

"Horny bastard." She glanced at the clock. "It's one in the morning. I have lab tomorrow at nine. I need to get some sleep." She pulled the sheet around her and sat up like she was going to get out of bed.

"Where are you going?"

"To get a nightgown or a shacker shirt."

"No, El. You don't need a shacker shirt. Sleep naked with me tonight." At the thought, his dick grew hard again.

She looked at it and smiled. "Are you going to poke me with that thing all night?"

"Not *all* night."

El straddles him. She's never ridden him like this before. Her bellybutton ring sparkles in the moonlight. A glint of peridot green. Her long blond hair falls down around her face, a cascade of silk he runs his fingers through.

She's hot and wet. He's on the edge already, fighting to maintain control, but wanting to let loose with her.

Her naked breasts bounce. They're so perfect. He reaches to caress one. It's full and heavy in his hand. Just the way he likes. He can't get enough of touching it. It buds beneath his touch. He takes the nipple between his fingers, rolling it and playing with it until it's long and hard.

She moans and moves expertly on him. Squeezing him rhythmically.

Just as he's about to tumble over the precipice of climax, she leans down to kiss him, her hair obscuring her gorgeous face. As her lips are just about to meet his, a terrifying sense of dread overcomes him.

It isn't El who's riding him. It's Dr. Rogers.

Logan woke with a start in a cold sweat.

"Logan? What's wrong?" El popped up next to him in bed and put her hand on his arm. "You're clammy. Are you sick? Do you feel like you have a fever?"

Too many questions. He fought to come out of the fog of the nightmare and realized El really was beside him. "Bad dream."

She gave his arm a squeeze. "Hang on. Stay there." She propped a pillow up behind him, fluffed it, and slid out of bed.

He watched her stroll naked to the bathroom in the dark, her sexy form like a shadow. The raging anger at Dr. Rogers pulsed in his temple. *Damn Her.* He wouldn't let *Her* ruin him and El. He wouldn't. He'd fight *Her* with everything he had.

She'd ruined things with Kels. Shit, Kels had deserved better. He wouldn't let *Her* destroy what he had with El.

The sound of water running in the bathroom was soothing. El returned a minute later with a glass of water. She slid into bed next to him and handed it to him. "Drink. You'll feel better. It will help you wake up and bring you back to reality."

He nodded and downed the water in three gulps, feeling the cold as it slid down his throat, hoping El was right. If she was, this water was a miracle. El was a miracle.

She took the glass from him and set it next to the bed.

"It was *Her*," he said. "Again."

"Oh, Logan." El wrapped him in her arms and coiled her legs around him, intertwining herself with him as if trying to shield him against the misery. "It wasn't real."

"It was the first time." As he pulled her to him, he brushed something warm and sticky on his stomach. Shit. He'd hoped that had been part of the dream, too. His face flamed in the dark. He had an overwhelming desire to punch something. He rubbed the stickiness between his fingers and looked at El's shadowed face, feeling like this was make-it-or-break-it time.

If she reacted with pity or horror like Kels had, it was over. He couldn't face her.

El grabbed the corner of the sheet and wiped the stickiness away with it. Her voice was a reassuring purr. "Don't worry about that. I was sleeping naked next to you. How could your body not react?" She laughed softly and ran her fingers through his hair. "The stress gave you the nightmare. *I* gave you a wet dream."

Shit. She was exactly right. She'd described the dream without knowing exactly what it was. He stroked her cheek. "I don't deserve you."

"Oh, I know. No one does." She kissed him lightly. "Feeling better?"

"Yeah. You were right. The water did the trick." He held her tightly against him, pulling her head to rest on his chest. "El?"

"Yeah?"

"Don't ever leave me."

"Leave you? You saved my life. I owe you a debt of honor. You're stuck with me until I save yours."

"Then I'm going to live very carefully so you never have to." But he had the feeling she already had.

CHAPTER NINE

Ellie

I didn't know if I'd said the right thing to Logan until he pulled me against him and the beat of his heart became steady and sure again as I rested my head on his chest. I just knew he didn't want to be pitied. And he was feeling guilty for something he had no control over, like a stupid nightmare. Like being sexually assaulted. And I couldn't lose him. I wouldn't let him be embarrassed. Not around me.

He had a similar nightmare the next night. And the next. I got up and got him water. I ran my hands over his forehead and held him to me and tried to make him laugh. I vowed I wouldn't lose him to *Her*. Not this way. She was like the demon between us, a horrible succubus that found a way into his dreams.

I vowed I'd get up every night for the rest of my life if I had to. But I would not lose. I couldn't ask him not to testify. I couldn't even hint. He needed my strength now more than he needed anything. If we could only get past the nightmares.

They were because of the stress of the upcoming trial. On an intellectual level, Logan knew they were, too. Just manifestations of stress and anxiety. But dreams have such emotional power that it was hard to combat them. I worried they'd affect our relationship.

Logan wouldn't tell me the content of the dreams. I had the feeling I knew the reason—I was somehow part of them. And you know how that goes. You have a dream someone did something to you, treated you badly, ignored you, or embarrassed you. Laughed at you. And the next morning you wake up mad at them, even though you know it wasn't really them. It was only a trick of your own traitorous mind and insecurities.

But worse yet, I couldn't let go of it. I imagined all kinds of horrible scenarios that might have been tormenting him in his dreams. I went over and over the few details Logan had told me about the assault. I thought so hard about them that I almost chased the memories away. And then in a moment of silence, when I wasn't thinking of anything in particular, Logan's words came back to me, indelibly etched in my mind so perfectly I could hear his voice in my head as clearly as if he was speaking aloud.

I felt an overwhelming sense of dread and revulsion. Violation. Images, just snatches, like scenes from a nightmare. The kind where I'm making love with a girl

I'm hot for and she suddenly morphs into someone repulsive popped up out of nowhere and made me break into a cold sweat. Dr. Rogers naked. On top of me. A cold nausea swept over me. I wanted to cry and sweep back my triumph of discovery. In his nightmares, Logan was making love to me, until I morphed into *Her*. I was battling not only *Her*, but me. There had to be a way to win and conquer both demons. I didn't know who to talk to about it. I loved Jason and Lyssa. But I couldn't talk to them about this. I was lost. I needed help.

On Wednesday, I got back to the apartment before Logan.

Collin walked in the front door with a handful of mail. He tossed it on the table. A large envelope with Logan's name on it slid free from the rest.

"Another job offer, lucky bastard. My dad's going to have my head if I don't get one soon. I'm going to end up bored, miserable, and unhappy in the family biz, just like dear old Dad. If you repeat this, I'll deny it, but I should have listened to him and paid more attention to my studies. But partying was just too damn fun."

I barely heard his ramblings. "Another one? As in more than one?"

"Oops! You mean Logan hasn't been bragging about all the companies who are hot to have him work for them? The modest bastard." Collin shrugged. "Thought you knew about the others."

I didn't give up. "How many more than one?"

Collin shrugged again. "I haven't been counting. You'll have to ask him."

Just then the door opened and Logan came in. His gaze bounced between Collin and me. "Am I interrupting something?"

Collin laughed. "Look who's here. We were just talking about you."

"What the hell are you talking about?" Logan looked puzzled.

"Another company vying for your considerable talents." Collin pointed to the envelope on the table. "Hope it's a good offer." He grabbed a beer from the fridge. "I'll leave you two kids to talk it out."

Logan scowled, scooped up the envelope, and shoved it into his backpack with barely a glance at it.

"Aren't you going to look at it?" I asked.

"Later."

"Logan, don't. It's not like I don't know you've been interviewing. This is important. This is exciting. This is your future." My heart pounded in my ears. I fought to sound reasonable and happy for him, but I wanted him to stay. And he knew it. These job offers would take him away from me—physically, at least. And maybe forever. "You should look at it. See if it's as good as the others."

"You know about those?"

"Collin spilled about them. He didn't mean to. He thought I knew." I paused. "I want you to feel comfortable telling me about them."

I pulled a chair out from the table, trying to keep my heart from showing. The thought of him leaving made me unreasonably panicked. "Sit. Look it over. I'll go into the other room if that makes you more comfortable." I forced myself to joke. "Salaries are private things. No one talks about them, right? But, you know, I could get on salary.com and get a good idea of what they might be offering."

He set his backpack on the floor, took a seat in the chair, and grabbed my hand, pulling me next to him. "Smartass." His hand was warmer than his voice. "Let's look together." He glanced at me for confirmation.

I nodded and forced a wobbly smile, trying to play supportive girlfriend.

He leaned down and pulled the envelope back out of his backpack.

I stood behind him and looped my arms around his neck, peering over his head as he opened it. When I got a look at the salary they were offering him, I whistled. And my heart plummeted into near-despair mode. How could I compete with that? Logan wanted out of this university town and out from his dad's control, and here was the ticket right in front of him.

"Wow! You'll be loaded. Engineers make the big bucks. No wonder nerds are hot."

"Shut up," he said.

"So? Is it a good offer? I mean, compared to the others."

He was silent and obviously reading. "It is a good offer."

"The best?"

"Maybe."

"You're awfully tightlipped. Do you like the company?"

He nodded. "Yeah."

I kissed the top of his head, trying to blink back a sudden assault of tears that were both happy and scared. "I'm happy for you."

He grabbed my hand and pulled me beside him. I plunked into the chair next to his. "I don't know what I'm going to do yet, El."

I kept a smile plastered on my face. "I know. You'll make the right choice."

He didn't look convinced. "For who?"

"I want you to be happy," I said, totally meaning it. I hesitated. "I don't want this to sound like blackmail or something, but I have to stay here for another year. I want to get to know Jason and Mia and Lyssa better. And meet the new baby. And finish my degree. I can't keep changing schools and losing credits."

His steady stare unnerved me.

"And after that, I'll have to get a job. Somewhere. And I don't know if I'll be able to follow you. I don't even know if that's best."

"I know," he said. "Believe me, I know." He looked away.

I knew he did. We both did. I didn't want him to feel the pressure. But somehow it was all on him. My plans were firm. I didn't have as many options as he did. He was the one with the decision to make.

We ordered in pizza to celebrate. Collin and Zave drank too many beers and got obnoxious, ribbing Logan too hard about being the golden boy. At the height of their rowdiness, Logan's phone buzzed.

He glanced at it. "Sorry to bail, but I gotta run."

I frowned, puzzled.

"Sorry, El. I forgot to tell you—I'm on call with CAPSA tonight. A girl just called for an escort to walk her home from her ten o'clock lab." He grabbed his car keys.

"And our superhero rushes off." Zave saluted him.

Collin sniggered. "Don't forget your cape."

He addressed me. "I'll be back soon." He turned to the guys. "Behave yourself and treat El nice."

Zave and Collin exchanged mock-puzzled looks and shrugged.

"Don't we always?" Zave said.

Collin nodded. "I thought we did."

Logan brushed my lips with the barest of kisses and was out the door, leaving me with an insane rush of jealousy. I couldn't help imagining girls calling just to get Logan as their safety escort. I felt abandoned, and knew it was unreasonable of me. But piled on top of that job offer, I felt Logan slipping away from me.

"Cheer up, Ellie. Now you can spend some quality time with us," Zave said.

Collin threw a pillow at Zave. "Shut up, douche. Ellie's upset."

It was that obvious? The thing was, I couldn't help seeing the relief on Logan's face when he got the call. Like he needed space and, most important, time away from me. I thought about his need to play hero and suppressed a shudder. I tried to laugh off my unreasonable feelings.

"It's nothing. It's important for him." I paused, realizing I knew hardly anything about what Logan had done during the months we were apart. "How often does he get calls like this?"

Collin hesitated, too, like he didn't want to tell me. "A lot. When you two were apart, he took as many shifts as they'd let him have." Collin set down the beer bottle he'd been holding. "Don't worry, Ellie. You're the only girl for him."

Maybe. But was I enough? Could I compete with his hero complex?

I made a decision. I needed to talk to a CAPSA counselor. If anyone knew how to deal with this, they would.

The next day, I made an appointment. They got me right in for an afternoon consultation with a counselor, Dr. Koin. The CAPSA offices were in the basement on the SUB, along with the study-body offices and various other club and campus organizations. I hadn't told Logan about the appointment. I found myself slinking into the offices once again like I was on a top-secret mission. Fortunately, I didn't have to wait. I was ushered immediately into Dr. Koin's office. She was kindly and no-nonsense, but had a sympathetic air. In her mid-forties, she wore little makeup and comfortable sandals. She put me at ease right away and offered me a seat.

She glanced at a note on her desk. "You're not a victim yourself?"

"No," I said. "My boyfriend is. Logan Walker."

The name sparked recognition. She nodded. "The Dr. Rogers case."

I nodded.

"I commend you for coming in," she said. "It must be difficult for you, too."

"It is. And I want to be supportive." I knotted my hands. "Logan doesn't like to talk about it. And I don't blame him. But I don't know how to help him. And with the trial approaching, he's having dreams. Well, nightmares, really. He won't tell me what they're about. But I think I know what they're about—me and *Her*.

"The dreams are coming between Logan and me. And he's hurting. And I don't know what to do." Tears stung my eyes. "I just don't know what to do or who to talk to."

Dr. Koin handed me a tissue. "That's why I'm here. Talk to me. Tell me about the dream and why you think you know what it is."

I looked at her sympathetic face and knew I could trust her. And so I told her everything—about the dream, about what Logan had told me about the rape, about everything I felt and felt Logan felt. She listened to the story without interrupting.

"He feels like should have been able to stop her. Like it's his fault," I said finally.

She nodded. "That's typical, Ellie. And completely understandable. Male rape victims often feel emasculated. Like they've lost control. Due to confidentiality, I can't speak specifically about Logan. I'm just your counselor now and I'm weighing everything as if I'm just helping you. Understand?"

I nodded.

"Now, this may not be true of Logan, but generally, men react by trying to regain control in all aspects of their lives, particularly their sex lives. It sounds to me like Logan is feeling he's losing control when he's with you. And it's frightening him. He's equating it with the loss of control he felt when he was raped by Dr. Rogers.

"You have to find a way to show him it's okay to lose control with you. That it's natural. Desirable. Our bodies are made to react sexually and have a mind of their own. You need to find a way to disassociate your sex life from his experience with Dr. Rogers."

"How do I do that?" I was desperate.

Dr. Koin looked at me kindly. "I wish I could give you specifics, but I can't. Not without knowing both of you and the inner dynamics of your situation better. Even then I could only offer suggestions that may help. If you'd like to bring him in, we could do couples counseling and go from there."

I shook my head. "He won't go for it."

She nodded. "The main thing is to remain supportive and open to communicating with him." She paused. "I know it's hard. Really hard. Please feel free to come talk to me again. Anytime."

I left Dr. Koin's office, trying to digest what she'd said. She made sense, but I didn't know if I was up to the challenge. How did I let Logan know he shouldn't be afraid of his feelings for me? Or his sexual response to me? That I wasn't *Her*.

As I left her office, I realized exactly whom I needed to talk to. I don't know why I didn't realize it before. I texted Dex that I was on my way to see him.

I found him in his dorm room. The door was open, so I walked in and caught him with a plastic tube—like fabric paint comes in—in his hand, an array of chemicals fanned out around him, and a sweatshirt spread out on his desk with a ruler on it.

"What are you doing, practicing your penmanship?" I asked as I closed the door behind me.

He held up one finger to let me know to give him a minute. He finished writing something in invisible ink and stood back, grinning evilly at his work.

"Did you actually find invisible-ink fabric pens?" I squinted, trying to see what he'd written.

"Yeah, but they sucked. Most of them were the kind you have to use a black light to see. There were a few heat-sensitive ones that changed color when warmed. But they didn't actually disappear. No humidity-based inks.

"I had to create my own unique blend. I'm trying it out on this fifty-fifty fabric blend to see how it holds up and reacts. And to make sure it really is invisible when it's supposed to be. What do you think?"

I walked over and studied the sweatshirt. He'd written *Dex rules.* "You rule? Really? It's not very invisible. That won't prank your mom. She'll see right through it."

He rolled his eyes at my pun. "Give it a chance to dry."

I shrugged and looked doubtful, but it felt good to be with Dex in the normal world. "Make sure she can't feel it, either. You don't want it tactile, or when she hugs you, she'll know you're up to something."

"Think I haven't thought of that? That rules out a lot of fabric paint. Puffy paint just won't work."

I shook my head at his folly. "Cheer up. You have another week to perfect your diabolical sweatshirt prank."

"Yeah, but it would be better if I had access to a lab."

"Since when has having access stopped you?" I asked.

He grinned. "You're right about that." He paused. "You should prank your mom, too. It's fun. I could help. I'm full of ideas."

I did the heavenward glance. "I'm sure you are. I'd take you up on it if I thought it would do any good or make any difference. Can you make me prettier and sexier than her?" I shook my head at his giving-it-serious-thought look. "No, I thought not. If I suddenly turned into Snow White and was the fairest of them all—fairer than her, at least—her life would be over. *That* would be worth seeing."

"Yeah, but you don't want her sending the evil huntsman after you."

"You're right about that." I sighed. "You know she's going to be on the prowl while she's here. A cougar on the make for a younger guy. I'd pay anything to see her taken down a notch. Vanity, thy name is mother."

"Stranger things have happened." Dex got that thinking-up-pranks look in his eyes. "You know, I could probably whip up some invisible face paint while I'm at it. The kind that's invisible until it gets moist or heats up when she blushes."

"Mom never blushes. She's completely immune to embarrassment. Nothing fazes her." She hadn't had the decency to blush when I caught Austin on top of her.

Dex ignored me. "Here's the plan—you get her wasted Friday night. While she's out, you draw a hideous face on her. You know, cat whiskers or something. It's invisible until you're walking around campus and she breaks into a sweat—"

"It would have to be waterproof or she'd wash it off in the shower. And wouldn't that humidity give it away? And someone would probably point it out to her."

"Killjoy. We're just brainstorming here. You're killing the creative genius."

"Sorry. My bad. Want to go together to pick up the sweatshirts next week?"

He shook his head. "And be seen in a crowd of girls as a whipped mama's boy? I'll give you a twenty to pick them up for me."

I shrugged. "Done. I could use the money." I held out my hand.

"I only pay on receipt," he said.

"Talk about trust issues." I laughed. "I wasn't asking for payment. I need your receipt so they'll give them to me."

He hit a button on his laptop and his printer came to life, spitting his order confirmation out. "What brings you here?"

"I needed to talk to someone normal."

"And yet you came here." His eyes danced with amusement.

"Yeah, well, you're not in the middle of bad-breakup depression. You aren't stressed out about testifying at a trial—"

"Now the truth comes out," he said. "Problems with the boyfriend."

"No, just worries. Doctor—" I cut myself off just in time before I spilled something confidential. "Can we lock the door? I don't want to be interrupted."

Dex shrugged.

I took that as a yes and flipped the deadbolt before turning to face Dex again. "All the articles I've read say male rape victims feel like they should have been able to defend themselves. Some of them cover it by bragging about their sexual exploits and how sexy they are. But deep down..."

I hesitated, knowing I could alienate Dex, too. But I had no choice.

"You lied to me," I said.

Dex frowned, perplexed. "What are you talking about?"

I swallowed hard. "You told me you didn't see Logan's picture when you found the rest of the naked photos on Dr. Rogers' computers. But that's a lie. You did." I bit my lip. My mouth went so dry I could barely get the words out. "Dex, please. I need to know *everything* you saw."

CHAPTER TEN

Dex stared at me. "Come on, Ellie. How do you know I saw anything?"

Logic was the only way to appeal to Dex. He didn't make decisions based on emotional appeals.

"Logan was Dr. Rogers' favorite victim. She told him she was in love with him. She was obsessed with him. That was clearly evident the day we pranked her class. When Logan came in, she looked like she wanted to do him right there.

"He told me she confronted him with a naked picture of himself. It doesn't make any sense she wouldn't have kept at least that one. If I have to guess, I'd say she had more than one picture. More than still pictures. I'd say she had a sex tape. And you know what's on it."

"I'm not a perv, Ellie." His eyes and voice were hard. But he bit the inside of his cheek, which meant he was nervous.

"I never said you were. I think something totally different—you're a true friend. You saw something, however brief, and you want to spare me and forget you ever saw it. But it's important to me now. What did you see? And what did you do?"

He took a deep breath and sat down on his bed. "Shit, Ellie, I never would have blackmailed you into being in my study group if I'd realized you were so damned smart."

"Is that a compliment?"

His grin was almost sad. "You'd better sit down."

I sat on his roommate's lumpy, rumpled bed across from him, trying not to think about the last time these sheets had been washed.

"I'll tell you the truth, but I will deny ever having said it."

I nodded. "I'm not a court of law. I want to know so I can help Logan. That's all."

"And what if you can't push the images I give you out of your mind?" he asked. "What if knowing causes you to turn away from him? And me."

"It won't. But that's a chance I'll take. And I won't tell Logan ever, either."

Dex continued to stare at me, looking like he was still thinking it over. Finally, he spoke. "You're right. There was a video. I erased it and the pictures of Logan. To protect you. And by default him. There was more than enough evidence to convict Dr. Rogers without it. I'm good. I covered my tracks thoroughly. If anything ever comes to light, I'll claim Dr. Rogers deleted the files to protect herself."

I nodded and let out a breath I'd hardly been aware of holding. I couldn't say I was relieved, exactly. But I was hopeful. "Thank you. Really, Dex. For everything you did."

"Shit." He looked away, obviously embarrassed. "Why do I feel like I could use a drink?" he said. "I don't like talking to girls about perverted shit like this."

"It's not my favorite topic, either. If it helps, I won't look at you."

He shook his head again. "You're funny, Ellie."

"Look," I said. "I'm fighting a succubus who haunts Logan in his dreams. It's like boxing with shadows. I need ammo. Just give me the basics."

He shrugged. "The tape was short and shot from a camera she must have hidden somewhere off to the side of the bed. The picture wasn't super clear."

If that was another lie, I let him get away with it.

"It opens with her leading Logan to the bed. He's leaning on her heavily, as if he can barely stand, and protesting that he feels sick and needs to leave. He's mumbling like talking is a real effort and stumbling and dragging his feet.

"She helps him on to the bed just in time and it looks like he passes out." Dex paused. "Shit. You really want to hear this?" He studied me like he was trying to determine if I was okay.

I nodded and swallowed hard. "If Logan has to live through it at trial, I can live through it here. Logan isn't going to tell me. I'd rather hear it from you than the hostile opposing lawyers for Dr. Rogers' defense."

Dex nodded and pursed his lips, looking like I'd made a good point. "Okay, then. She undresses him, slowly, like she likes it, running her fingers over his body, squeezing his muscles, telling him how hot he is and how much she wants him. His breathing gets heavier, but he doesn't move.

"Then she does a striptease for him, even though he's out cold. And gets herself off as she lies next to him, stroking his dick." Dex shivered like he was totally revolted. "It was horrifying and I fast forwarded through a lot of it. But my morbid curiosity got the best of me and I saw enough of it. Too much."

I nodded. "I know. Keep going."

Dex looked out the window as he spoke. "She strokes him and plays with him until he's hard. Then gets a condom out and rolls it on him. Climbs on top of him and puts him in her. She's riding him, calling his name, trying to wake him. Finally, he rouses just a little and murmurs a girl's name."

Dex glanced at me guiltily. "Don't ask me the name because the sound quality was bad and he mumbled. I couldn't hear it, but it sure as hell wasn't Dr. Rogers' name. That much was clear. He thought she was some girl he was into, okay?"

"Okay."

"Just so you're clear—he was obviously confused. He was in no way into Dr. Rogers. I have to make an editorial comment here—she was not sexy. Her breasts were baggy and her skin wrinkled. Her belly was flabby. She looked like an old crone getting off on a hot young guy. It's important to keep that in mind. If Logan had been conscious, he would have been as repulsed as I was."

My heart was racing as I nodded. "I know. Believe me, I know. It's just that he doesn't see it that way."

Dex looked stricken. "Maybe I shouldn't have erased it. At the time I didn't think. I was shocked and sickened. I never thought..." He took a deep breath and let it out. "I never thought it would be healing for Logan, or any victim to see that. Maybe I was wrong."

"It's okay, Dex. You had every good intention. Is that the end?"

He shook his head. "She rides him until he climaxes, but it was clear he was never fully awake and aware. He was hallucinating or dreaming. He thought she was someone else.

"Just after he comes, he starts like he's waking up and realizes for a second who she is. He looks horrified. Then he passes out again." Dex stared at me. "Ellie? You okay? You look pale."

"I'm fine. Just..." It happened exactly like Logan's nightmare. He was reliving it and substituting me for the girl before.

"Icked out and feeling like you need a shower?" Dex asked.

I finally managed to nod and smile. "Yeah."

He sighed. "I know the feeling." He was silent. "I know the last thing he wants is pity, but I feel for Logan. That's some serious shit to have to deal with."

We fell silent.

Finally, Dex spoke again. "If it ever comes up, reassure him that he didn't really regain consciousness. He had no idea what he was doing."

"I know. I will," I said, relieved by that part of what Dex had told me. "He won't bring it up. And I can't. He doesn't want me at the trial because he's afraid of the images getting to me. So how do I convince him?"

"Shit, Ellie. I have no idea." Dex actually gave me a hug.

The day was warm. When I got back to the apartment, the windows were open, Spartacus was swimming happily around his bowl, and the guys were lounging around the living room making plans for the weekend. I entered in the middle of their conversation.

"It's too late to plan a really epic party," Zave said.

"Spontaneous parties can be epic, too." Collin was drinking a beer. He took a swig before he spoke. "We have to do something. Live a little. Next weekend we'll be tied down with the moms." He rolled his eyes in disgust.

I hadn't really thought about their moms coming. Truthfully, I wasn't thinking about much more than Logan and my own troubles with Mom coming. I realized I'd have to move back to my dorm room, at least for that weekend. And I didn't relish the thought of going back or stopping by and talking to Bre about it. I still didn't know if her mom was coming, too.

Zave shrugged. "Yeah, your mom's a party dud."

"What are you talking about? Yours is worse. Mine's decent at beer pong. Logan's sucks."

Logan didn't come to his mom's defense. He remained silently amused.

"Let's have a mom beer pong tourney." Zave noticed me. "Oh, hey, Ellie. Think your mom would be up for it?"

"Probably. But she'd be more up for strip poker and I'm not letting her take advantage of you guys." I liked teasing and egging the guys on.

"That sounds dirty," Zave said.

"Does it? I didn't mean it to," I said, all innocent-like. Then I winked as I walked over and gave Logan a kiss. He pulled me into his lap.

"Don't worry about us, Ellie," Collin said. "We heard your mom is hot and not all that old. We'd let her take advantage of us. For your sake."

"I'm touched, boys, really. But no thanks. I'm going to take her dancing at Up All Night and let her pick her victim from a pool of willing strangers."

"Cruel girl," Collin said to me, but it was all in good fun.

Logan wrapped his arms around me and nuzzled my neck. "You always smell good." He kissed my neck. "Where've you been? I was expecting you earlier."

My heart raced, but I reverted to my cool lying techniques and told a good partial truth. "I stopped by to see Dex. He wants me to pick up his Mom's Weekend sweatshirts and I had to get his receipt. Did you order matching sweatshirts?" I ribbed Logan.

Logan shuddered. "Not even Mom could make me do that. So what do you want to do this weekend, El?"

Zave cut in. "Let's go to the cliffs and do some jumping. We haven't been since last summer."

I froze.

Logan noticed and hugged me tighter. "No thanks. I don't think I'm up to saving El's life again." He kissed my cheek.

"Shut up." I punched him playfully, happy he'd come to my defense. But sensing that he was telling the truth—until Mom's Weekend and the trial were over, he was distracted.

"Sorry, Ellie. Didn't mean to upset you. Almost drowning has to be a once-in-a-lifetime event, right?"

"Not if you really drown the next time," Collin said.

"I'm with Logan," I said. "I'm a fair-weather jumper. It's not hot enough yet."

"We're out," Logan said.

Collin lifted his beer bottle toward me. "She has a point. It's more fun to drink beer and jump off cliffs in the heat."

Zave conceded defeat. "Okay, so what do you want to do?"

Logan slid me off his lap and took me by the hand. "You guys figure it out. El and I have to study." He pulled me toward his room.

"Anatomy again?" Collin smirked.

"Shut up." Logan pulled me into his room and closed the door. "I missed you."

"Are we really studying?" I asked.

"Yeah, anatomy." He got that wicked look in his eyes as he pulled me close and ran his fingers through my hair.

His back was toward the bed. I was facing him and it. I had a delicious idea, something I hoped would work to rid him of *Her.* And give him nothing but happy, erotic thoughts of me.

We'd made love fewer than a dozen times, always with him on top. My inexperience, especially with being on top, put me at a disadvantage. But love, determination, and complete enthusiasm for the job had to count for something.

I had a hard time focusing as his lips inched toward mine. I braced my hands against his chest and matched his grin, playfully pushing him backward toward the bed, taking full command as I pulled his T-shirt over his head.

He matched my move and ran his hot, talented hands beneath my blouse. He removed my blouse in a single, fluid move.

He dropped it to the floor with a flourish. "Now you see it. Now I see you." His grin practically stopped my heart. "I want you, El." He pressed an urgent kiss on my neck, sucking gently and pressing me against him.

I held back a sigh. Seducing Logan was the easy part. Playing aggressor was trickier. He stripped me of command too easily. And I was sure it was purely intentional.

He trailed kisses, hot, wonderful kisses, down my neck to my shoulder. He coiled himself around me, pressing me against the hard bulge in jeans. I was thrumming with lust and already wet for him as he nibbled and raked his teeth over my skin. I momentarily surrendered and spoke his name on a sigh. "Logan."

"I need you, El. *Desperately.*"

"Only desperately?" I whispered back on a ragged breath. "I need you tragically."

"Tragically?" He kissed the hollow of my neck. "Achingly."

"Are we engaging in a corny adverb war?"

"Yes, definitely." I ran my fingers through his hair. "Your turn."

He whispered in my ear. "I *love* you."

"Cheater! You win." I caught him off guard and pushed him backward to the bed until he butted up against the mattress. "You're going down, Walker."

"Is that an invitation? Because I'll go down on you any day."

I felt a rush of wetness and heat between my legs. "Shut up." I playfully shoved him backward, hoping I had enough control to hang on and make my point.

He fell back onto the bed with an exaggerated bounce.

"I like the sight of you on your back. Under *my* control."

"Under your control?" He spoke like he was issuing a challenge. "Power hungry?" His eyes danced.

I grinned and climbed on him, straddling him, rubbing my crotch against the obvious bulge in his jeans. I bent and sucked his nipple. "Anyone ever tell you you're a hot anatomy subject?"

He laughed. "No. No one. You're the first."

"Glad I'm first at something." I licked the hollow of his throat, feeling his pulse leap beneath my tongue.

He unhooked my bra. I sat up and let him pull it off, holding his gaze, daring him to turn me on even more. He dangled my bra from one finger before dropping it off the side of the bed. He took my breasts in his hands and ran his thumbs over my nipples until they were so hard and erect I thought they might shatter. "Now we're even."

We were *so* not even.

His eyes were dark with lust as I reached for his fly. "Are we?"

It had all been fun and games up until now, but now he froze as I unzipped his jeans.

"That's right. Just lie there and let me turn you on."

His breathing became shallow as I pulled back the fly of his jeans and slid his pants slowly to his ankles. He kicked them off as I reached for a condom.

I pulled his dick out from his briefs, stroking it slowly before rolling a condom onto it as expertly as my inexperience let me. I was wearing thong panties. There was no need to shed them. The thought of him sliding in around them made my breath catch. I should have talked dirty to him then, but I was afraid of being too obvious. Too similar. And it wasn't really like me.

I got up on my knees, took his dick in my hand, and poised myself about him, ready to plunge him into me. "I want to feel your big, hard—"

Before I could sit on him and take him into me, he grabbed my wrist, squeezing it so hard my hand turned almost instantly purple.

"Not like this, El."

I gasped and reflexively let go of him, stunned.

He took advantage of my moment of weakness and flipped me over, pinning me beneath him. His chest heaved. He was breathing hard and fast, excited, but he looked pale and wild. "Now who's in control?" His voice was excited and hard.

He plunged into me before I could answer, driving so hard and deep I could barely breathe, let alone speak. I wrapped my legs around him as he drove again and again, harder and harder, deeper and deeper until the headboard banged against the wall in time with us. And someone in the next apartment banged back.

"Logan!" I cried on a wave of pleasure as we climaxed together.

When it was over, he lay on top of me, breathing hard as I the aftershocks of my climax ebbed away. Finally, he pulled out and flopped next to me on the bed.

I rested my head on his chest. His heart was hammering and pounding as I mindlessly rubbed my right wrist.

"Shit! That was...some powerful orgasm. Like *nothing* before."

Although I was in total agreement, my experience was limited. I didn't reply. I was lost in my thoughts. I'd tried to replicate the dream and replace the outcome. And failed. As long as he had to be in control, *She* was still winning.

He leaned up on an elbow and stared at me. My face must have given me away.

He frowned like he was concerned. "You okay? I'm sorry, El. I don't know what the hell came over me. Was I too rough?"

Logan brushed my hair out of my face. He took my wrist, bringing it to his lips to kiss. Halfway there, he froze. He frowned as he stared at my wrist. "I *was* too rough. *Look* what I've done to you." His voice broke.

I glanced at my wrist. It was circled with finger-size bruises.

"Shit. Sorry, El. I can't believe I hurt you." He sounded truly stunned.

"I bruise easily," I said fiercely. "It's nothing. I get bruises all the time and I don't even remember bumping myself."

The look in his eyes said he didn't believe me. "Shit."

"Don't worry about it. I heal quickly, too." I paused, going for broke. "I know how you can make it up to me."

"How?" He looked intrigued and relieved.

"Next time, let me be on top." I smiled suggestively at him. "It's a fantasy of mine to have you totally in my power."

Logan's cell rang from his jeans pocket on the floor, saving him from answering. He looked away too quickly for me to read his face and didn't answer me. "I have to get that." He rolled off the bed, slid the condom off, and grabbed his briefs, shirt, and jeans.

He pulled the phone out of his pants as he walked to the bathroom and picked up. "Amber, hey," he said just before the door slid shut and cut off his conversation.

A wave of jealousy crashed over me. I hated that predatory Amber. I felt like a knight protecting his castle while a different enemy stormed it from every side. I was losing more than one battle at once. And I didn't have enough defenses.

I needed reinforcements. But I had no idea where to get them. None.

CHAPTER ELEVEN

Logan

Logan closed the bathroom door and held the phone to his ear with his shoulder as he got dressed. That was a close escape. How could he explain to El that the thought of her on top caused him to go cold with nausea?

He didn't do that position. Ever. Not since *Her*. El could poll all of the girls he'd slept with since, and if they thought about it, they'd realize he not only liked it on top—he insisted on it. Or behind. Or any of another zillion positions. But not that one.

"Logan, glad I caught you." Amber exuded her usual confidence.

He held himself in check, irritated with Amber for calling, yet grateful for the interruption at the same time. El hadn't known what she was asking of him. And he couldn't tell her without cracking and looking like a coward and a sexual failure.

"What's up?" he said.

"We've hit a minor snag with the IPO." Amber's tone was so casual she may as well have been talking about the weather.

Which put Logan immediately on edge. He swore beneath his breath. He needed *one* thing to go right. *One damn thing.*

"It's nothing on our end. I'm already on top of damage control. But I thought you should know—Core Technologies is rattling their sabers and claiming to have a technology similar to ours that they're planning to release within the month."

"What!" The word exploded from his mouth. "They're lying. I did the due diligence. Core has nothing like ours."

"Of course they're lying." Amber laughed. "They're trying to mess with our IPO while they play catch-up. It's nothing more than corporate politics. I wouldn't even think twice about it, except Harlan has connections there."

Logan took a deep breath. "You think Dad's behind this? How would he even know about the deal?"

Logan could almost hear Amber shrug. "I have no idea. I only know he's unhappy with you. And I know what he's capable of if you cross him."

Logan jostled the phone as he pulled his shirt on. "Yeah. That's an understatement. He doesn't want me to testify, but I'm not backing down on that. I can't now, anyway. Too many people are counting on me. What do you want me to do?" He had a feeling that whatever it was, he wouldn't like it.

"He'll be on campus for the College of Business' annual advisory board meeting, right?"

It was rhetorical question. Amber knew the answer, so he didn't bother answering.

"Play nice and try to placate him. We may need him to use his influence to get Core to back off."

Logan swore again. "Only as a last resort. That would mean I'd have to tell him about the deal. It's even odds he'd go ballistic."

"The first rule of business, Logan—play the politics. Dirty politics if necessary. Don't think of it like owing your dad one. Keep the endgame in mind. Think of it more like using Harlan to get back at him. The ultimate double cross. Once you have your cash, you can tell him to go to hell. Isn't that the goal?"

She'd made a good point, but he didn't reply.

Finally, she laughed into the silence between them. "I'll do what I can on my end and keep you posted. In the meantime, don't worry." She paused. "Changing the subject to something more pleasant—I'm coming for Mom's Weekend. One of the speakers at the moms' breakfast had to back out. As a regent, I'm stepping in for her. Leave some room in your schedule for me. We have a lot to catch up on."

Shit.

"I'll be in town a week from tomorrow. Oops! I have another call coming in. Got to run. See you soon."

The line went dead. Logan ran his hand through his hair and leaned back against the bathroom counter. He'd put all the money he'd inherited into this deal last fall, when all he wanted was to prove to his dad he could make something of himself. Money he could have used to go to grad school. Money to set up an apartment in the real world. Money that gave him some independence from Harlan.

He took a deep breath. Grad school. He couldn't believe he was even entertaining the idea. He wasn't ready to leave El.

El!

She was going to be pissed at him for taking a call from Amber. And acting like he didn't trust her to overhear it. He couldn't tell El the real reason he'd run—he couldn't tell her the truth. His slid his phone into his pocket, steeled himself, bracing for backlash, and stepped into the bedroom.

El sat on the bed, fully dressed, working on her laptop. She didn't look at him when he came in. "Done with the top-secret call already?"

Yeah, she was pissed.

"It was just boring business crap." He sat down next to her on the bed. "Hey, I'm sorry. My business with her will be done soon. Don't be upset with me."

"Me? Upset?"

"Don't be like that, El. Please."

She sighed and finally looked at him. "Is everything okay with Miss Double Deltsie?"

"Yeah, she's great," he said, resolving to come clean. "And coming to town for Mom's Weekend."

Beside him, El stiffened. She was definitely upset. "Of course she is. She can't seem to stay away." El's tone made it sound like an indictment. *Of him.*

Logan tried to deflect. "She should be easy to avoid. Just don't go the university-sponsored moms' breakfast. She's filling in as the speaker."

El shut her laptop. "Thanks for the heads-up. Lucky for me that breakfast is the *last* place you'd catch my mom. Now, a frat-house breakfast would be entirely different." She sighed. "Your mom, though? That kind of event sounds exactly like her thing."

"If she goes, she'll be going on her own. I'm not going with her." He touched her arm.

She didn't seem placated. "Speaking of Mom's Weekend, I should go." She slid past him and put her feet over the edge of the bed. "I need to work the details for Mom's Weekend accommodations out with Bre. I don't even know if her mom is coming."

El was still upset. Logan couldn't stand for her to leave like this. "Don't go." He grabbed her arm.

She stared at him.

He dropped her arm. "I'm sorry." He took her hand gently in his. "Let me make it up to you. What do you want to do this weekend? Whatever it is, I'm in. We'll do it."

As she studied him, the look in her eyes scared him. She was calculating something. But he couldn't figure out what. Whatever it was, he didn't measure up. His mouth went dry. He'd promised too much. There was one thing he couldn't do and he had the awful feeling she was about to ask for it.

"I want to party." She smiled suddenly and squeezed his hand like he was forgiven. "The guys are right. We need to live a little this weekend."

Ellie

I spent the night with Logan. He had the nightmare again and woke up in the middle of the night in a cold sweat. I tried to calm him and joke about it, saying I was going to start putting a pitcher of water by his bed. He didn't think it was funny, so I shut up. I cuddled into him and ran my hands between his legs like I was interested in some late-night action.

He pushed my hand away. "Not now, El." His tone was apologetic.

I let it drop, because what else could I do that wouldn't make it worse? But turning me away was a first. It didn't hurt, not really, because I knew the reason for it. But it scared me. It felt like the first step down a slippery slope. Logan Walker didn't turn down a chance for sex unless he was so sick he couldn't perform. This was something worse than a physical illness. This was psychological. I had to act. Soon. I had to make another attempt. Before things got worse.

While Logan had been in the bathroom talking to Amber, I'd been thinking I'd taken the wrong approach. I needed to get him when his defenses were down. Which was why when he asked, I said I'd like to party. I'd never get him drunk, but if he had a few beers in him—better yet, a few hard drinks—then maybe he wouldn't fight me. Maybe he'd let me show him I wasn't Dr. Rogers. Maybe I could replace the nightmare with pleasurable reality.

It took him a long time to fall asleep again. I know, because I pretended to fall asleep again right away, but I was worried about him, waiting for him to drop off first.

He took me to breakfast at a local pancake house. Then I made him drop me off at the dorm, using a flimsy excuse. "I have to do my laundry and talk to Bre."

"You can do laundry at my place. And we have this modern invention called a cell phone."

I shook my head. "You are pathetically obvious. I don't have any good party clothes at my place."

He made puppy eyes at me. I remained unmoved. "Most of my laundry is in my room. And I need to do my roommately duty of checking on Bre and getting her out in the world again."

Logan rolled his eyes. "Tell me you're not going to invite her to party with us tonight."

I laughed. "I'm not that cruel or masochistic!"

"Good to hear." He made a comical face and kissed me goodbye before I slid out of the car. "I'll see you tonight."

I nodded. "Find the best party on campus." I bounded up the steps to the entrance. At the top of the stairs, I caught a last glimpse of his car as it turned the corner out of sight. I hadn't fully lied. I did need to check on Bre. But I also wanted to talk to the girls and get their advice.

I took the stairs to my second-floor room, slowly, and paused in front of my door. *Buck up,* I told myself, as I listened for music or movement inside my room. I gave up and plunged the key in the door.

Bre sat at her desk with her laptop open and her headphones on. She glanced up when I walked in and took her headphones off. "You're back."

"Yeah, the prodigal roommate returns."

"Tired of Logan already? Ready to join the Men Suck Eggs Club?"

"Not quite. You're up and dressed." I nodded toward her desk. "And studying. Are you back among the living?"

"Not quite." She smiled.

"You look like it to me. Welcome back," I said as I threw my stuff in the closet and took a seat on my bed. "What made you turn the corner?"

"I haven't turned the corner. But if I flunk out, my parents will kill me." She sighed. "Mom is coming next weekend to give me a pep talk and make sure I'm okay. I'm just practicing seeming normal."

"Good idea." I nodded. "Practice is always good."

Bre got an evil grin on her face. "And Dan totaled his car, wrapped it around a streetlight, got picked up on a DUI Thursday night, and spent a night in jail. The new girl dumped him. I guess she was more into his car than him. He's in a ton of trouble with his parents."

"Don't sound so upset," I said.

She grinned back.

"And you know this how?" To say I was suspicious of her sleuthing methods was an understatement.

"Social media."

I didn't ask for more details. Last I heard she'd un-friended him, disconnected with him, taken him out of her circles, linked him out, unpinned him, basically excised him from any of her online accounts. But there were always ways to stalk people online, as I knew full well.

"Thank goodness for online connections," I said, and took a deep breath. "Speaking of Mom's Weekend, I have some bad news."

Bre shot me a worried look, like more bad news was the last thing she needed. "*What?*"

"My mom is coming." I made a face that showed my disgust.

Her mouth dropped open.

"I thought Nic and Tay would have told you by now," I said.

"You caught me on a good day," she said. "I haven't talked to anybody since..."

I nodded, knowing what she meant.

"Holy crap! Your mom is coming for Mom's Weekend! How did you let that happen?"

"She blackmailed me into it." I gave Bre the quick rundown. "Worse, she's insisting on staying here with us." I took a deep breath. "There aren't any hotel rooms anywhere. She wouldn't stay in one if there was. I'm really sorry. Your mom is going to hate her."

"I'm finally going to get to meet the infamous man-eating Melissa." Bre actually sounded excited. "I hope she lives up to the hype. I can't stand another disappointment." She nearly broke into an actual smile. Well, at least the edges of her lips curled up slightly.

I made a point of shuddering. "Let's hope *not*. Why are you smiling?" I asked, relieved she was taking the news so well.

"This is a stroke of good luck—she'll divert Mom's attention away from me."

"Yeah, maybe. But this means we're both going to have to sleep on the floor," I said. "Know anyone with a spare sleeping bag?"

"Why don't you just sleep with Logan?" Bre asked. "Your mom probably expects it anyway."

"Yeah, but his mom will kill me. Remember Thanksgiving?"

That great memory got a full smile from Bre. "I guess you could be right. But it seems like you could put your mom up on Logan's couch."

"Collin's and Zave's moms will be in Logan's apartment, too. I think they've already called the couch. And I'm not keeping Mom in Logan's room."

"Yeah, I see your dilemma." Bre took a deep breath. "I'll ask my mom to bring two sleeping bags with her and the camping pads. I'd guess your mom probably doesn't own a sleeping bag?"

"You'd guess right." I got up and gave Bre a hug. "It's good to have you back. Hang in there."

"Oh, I will," she said.

The hair stood up on the back of my neck. Something about her tone put me on guard.

I hung out with Bre for a while, then grabbed my laundry bag and headed to the basement to do my wash. Tay was working, but Nic was in her room. I tapped on the door and walked in.

"You're back!" Nic jumped up and gave me a hug.
"I'm off to do my laundry. Care to join me?"

"Wow, make me an offer I can't resist!" She laughed. "It's a nice day outside. I was actually thinking of heading to the sunbathing porch and getting some color before party time tonight.

Nic was already half a dozen shades darker than ghostly pale me.

"Don't look at me like that. Beautiful caramel latte girls like me get pale after a horrendous winter, too." She eyed me. "Let me grab my stuff. We'll throw our clothes in the machines and take in some sun. Go get your suit on."

We stopped by my room so I could change into my bikini, then headed to the laundry room and loaded up the machines. I made her swear not to repeat anything I told her and filled her in on everything, including Logan's nightmares.

"That's heavy, Ellie." She paused. "I don't need to tell you to be careful. This could backfire on you."

"I have to do something. Or I'll lose him."

She raised one eyebrow. "But getting him drunk and taking advantage of him?"

"I'm not getting him drunk. Just, you know, taking advantage if it happens."

"Well, you've come to the right place. I'll help you get ready for tonight. He won't be able to resist you. First, let's catch some rays. My mom would say you look like milk poured through a bathing suit."

"Your mom would be right."

The sun porch wasn't really a porch at all. It was the roof to the dining hall. You had to climb through a dorm-room window to get to it. Only certain rooms had access. Fortunately, we knew the girls on one of the rooms that did.

We settled our towels on the heat of the asphalt roof. I plugged my iPod into a speaker, turned up the music, slathered on lotion, and settled in—ostensibly to study—while we baked.

CHAPTER TWELVE

Logan was late. He knew how much I hated late. But he showed up with an apologetic smile and a bouquet of flowers.

"Bought specially for you from the grocery store." He handed them to me and brushed my lips with a kiss. "You look so hot, El."

"And possibly sunburnt." The way his gaze traveled over me gave me shivers of pleasure and was worth the extra time it had taken me to get ready. I took the flowers he held out to me. "What's the occasion? I hope you aren't trying to bribe me into forgiving you for being late."

Logan being late was kind of a joke between us. He'd been late the first time we'd met for dinner and I'd almost left without waiting for him.

He looked charmingly guilty, like a bad boy who was caught. "I'd never do something as obvious as that." He pulled me into his arms and kissed me. He tasted deliciously just like himself and smelled like the cologne he always wore and the soap he scrubbed with.

But I recognized diversionary tactics when I saw them. I let myself get lost in his kiss, but he wasn't off the hook. When we finally pulled apart, I smiled into his eyes. "What are you *not* telling me?"

"There are a ton of great parties that have already started right in my building. Collin and Zave headed out before I left and swore to report back on the best of them. I'm waiting for their texts even now."

"Party scout, excellent," I said. "Creative. Thoughtful. Smart, sending out the experts. And?"

"There has to be an 'and'?" He stroked my bare arm.

"The 'and' is in your voice."

He sighed, putting on an exaggerated expression of being defeated. "I'm on call for CAPSA as a security escort tonight. No drinking for me." He hesitated, looking so guilty.

I stared at him like I could not believe what he was saying. "On call, meaning at a moment's notice you'll ditch me to run across campus and walk another girl home? Leaving me to what? Party on alone and call for my own security escort?" I was so surprised that I didn't have time to mask my surprise or unhappiness.

"When you put it like that." He looked totally sheepish, but he sounded defensive. "Look, I won't let you walk home alone, okay?" It was clear he wasn't going to back down.

"I thought that was a weeknight thing?"

He shook his head. "I've had the Saturday night shift since we broke up before Christmas." His eyes pleaded with me to understand. "It was the only way to keep myself sane. I needed something to do on Saturday nights so I wouldn't think about you and go crazy with loneliness. I was dealing with all the fallout from *Her* arrest. I couldn't talk to Jason. There was no way I was going back on my girl binge, because I only wanted you." His voice broke with emotion.

My heart cracked, too. What had we done to each other? I stared at him blankly, trying to listen with an open mind.

"I needed something to keep me from falling back into an alcoholic haze. Helping others was healing. Protecting girls in a platonic, friendly way kind of made up for sleeping with so many so callously before."

He grabbed my hand and ran his thumb over the back of it.

"The CAPSA office was shorthanded." He squeezed my fingers. "Not many guys volunteer for the weekend shifts. I didn't have anything else to do. So I took Saturdays because I could be of the most help then." He took a deep breath. "I only took Fridays when you weren't playing video games with Falcon26."

"When you put it like that," I said. He was breaking my heart. How could I be upset with him for being such a great guy? And for holding things together and helping others rather than falling into a tailspin again? And yet I felt betrayed.

I pulled away from him, shocked by how little I knew about our time apart. "Why didn't you tell me before? Why did you plan this date and let me pick the activity when you knew you were already busy?"

He stuffed his hands into his jeans pockets and looked so contrite my heart clenched. "I'm sorry, El. I told the office on Monday that I couldn't do the weekends anymore. I thought I was in the clear. But one of the guys called in sick tonight and they couldn't find anyone else to take his place. So they called me less than half an hour ago, desperate."

"And you took it even though we had plans?" I couldn't keep the accusation out of my voice. Unreasonable jealousy is a callous bitch.

"They were in a bind, El. I couldn't live with myself if some girl called for an escort and ended up walking home alone and getting attacked."

When he put it that way, I felt like the world's most selfish girlfriend. "You aren't responsible for saving the world."

"Maybe not. But it's just one evening." He wasn't going to budge.

One evening out of the dwindling few we had left. In just a few months, he was graduating. I pushed the thought away.

He held his hand out to me. "We're wasting valuable party time. No one will be calling for a few hours."

I took his hand, pushing away my disappointment. I couldn't tell him I wasn't being *entirely* selfish. That I had a nefarious plan to wear down his defenses, with the help of a few drinks, and rid him of that nightmare.

That his security-escort duties just ruined it. Then again, maybe I was being ridiculous about that anyway. Maybe there was no cure. Or maybe doing good was it.

"The perils of dating Batman."

"You mean Bruce Wayne." He pulled me close.

"Maybe I mean both."

He pulled his phone from his pocket. "Zave says the best party is at the clubhouse." Logan shrugged.

"What?"

"Usually the clubhouse parties are lame. Either all the other parties are lamer or this is a freaky anomaly."

"What are you saying?"

"Don't set your expectations too high." He unlocked the car for me.

We drove with the windows down through Greek Row, which smelled like cheap beer owned the block and pounded with loud music and drunken laughter. Down the hill off campus and back up the hill on the other side to Logan's apartment complex. He parked in his usual spot. He waited for me behind the car and took my hand, leading me to the party.

Just like Greek Row, the area thrummed with music. The air held an overtone of freshly plowed fields that blended with the scent of alcohol, reminding me of the first time I'd come to a party at Logan's place. And how he'd taken me to the edge of the fields behind the complex to look at the stars. That was where I would have rather been now, gazing at the stars with Logan's arms around me. Just the two of us alone with the Milky Way and the universe beyond. Without the incentive to party to get Logan to loosen up, I wanted him all to myself.

The clubhouse was packed. The party spilled out to the surrounding area. Just as I was about to ask Logan if we could bag the party, Collin spotted us in the crowd and waved us over. He was hanging with Zave and group of friends, including a gorgeous blonde. I should have known Kelsie would be there. She looked stunning, like always. And confident. Even in the dim light I could see her eyes light up when she saw Logan. And the subtle frown she was fighting at the sight of me.

She'd been friendly to me at Thanksgiving at Logan's. I hadn't seen her since. She was Logan's friend, not really mine. But now she looked past me to Logan with barely concealed longing in her eyes. They'd been friends forever. More than friends for a while. I knew they'd been hanging out while Logan and I had been apart. I realized our split had given Kelsie hope. No matter what she said, she wasn't over Logan. She could have had just about any guy she wanted, but she wanted mine. I shivered.

She gave Logan a huge, lingering hug and yelled over the music. "What are you doing here? You're on call."

My heart stopped. Kelsie knew? He'd told her and not me.

Zave interrupted, handing me a red plastic cup of freshly tapped beer. "Drink up, Ellie. It's the only way to tolerate this party."

I gave Zave a wobbly smile. He usually wasn't perceptive or sympathetic. Then I noticed the way he was looking at Kelsie and I understood. We were comrades in the battle of love, each fighting a shadow demon of our own. I wondered how I'd missed Zave's feeling for Kelsie before. Maybe they were new? Or maybe he'd masked them around Logan. Did Logan even realize?

Logan laughed. "Yeah, Kels, thanks for twisting my arm."

Kelsie laughed in reply. "What are friends for? Anyway, you know how much we need you and the girls trust you." She swung her gaze to me as if her sense of politeness wouldn't let her ignore me forever. "Ellie, it's been forever!" She gave me an air hug that held all the warmth of a cold shower.

It hit me full force—she was the traitor, the one Logan couldn't refuse when she called and asked for his help. I was sure it was intentional on her part. I had to force myself to answer and make small talk. But the whole time, my blood pounded in my ears. I was angry with Kelsie and her machinations. Furious with Logan for letting himself be manipulated by her.

Logan didn't notice. "Come on, El. Let's dance." He pulled the beer out of my hand, set it on a nearby table, and guided me to the center of writhing dancing crowd.

Logan knew how to dance. But he completely ignored the fast beat of music and pulled me into him.

I had to let it go. I had to or risk pushing him away. I wrapped my arms around his neck and rested my head on his shoulder as bursts of drunken laughter erupted around us. I shut them all out, trying to be in the moment with Logan. For a moment, I was happy and calm. Then his phone buzzed in his pocket. I felt it through both of our jeans. He ignored it.

"Logan?"

"Yeah, I know. I just don't want to let you go."

He knew how to melt my heart. I reluctantly let go of him as he reached into his pocket and glanced at his phone. "Duty calls." To his credit, he sounded incredibly disappointed. "I'm sorry, El. I thought we'd have a few hours together. This is the earliest I've ever been called out."

I shrugged, like what can you do? "Take me home on your way."

"What? You don't want to stay at this fabulous party and hang with Collin and Zave?"

"Stop teasing. I'm not dumb enough to depend on those two to get me home safely. Let's go." I took his arm.

"It's just a short walk through the complex to the apartment. I should be back soon."

I just stared at him.

He took a deep breath. "*Seriously*, El, you want me to take you home like back to the dorm?"

I nodded. "Yeah."

"Wait for me at my place?" He looked hopeful to the point of pleading.

But I couldn't. I knew I would just be there waiting way too eagerly for him to return. And getting more upset by the minute when he didn't. It was better to be unreasonable in my own space. But I couldn't help firing a parting shot. "I'd just be in the way here. I think Zave has a thing for Kelsie."

Logan looked shocked, snorted, and laughed like I was crazy. I stared back at him, totally serious.

"No *way*." He went serious, too, when I didn't back down. He shook his head. "He doesn't have a chance." I held Logan's gaze. "Not with you in the way." I started walking to the car with my heart pounding so loud in my ears it drowned the music out.

Logan had to run to catch up to me. I kept walking, finally waiting for him at the car. He unlocked the door. We both got in in silence.

He stuck the key in the ignition, turning to me before starting the engine. "There's nothing between Kelsie and me."

I nodded. "I know you believe that. And I believe you when you say you don't have feelings for her. But she still has feelings for you. You'd see them if you weren't so busy trying to ignore them. Every time you hang out with her or share your troubles with her. Or jump when she asks you to be a security escort—"

"El, that's not fair—"

I held up a hand to silence him. "Since when is the truth fair? I know you volunteered because it's important to you. I'm sure it's important to Kelsie, too."

And I wondered if she was the one who'd gotten Logan involved with CAPSA in the first place. "But it's more than that to her. She sees it as you doing it for her as much as for the girls who need your help.

"You have to cut her loose, Logan. Hard as it is. As much as her feelings aren't your fault, they aren't really hers, either. She needs distance and space from you. She needs to realize there's no hope. Let her go, and guide her into Zave's arms. He could use her steadying influence."

We didn't speak for the rest of the drive back to the dorm. I couldn't tell whether he was upset with me or just thinking things through. He pulled to a stop in front of my dorm and gave me a quick peck. "I'll call you tomorrow."

"You better." I kissed him back, trying to show I wasn't being unreasonable or pushing him away. "Be safe out there."

He waited until I was inside the dorm before he pulled away. I watched him drive off from the side window by the front door. Just as he pulled out of sight, I realized I'd left my flowers on the seat. But I wasn't going to call him back for them.

Bre was sitting on her bed in our room, watching television in her sweats. Her hair was swept up in a ponytail with strands randomly falling free. She wasn't wearing any makeup, either.

She physically jumped when I came in, that was how surprised she was to see me. She muted the TV. "You scared me!"

"Yeah, I have that effect on people," I said.

"Only when you sneak up on them. What are you doing back? I didn't expect to see you until next weekend?" She gave me a concerned look, probably hoping I wasn't going to go into depressed mode, too. One of us needed to be somewhat up.

"Logan got called to security-escort duty." I plopped onto my bed across from her, all dressed up with no place to go.

"That's crappy." Her voice was full of commiseration. "You spent all day getting ready to go out."

"I know. I even braved sunburn." And was paying for it now.

She stared at me, waiting for the story to come out. Finally I explained, briefly.

"This is important to him."

"Okay," she said. "And you're playing the selfless girlfriend. I get it."

"Not so selfless. I'm kind of pissed, actually."

Bre laughed. "Yeah, that's obvious. What else did he do?"

"Nothing." I took a deep breath. "It's what Kelsie did." I gave Bre my theory.

"That is really crappy. Did she know you two had plans?"

I shot her my deadpan look. "What do you think?"

"Yeah, that's low. Jealous bitch. She had her shot and lost him." Bre's phone sat on the bed next to her. It buzzed. She picked it up and glanced at it. "Email." She shrugged. "Want to get her back? We could pose as an admirer on Missed Connections. Kill her with curiosity."

"No." I grinned at the thought, though. I was so not a good person at times.

"You're no fun. Want to watch a movie? Or we could go to the dining hall and pig out on ice cream." Bre kept checking her phone.

"Maybe a movie." I frowned, wondering what Bre was up to. "Are you expecting a text?"

Bre's brave smile faded and she sagged. "You caught me. Before you came home I was just going to watch a movie and do a little cyberstalking of Dan. Don't look at me like that. I just check my Twitter feed and Facebook and see if anybody mentions him. Or he posts anything interesting. I'm not going to *do* anything."

I didn't fully believe her. Not after the phone escapade. "Pathetic. Get dressed. Let's go for ice cream and a movie. It beats sitting here obsessing about guys." When she kept staring at her phone like she was ignoring me, I jumped from my bed and went to her closet. I got a pair of jeans and tossed them at her.

She deflected them with one arm and let them plop next to her on the bed. "Wait! This is interesting." Bre let out a whistle.

"What?" I turned back toward her, wary.

"'Hashtag Logan Walker is on security-escort duty tonight! Now's your chance to have a hottie walk you home. Hashtag Sweet. Hashtag sigh.'" Bre looked up at me.

"Logan's been hashtagged?" I rushed to the side of her bed. "Who tweeted that?"

Bre held out the phone for me to see. "@collegegirl25. Her profile is blank. No picture. She's a sock puppet."

I took her phone, frowned at it, and handed it back. Bre ignored me as she brought Facebook up and searched for something. "Whoa. Have you looked at

Logan's wall lately? He has a crazy number of fans. A few haters. But mostly fans."

I grabbed my phone and brought up Logan's profile, stunned when I saw what Bre had.

"Whoa!" she repeated. "Someone's created a fan page for him, too. See the link?"

I did. And I clicked on it. My stomach turned over. The page had thousands of likes. It was filled with adoring comments and selfies of girls with Logan dropping them off at their dorms, sororities, and apartments. Messages of thanks from girls he'd walked home. Messages from girls wishing he'd walk them home.

"'Logan Walker, you are so aptly named,'" Bre read. "'You can walk me home anytime. You can walk me anywhere.'" Bre made a gagging noise and rolled her eyes. She glanced at me. "Maybe you should be worried, Ellie. These are real fangirls."

"Logan," I whispered, ignoring Bre. I didn't know if I should be jealous or incredibly proud. The girls loved him, saying how funny and genuine he was. How he made them feel at ease and safe. How they supported him totally. And how they were going to cram the courthouse in support of him on the day he testified.

If I stayed away from the trial, like he'd asked me to, to the world I'd look like the biggest bitch of a girlfriend in girlfriend history. But how could I go?

Just by being Logan, he had charmed all these girls and made them fall a little bit in love with him. They adored him.

Maybe he was right. Maybe he'd never live down this trial. But not for the reasons he thought. He was becoming an object of hero worship. No one thought he was any less a man, at least not judging from this page.

I looked up at Bre. "Why didn't I know about this?"

"Because you never went looking." Her expression softened. "Don't worry. He loves you."

For now, I thought. Until fate and circumstance won.

"But it I were you," Bre added, "I'd keep an eye on him. Some of these girls are rabid."

THIRTEEN

Logan

El's flowers sat on the seat next to Logan as he pulled away. He noticed them too late. El was already out of the car and sliding through her dorm door. He thought about texting El to come get them before he took off, but she was upset with him and needed her space.

He didn't blame her. If he was honest, she was being amazingly sympathetic. If she'd blown him off to escort random guys home, he'd do something stupid. Like punching them out. He felt crappy about upsetting her. And worse about what El had said about Kelsie—was he really stringing her along? Was Kels still into him?

Shit, new complications were the last thing he needed right now with his grad school interview coming up on Wednesday, followed by Mom's Weekend and the

trial and the business deal with Amber at risk. Everything felt like it was about to spin apart and he was
barely holding it together.

He shouldn't have let Kels talk him in to taking this
shift tonight. He realized that now. It was just that he'd
hurt Kels in the past, too. He owed her. Until El pointed out the obvious, he'd thought he was just helping
out a friend for a good cause.

A lot of people thought he was cocky and arrogant.
But he wasn't all that vain. Not really. Maybe that was
why he had a hard time believing Kels still had a thing
for him after the way he'd treated her. Especially now,
when he was so obviously in love with El.

He was going to have to fix all this shit. He just did-
n't know how right now. He pulled into a spot in a
parking lot near the science library and put his security-escort pass in the car window before hopping out,
putting on his security-escort vest, and making the
climb uphill to the library entrance.

The girl Logan was supposed to escort was waiting
for him between the double doors at the entrance. The
library closed at eleven on Saturday nights. It was
shutting down now. Logan wondered why it was open
at all past about three in the afternoon.

The girl was short and chubby. His grandma would
have said pleasantly plump. Her hair was a mousy
brown, cut in a style that didn't flatter her round face.
The heavy backpack she had slung over one shoulder
looked like it was threatening to tip her over backward.

"Amy?" he asked, though it was obvious she was
waiting for him and it was hard to miss his neon securi-

ty vest. He extended his hand. "Logan Walker. Your security escort tonight."

"Logan Walker. *The* Logan Walker?" She hesitated like she was surprised.

"I don't know about *the* Logan Walker. Last time I checked there were hundreds of us in the country. Maybe thousands. Walker is a pretty common name. I think I'm the only one on campus, though. If that's what you mean."

"Sorry. You're kind of famous." She didn't sound horribly awed, but she did act flustered.

"Infamous, you mean."

She regarded him with round eyes. "No, I think you have a pretty good rep."

"I don't know where you heard that. You'd better check your sources." He stretched his hand out to her. "Let me carry that backpack for you."

"A gentleman, too? Is carrying my backpack part of the service? Or are you trying to earn a tip? FYI, I don't have any cash on me."

He laughed. "No tips. We aren't allowed to take them. But it would make me feel better if you let me carry that thing. You're going to give yourself back problems hauling that thing everywhere."

She slid it off her shoulder and handed it to him. It was just as heavy as it looked. He slung it over his shoulder and held the door open for her. "Where are we going?"

She gave him the name of her dorm. From where he was parked, it was just as easy to walk her home as to walk to the parking lot and drive her.

"Why isn't a guy like you out partying tonight?" Amy asked as they walked toward the footbridge that crossed the street to her dorm.

He grinned at her, but the question cut him. "How do you know I wasn't?"

"You seem to be sober enough," she said. "I don't smell alcohol on your breath and you aren't weaving."

He shrugged. "As a matter of fact, I was partying when you called. With my girl. Do you want me to put my finger on my nose and walk a straight line?"

Amy smiled at him and giggled. "Proof not needed." She was beginning to puff and wheeze. "She must be really understanding."

He slowed down. He had long legs and a habit of accidentally walking too fast for the girls. "Yeah, she is. She understands it's important to me to protect others from being victimized." It was only a partial lie.

"Even if it means leaving her to party alone? That's a *really* great girl. And you're a trusting guy. You better hang on to her. Most of the girls I know would tell you where to go, as in someplace really warm. And I don't mean Hawaii."

He laughed, but Amy had pricked his conscience again. Running out on El, no matter how just the cause, wasn't fair to her. He changed the subject. "Tell me—why is a cute girl like you studying on a Saturday night and not out partying?"

They passed beneath a streetlight. Amy blushed. He'd flustered her.

"I'm trying to keep my scholarship."

"Wise plan," he said.

They chatted about nothing until they reached Amy's dorm. He waited while she got her key out and unlocked the door. Then he handed her backpack to her.

"This really isn't just PR for you, is it?" Amy sounded surprised by the realization.

Logan wasn't sure whether he should be offended or not. Instead, he laughed. "No."

"Sorry!" She blushed again. "I didn't mean to insult you. It's just, a guy like you giving up his Saturday nights isn't typical. And with the trial coming up, I thought...I thought wrong, obviously." She stared at her feet a moment and laughed at herself before meeting his eye. "Thank you, Logan."

He nodded. "Anytime." He turned to leave.

"Logan?"

He stopped and turned to look at Amy over his shoulder.

She was holding her phone. "Good luck at the trial. It's really brave, what you're doing. We're all on your side. I hope they put that *bitch* away forever." She hesitated. "Would you mind if I took a selfie of the two of us?"

Logan answered a steady stream of calls. He took the last one at four in the morning and finally headed home to crash, wondering if at this point he should pull an all-nighter. A wave of sleep passed over him as he entered his apartment, and he decided sleep was the better option.

He stumbled toward bed, pausing to pull his phone out of his jeans. He was dead tired, but that didn't stop him from checking his fan page. Sure enough, half a dozen new selfies with him and girls he'd walked home were posted. He was becoming more and more of a campus celebrity. And that wasn't the point. He didn't want celebrity to interfere with the job. Maybe he should give the security-escort gig up. He wished he knew who had started the page. It embarrassed him. If he could, he'd take it down. He hadn't even mentioned it to El, fearing it would upset her.

He stripped off his jeans, pulled back the covers, and fell into bed.

He slept until two in the afternoon, only waking then because Collin was playing his music too loud in the living room and the neighbor was banging on the wall in a vain attempt to get Collin to turn it down.

Logan threw his arm across the bed, reaching for El. The disappointment of being alone struck him hard. He'd been a shitty boyfriend. He couldn't blame El for going home. But he missed her. She was like air to him. He needed her, but sometimes he took her for granted.

He took a deep breath. No El in his bed with her cute, messy bed hair and sweet, sexy morning eyes next to him to greet him with a sleepy smile. No nightmare of El morphing into *Her*, either, for the first time in a week. He'd have to be stupid not to worry that there was a connection his mind was making between El and *Her*. He'd lost control with both women, but with El it was pure pleasure. He had to get rid of that damn nightmare.

El. He had to make things right with her. The date last night was supposed to end in hot, urgent makeup sex. There was no one else to blame—he'd blown it by being terminally helpful and playing hero to strangers when he should have been El's.

He'd hurt her feelings when he'd pushed her away after the last nightmare. Even though she insisted she was fine, he knew she was stinging. He couldn't explain without describing the nightmare in frightening, embarrassing detail. Whatever that shitty dream revealed about him, it wasn't flattering. How would El feel if she knew his subconscious equated her with *Her*? He couldn't chance her knowing.

Running off to do Kels' bidding for CAPSA was asininely insane, too. Yeah, he was a douchebag. He sat up, determined to shower and take El's flowers back to her. Wishing El was there to shower with him.

As he slid his legs over the side of the bed, his cell phone rang. He glanced at it. Amber. Again. He picked up reluctantly. This had to be more crappy news. "Hey."

"Logan? You sound hung over."

"Sleepy. I just woke up."

"At two in the afternoon? Sorry, I've forgotten what it's like in college. Two is early after a Saturday night. I should have called later. My apologies." She laughed. Amber was always laughing, even when things weren't funny. Her laugh had an edge to it this time, like she was hiding something—bad news, probably. Why else would she be calling?

"Now's fine. I had to get up to answer the phone an-yway," he said, although he'd been awake before it rang. "What's up?"

"A bit of bad news, actually. I can wait until you're more awake? Want to grab a cup of coffee and call me back later?" For the first time since he'd known her, Amber sounded tentative.

"You have my attention. I'm awake now. Give it to me straight."

"I just got back from an emergency board meeting. The board feels it needs more time to control the ru-mors Core is spreading about our IPO. I tried to reas-sure them, but my arguments fell on deaf ears. Sometimes that old gentlemen's club is just a bunch of bastards." She sounded upset. Angry. Amber rarely lost her cool. She took a deep breath. "Sorry. I should-n't let my meeting frustration show through. The board believes if we go ahead with the IPO as planned, it won't be as successful as we'd like." Amber, always the politician.

"They want to cancel it?" Logan's head spun.

"No, just delay it."

"Delay it!" He sounded like a damn parrot. "How long? A week? Two weeks?"

Amber hesitated, and he knew it was *really* bad news. "Four to six months."

He swore beneath his breath and his mouth went dry. He didn't have four to six months.

"You'll get your money, Logan," she said. "I swear to you I will. This will be the best investment you've ever made. It's just..."

She hesitated again, a long, drawn- out pause that was so pregnant it was about to give birth. "They're running low on the capital we've given them. They need more money to keep running and meeting payroll and paying suppliers and making product improvements.

"Without an infusion of cash, they'll go under. We'll all lose everything. All the venture capitalists are being asked—required, really—to contribute more cash to the cause."

Logan felt nauseated and dizzy, as if he was hung over, but without the pleasure of having had a drink. He didn't have any more money. He'd invested everything. "How much more?"

"Twenty thousand should cover your share."

It may as well have been a million. He didn't have it. "And if I can't pay?"

"That's not an option, Logan. Sorry. You either pay and play with the team, or you're out. That's the way these guys operate."

He had been hoping she'd offer to buy him out. At this point, he just wanted his money back. He opened his mouth to ask but she cut him off.

"I'd chip in for you if I could, Logan, but I'm strapped right now, too. My share is going to tap me out. We're all bleeding money right now. Is there any chance you could ask Harlan for a loan?"

"No fucking way!" The words burst out of his mouth automatically.

There was another long pause. "Think it over, Logan." Amber's voice remained smooth and calm, almost sympathetic. "You have some leverage with Harlan right now. Use it. You have a week and a half to come up with the money."

Money, money, money. It always came down to money. How was he going to get it without going to his dad and admitting what a huge mistake he'd made?

Logan had a few ideas, none of them particularly palatable. He rifled through his desk and pulled out the stack of job offers he'd been ignoring. He had until the end of May to respond to most of them. Time to figure things out. Until Amber forced his hand. The offers all came with signing bonuses. All he had to do was agree to take one of these jobs and the money was his. Not the full amount he needed, but enough to stall until he could come up with the rest. Just take a job far away from El and his problems would be solved.

Grad school seemed out of the question now with possible salvation staring him in the face. But what would he do about El?

Logan showered and dressed. Collin was sitting at the kitchen table as Logan grabbed a bowl of cereal. He'd turned his music down.

"Quiet in here," Logan said.

Collin grinned. "I like tweaking those assholes next door." He laughed. "You're up early. I didn't expect to see your smiling face for another couple of hours."

"Yeah, I was gently rocked out of bed by some heavy bass."

Collin laughed as Logan sniffed the bottle and poured the last of the milk into his cereal.

"Hey, dude," Logan said, "You wouldn't have some cash you could lend me?"

Collin shrugged. "Yeah, sure. What do you need? Twenty? A hundred?"

"Twenty thousand. I'd pay it back with interest in six months."

Collin whistled. "Dude, you know Dad has put me on a tight budget. If I had it, I'd give it to you. What do you need it for?"

Logan took a bite of cereal, trying to play it cool. "That deal with Amber."

"Oh shit, man. Amber is screwing you over? That's brutal."

"We've hit a snag. Things will work out."

Zave staggered out of his room and joined them.

"You got any cash, man?" Collin asked him. "Logan is short on funds."

"You've come to the wrong bank," Zave said. "The old man froze my assets to curb my reckless spending. I can lend you a twenty."

"He needs about a thousand times that. Amber," Collin said.

"Amber, that little minx. You didn't knock her up, did you?"

Collin shook his head and rolled his eyes. "Wake up! An abortion doesn't cost twenty thou. It's that business deal she sucked Logan into last summer. We would have been in, too, if we'd had the money."

"Oh, yeah," Zave said. "I remember now. Sorry, Logan. Wish I could help."

Logan nodded. "Yeah, it's probably best this way. You know what they say—never a borrower or a lender be. Borrowing from your friends is a great way to kill a friendship."

Logan had left El's flowers in the car overnight. They were looking sadly in need of water as he unlocked his car and got in. He thought about stopping to get fresh ones, then thought of El accusing him of buying her another bribe.

He got lucky and found a parking spot on campus not far from her dorm. He texted her as he bounced up the steps with the droopy flowers in hand, hoping acting confident would give him confidence. To the world, Logan was never short on it. Inside himself, he was sadly lacking.

She met him at the door, her hair tumbling around her face. Her chest rising and falling rapidly as if she'd taken the steps two at a time in an effort to get to him as quickly as possible.

He had that gut reaction he'd gotten since the first time he'd seen her. His skin tingled, on fire for her. She was hot, but she made him burn. Deeper than that, an emotional connection sizzled between them, even when tensions were strained. It was crazy, really. It seemed like he should have more in common with Kels—their shared childhood, economic status, shared experience of rape. But he'd never clicked with her like he had with El. Never needed Kels like he needed El.

El tucked a strand of hair behind her ear as her gaze ran from his face to the flowers. "Secondhand flowers? For me? You shouldn't have."

Her smile lit up his day and his dick went hard at the sight of her. He knew he'd made the right decision in not buying new flowers. "Returning them to their rightful owner. You forgot them last night." He put on his most apologetic look.

She shook her head like she could see through him and his apologetic looks, to the core of him that was uncertain and eager. "I realized I'd forgotten them just after you pulled away to play hero."

Was it his imagination or had she emphasized the words *pulled away?*

"El, about that—"

"Don't, Logan." As she took the flowers from him, her fingers brushed his, lingering a second longer than necessary, adding to the flaming heat he felt for her. "Poor, thirsty bouquet." She glanced at him. "Come in while I put them in water." She turned and walked away, expecting him to follow her.

He was the one who was thirsty and parched for her. He followed obediently.

She led him to her room, not giving him an opening to kiss her.

When she paused with her key in the door and her back to him, he pressed up against her, grinding his hard dick into her cute little ass. When she didn't move away, his breath came faster.

She ignored him while he pressed his advantage. But she didn't swat him away, either. She swung the door open. "Don't worry. Bre's out. We have the place all to ourselves."

Was that flirtation in her voice? Was she giving him permission? Issuing an invitation?

She let him in, stepping quickly away from him. Before he could reach for her, she went to her closet and rummaged for a vase, leaving him standing hard and ready in the doorway.

"Shut the door. And lock it." She bent over and pulled open a built-in drawer at the base of the closet.

He did as she commanded and watched as she got a cheap glass vase from the drawer and smiled to herself.

"I don't blame you for being upset." His heart was hammering so hard he could feel it all the way to the bulge in his jeans.

"Am I?" She went to her desk and grabbed a pair of scissors. Then she walked past him to the sink, cutting so close to him he caught a whiff of her perfume as her hip brushed his.

The agony was sweet. He was bound up and getting more uncomfortable by the minute.

"Are you what?" He fought to keep his breathing even. He itched to touch her and show her how sorry he was.

"Upset." She filled the vase with water and set it on the edge of the sink. "I'm not, Logan. Not really. I'll tend to you in a minute. These flowers need me right now."

Shit. Like he didn't?

She pulled the plastic wrapping away from the bouquet and frowned like she was looking for something. "There's no freshness packet." It sounded like an indictment.

He almost laughed. Her concern was so sweet and ridiculous at the same time. The flowers were way past fresh, almost past redemption. A lot like him.

"I'm sorry," he said again. At that minute he would have apologized for anything to get her to forgive him.

She shrugged. "Wish I had some sugar for them."

He could use some sugar, too. Shit, he was desperate.

She cut the bottoms off the stems over her wastebasket before shoving the whole ensemble into the vase. She brushed past him again, too close. It had to be on purpose. Her breast brushed his arm, tantalizing and firm. She was wearing his favorite lace bra. He knew she was. He could tell by the natural feel of her.

She set the vase on her desk. She had her back to him, but he imagined she was staring at the flowers. Or maybe out the window. She bent and opened her laptop. Tapped on the keys while he ogled her.

When she turned around to face him, she had tears in her eyes. But she didn't look exactly sad or angry. He couldn't figure her out.

"How come you didn't tell me about this?" She stepped aside so he could see what she was talking about.

His fan page glowed on her screen. Amy's selfie was pinned to the top over dozens of others. He had his arm around Amy like they were palling around. He was flashing what he thought of as his disarming grin. It covered a multitude of situations and sins and masked his true emotions when needed. Easygoing Logan, that was what the grin made him. Amy was blushing like a girl who had a crush on him.

He was in deep shit now. "I didn't do that. I didn't post that page. The damn thing embarrasses me. I wish the owner would take it down."

"Don't be embarrassed. You're a hero. Your fans adore you." Her voice broke with emotion.

But for the life of him he couldn't tell what the emotion was—good or bad? He swallowed hard, wanting her to understand. Wanting her period.

He took a step into her. She didn't move away. That was good sign. It had to be. He cupped her cool cheeks in his hands. "I love you, El. Just you. Only you. Always you."

"But you care about others, too." She looked at him with wide eyes. "And that's what I love about you." She wrapped her arms around his neck and played with the fine hairs at the back of it until he shivered with pleasure.

He lost control then, tipping her face to his and kissing her hard, inserting his tongue into her mouth and toying with it until she whimpered.

He cupped her totally grab-able ass, pulling her against his dick. She pressed her chest against his so tightly he swore he could feel the beat of her heart through his shirt and hers as it matched the wild, needy rhythm of his.

She unwrapped her arms from his neck and slid them down his chest, hesitating at his fly, skimming the bulge straining to get out, teasing him.

His breath caught. He pulled away from her kiss and cupped her breasts, mounding them in his hands, feeling the lace through her blouse. He bent and kissed the tops of them that peeked above the V-neck of her shirt. He felt the rise of her chest, shallow and excited as he licked the top of her breasts, and inserted his tongue in the valley between them. Her nipples popped up, erect beneath his touch through a layer of lace and cotton. He rubbed them with his thumbs as he licked and slowly moved down to suck on her nipples through her thin blouse.

"I want you, Logan," she whispered. "Now." She unzipped his fly and pulled open the warm denim of his pants.

He was long, hard, throbbing as she pulled him out. Wet at the tip and ready to enter her. Barely hanging on and hoping he didn't come in her hand as she stroked him. She walked him backwards to her bed while he unzipped her jeans and pulled a condom out of his pocket.

He had it unwrapped and ready by the time they reached they edge of the bed. She took it from him and rolled it onto his purple, throbbing dick, as he tried not to come into the condom. He should have taken her shirt off, but he was too far gone now to bother removing clothes that weren't an absolute impediment. Too close to embarrassing himself by losing control and being premature.

He pulled her jeans down around her hips and slid one finger beneath her panties and into her. She gasped and kicked free of her pants. She was so ready for him. As he tried to spin her around to take her on the bed, she dug in and resisted him.

"Let me be on top, Logan, *please*."

His heart beat a new rhythm, a beat called fear. It was irrational, but it was strong and ready to derail this reunion. He couldn't let it happen. He needed her so badly, yet her request was so simple. So reasonable. How could he refuse without looking like the world's biggest douche?

He sensed a pattern. She'd tried this before. He cursed whatever women's magazine had given her this idea that she needed to be on top. But deep down he worried she knew what she was doing, that she suspected what his nightmares were. He couldn't let her into them. He wouldn't.

He cupped her butt. "Climb up on me, El." He hoisted her and she jumped, wrapping her legs around his waist.

He slid her down onto him, entering her slickness with one great upward thrust. This was where he belonged—with her. With El.

She gasped and pressed her forehead against his. "Logan."

"Last night, walking those girls home, all I could think about was having sex with you. And what a douche I was for leaving you. All I could think about was this—pressing you up against the wall and losing myself in you."

Before she could protest, he bypassed the bed, pressing her back up against the empty wall beside the bed. Holding her still and firm as he thrust into her again and again. Fighting climax. Trying desperately to maintain control.

Her back banged against the wall with each thrust. She squeezed him and moaned. He thrust again, deeper, harder, feeling the fire build. Fighting it as every muscle in his body coiled hard. Sliding into her, wishing the condom wasn't between them. At the same time glad it was there because it dulled things just enough to give him some control.

She whimpered and gasped.

He took her shoulder in his mouth and sucked and gently bit, grazing it with his teeth until she gasped again. He felt her tipping over the edge, losing herself, felt her body tighten and relax against him. He lost control then, too, and flew over the precipice with her.

When it was over, he rested his sweaty forehead against hers, still pressing her against the wall. "Adventurous enough for you?" He kissed the tip of her nose.

"I don't know." She was breathing heavily and clinging to him, but there was a smile in her voice. "I can't think."

"Me either." He spun around, still cupping her butt and holding her up while she clamped her legs around him. He let go of her ass for just a second, teasing her.

She screamed and clasped him; pressed her head against his shoulder. "Don't drop me!" She was still breathing hard. "How can you even stand? My legs are jelly. If you set me down, I'll collapse."

He whispered in her ear, "Should I test it?"

She squealed again, laughing and holding on to him for dear life. "Don't you dare!"

He kissed her neck and bent his knees like he was going to collapse.

"No!"

"I can't stand any longer, either." He fell onto his back on her bed with El on top of him, still inside her. His hard-on wouldn't go away. She was so slick and wet he was tempted to go at it again. He arched up, thrusting into her, teasing, trying not to think about *Her.* Trying to push *Her* away. "Come on, El, have a ride."

"Shut up. Just shut up. I have to catch my breath. Why don't you? Are you some kind of mutant alien?"

"It's an athlete thing."

"Don't you have to, you know, first?" She arched her brow like he should fill in the blank.

"What, El?" He couldn't resist teasing her.

The way a blush crept up her neck and into her face was so cute it only kept him turned on. "You know, reload or something." She made a wilting motion with her finger.

He grabbed her hand and kissed it. "Not going to happen while I'm still inside."

She pulled her legs from beneath his back, slid off him and rolled next to him, resting her head on his shoulder. "So reload, then."

He laughed and wrapped his arms around her. "So you were spying on me last night. Because you missed me so much?"

She snuggled into him and tucked her head beneath his chin. "I wasn't *spying* on *you*. I found out *accidentally* while Bre was spying on Dan. Big difference."

"I don't even want to know how Bre found me while she was spying on Dan." He took a deep breath and ran his fingers through her hair. A wave of contentment washed over him. He wanted to drift off to sleep with his arms around her. But girls got offended when he fell asleep after. They didn't realize it was the ultimate compliment. Instead, he pulled the condom off and dropped it into the wastebasket nearby.

She sighed. "There was a moment last night when I was jealous of the girls who got to be with you. And missing you and feeling bad because I was jealous of what you needed to do. I thought about calling CAPSA for an escort and requesting you."

"Why didn't you?" he asked, flattered. He wished she would have. Then he could have spent the rest of the night "walking her home."

She lifted her head and looked him in the eye. "Would you have come?"

"In a heartbeat." He paused. "I felt so shitty about leaving you I almost bailed anyway."

"I'm glad you didn't." She sounded almost fierce. "As much as I missed you, if this is something you need to do to heal, then you need to do it." She pushed up and looked him in the eye. "Logan, you have so much support here. That's what I realized when I saw the fan page.

"I'm proud of you. All those girls you've helped. How safe you've made them feel." She didn't sound the slightest bit sarcastic. El was completely genuine, which surprised and pleased him.

"You belong here. Even if I have to fight off flirty girls and share your heroics with them." She chucked his chin playfully. "And put up with them posting pictures of themselves with you."

"I have my phone." He reached into his jeans pocket. "I'll take a selfie of us now." He pulled his phone out and held it out of her reach as she swatted at it, trying to get it away.

"Take that picture and I'll kill you."

"Why? I like the way you look after sex. You're dressed from the waist up." He wrapped one arm around her waist, enjoying the feel of her breasts rubbing against him as she struggled to get the phone.

She bent down and kissed him, taking him by surprise as she sucked on his lip and teased her tongue around his mouth. He relaxed. She pulled the phone from his grip, laughing as she broke away from the kiss. She studied him and her expression became suddenly serious. "Stay here for grad school where everyone loves you."

His heart stopped. He froze. He muttered. "El, I haven't made up my mind."

"I know." She rested her head against his chest again. "I promised not to pressure you. But I don't want you to go and leave me behind." She clutched his shoulder.

He sighed. "I don't want to leave you, either. But it's not that simple."

She nodded, but she looked so sad he just wanted to cradle her. He grabbed her and pressed her against him, feeling her heart beat with his again.

When El broke the silence, her voice was too bright, like she was trying hard to be normal. "What time did you finally get home?"

"Four."

"Early, then."

"Yeah. Early." He was a crappy boyfriend. "About grad school—"

"Yes?" She looked so damned optimistic.

He had to come clean. "My interview is Wednesday. I'm thinking of canceling it. Something's come up."

CHAPTER FOURTEEN

Ellie

"Canceling." I sat up and stared at Logan, looking away as a surge of panic coursed through me. "You can't be serious. You promised. You *promised*." I pulled my blouse down and straightened my panties. Then I slid off the bed and looked around for my jeans, trying to rein my emotions in before I said something I'd regret.

"El, come on. Listen to me. I have a good reason." He sat up and zipped his fly.

I found my jeans and pulled them on, zipping, still not looking at him. "Then tell me."

"Like this? Now?" He slid his feet over the edge of the bed.

"Yes. Why not? You just got what you wanted."

He jumped to his feet and grabbed me by the arms before I could move or think about running. "I'm in trouble, El. I don't have the money for grad school. I'm about to lose everything."

I stared at him, unable to grasp what he was saying. More trouble? Like we needed more.

"It's the deal with Amber." He started explaining.

I was so upset, I barely heard what he was saying until he said he needed twenty thousand dollars. He looked as close to despondent as Logan ever got. Which scared me.

"I'm obligated to contribute my share. If the company goes under, we'll all lose everything and I'm done. My original investment will go up in smoke."

I kept staring at him, trying to let it sink in.

"I can get the money, part of it, if I take one of my job offers and get my signing bonus. Then I'll stall them while I get the rest."

"No," I said, shaking my head. "No."

"There's no other way, El."

I kept shaking my head.

"What do you want me to do? Ask Dad for the money like Amber suggested?" He looked at me like he hoped I wasn't a traitor like her. "Admit I'm a failure?"

Like I would ever betray him like that. "No!" I wrapped my arms around him.

"I won't ask him to pay for grad school, either, El. I can't."

"Ask Caleb for the investment money. That's chump change to your big-shot big-league baby brother."

Logan stiffened. "I thought of that. But I can't ask Caleb. Going to my little brother for money is like going to Dad. Everyone hits Caleb up for cash. I don't want to be like everyone." His heart pounded in my ear.

"You aren't everyone. You're his brother," I said into his chest. "He owes you for all the years you played pitcher to his catcher. It was the two of you who made him what he is. Without you, there would be no major leagues for Caleb. He has to know that." I wasn't backing down. In my mind, Caleb owed Logan much more.

Logan sighed and rested his chin on my head. "Okay. You're right. Caleb owes me. But I'm not sure he'll see it that way." He sounded so defeated that it should have broken my heart.

I squeezed Logan, selfishly relieved, feeling guilty for pushing Logan to beg his brother for money and hoping I hadn't misjudged Caleb. That he wasn't a bigger douchebag than I thought.

I bit my lip and went for broke. "I'm going with you to your interview. For moral support. I'll wait outside and be there to cheer you on."

"Don't trust me?" he said, sounding more like the playful Logan I loved.

"Can't stay away from you."

Logan thought he'd won. Thought he'd outwitted me when he pulled me on top of him on the bed when there was no chance of completing the act. I'd been too transparent. Somehow he had caught on to my plan.

I kept hoping what he'd allowed me to do was enough. That just playing with me on top was enough to break the cycle of nightmares. But that night he woke in a cold sweat again. He blamed it on business worries, but I wondered.

Monday and Tuesday flew by. We made love like humping bunnies. We couldn't keep our hands off each other. But through it all, I noticed Logan liked to be in control. He resisted when I tried to take charge. And teased and played to distract me and regain control. I had to make him see I wasn't *Her*.

Zave gave us a celebrity name, Loganel, and used it until it was just plain annoying. I believed there was some passive aggression behind it. That Zave was getting subtly back for blocking his chance with Kelsie. I made up my mind to help Zave win her, if I could. Kill two birds. Though it would have been better if Kelsie found some guy totally out of the gang, it didn't look like that was going to happen.

Logan and I didn't mention the money he needed. If I had it, any portion of it that would have made a difference, I would have given it to him and never cared if he paid me back. I was getting by. Jason was as generous with me as I would let him be. But I was stingy with his money, not letting him spoil me.

He had offered repeatedly to pay my tuition or room and board. He felt it was his duty. The least he could do for not paying a penny of child support while I was growing up. Not that that was his fault. I refused to take it. Paying for college was my responsibility. It was not what I wanted from him as a dad.

If this had been a private university, as his daughter, I would have been entitled to free tuition. But it wasn't. I let him use his employee discount to help me out at the student bookstore and for software I needed. And buy me dinner and coffee now and then. I took the odd bits of fun money from him when he absolutely insisted. But that was it.

I was tempted to ask him for money now. But he had the new baby coming and I couldn't make myself do it. I hadn't found him because I wanted money from him. I didn't want the thought to even cross his mind.

On Wednesday morning, I stood in Logan's bathroom in my panties and bra, getting ready to go with him to his interview. I was preoccupied with dreams of Logan deciding on grad school and staying with me for my senior year. Thinking if he did we could move in together. Officially. Wondering how I'd tell Jason, my super protective, surprisingly conservative bio dad. I brushed my teeth on autopilot, poured a glass of water, and reached for my birth-control pill pack without thinking, just like I did every day.

As I picked up the pack, it shook in my hand. *Nerves for Logan*, I thought. I had trouble popping the pill through the foil. When I finally succeeded, I dropped the pill in the sink. It slid around the slick ceramic finish while I dove for it. I caught it just in time to keep it from slipping down the drain.

My heart roared in my ears as I stared at it in my hand, with its coating melting in my palm from the wetness of the sink. I shivered, cold and nauseated. Dumbfounded as I realized what my subconscious had known all along—I was staring at the last active pill in the pack.

In a few days, my period should hit. *Would* hit. But there was that element of dark, forceful doubt. That voice in my head. *You've been reckless, Ellie. You're going to turn out just like Mom. Bitter and alone.*

I pushed the voices away and swallowed the pill. *I haven't been careless. I haven't missed a pill. We used condoms every time.*

The fear may have been totally unreasonable and unfounded, but it was powerfully real. Totally reactionary. And completely uncontrollable and subconscious. Like Logan's. So real I had to sit on the toilet seat and put my head between my knees to fight off the lightheaded, dizzy feeling.

You'll be okay. You'll be okay. You'll be okay.

I took long, deep breaths, trying to get control of myself. Trying to think of ordinary things. Like, of course my period was due for Mom's Weekend. Of course it was. Perfect timing. I would be all fat and bloaty and broken out while my mom was skinny and hot.

My heartbeat slowed, trying to find its normal rhythm. Was this how Logan handled the fear that attacked from his subconscious every time I climbed on top of him and tried to take control during sex? I admired him more than ever. He handled it better than I did.

I swallowed hard. *You'll be okay. You'll be okay.*

I was going to have to attack when his subconscious was asleep and couldn't fight back. But how?

Logan pounded on the bathroom door. "El? Are you about ready? It's almost time to go."

"I'm fine," I said. "Give me a minute. I'll be out in a second."

You'll be okay. You'll be okay.

I stood up slowly and slid into the little sundress I'd hung to steam in the bathroom. I would not make Logan late for the interview I'd insisted he take. I put on some lipgloss and steeled myself. *You'll be okay.*

When I opened the door, Logan was sitting on his bed, looking so completely adorable my subconscious fears relented and subsided. I whistled. "You look hot. Totally sexy."

He was dressed in a pale blue fitted dress shirt and tailored suit with skinny slacks that showed off his athletic build and made me want to run my hands over his shoulders. Stylish leather shoes. Happy socks with a funky geometric pattern in shades of blue that complemented his shirt. No tie.

"That's too bad. I was going for professional." He flashed me a lopsided grin.

I knew him well enough to know he was nervous, even if he didn't look it. "You'll do great." I walked over and stood between his legs as I bent and kissed him. And ran my hands over the sleeves of his shirt, copping a feel of his biceps. "I could just throw you back on the bed and take you here."

"Fine with me." He fell backward.

I climbed on him and sat on his crotch, letting the skirt of my sundress spread out around us. I rubbed against his crotch, feeling his hardness through his slacks and my panties. His eyes were dark with desire, but his body was taut, ready to strike and his face was paling. If I had believed this was my moment to cure him, I would have taken it. But I knew his MO. In another second, he'd flip me over.

I went wet at the thought. "Nice try." I slid off him before I gave him an embarrassing wet spot on his crotch. "You're going to the interview."

"But not as a happily sexed man, evidently." He frowned.

"Shut up! I thought we're running late. There's no time."

"There's always time for a quickie. Two minutes is all I need."

"Maybe I need more time."

He slid a hand beneath my skirt and slipped a finger into my panties. "Doesn't feel that way to me."

I pushed his hand away and stood up. "Focus, Logan."

"I am."

"Not on me, on the interview."

He sighed like he'd lost this battle.

"We have a ton to do today. After your interview, we'll go pick up my Mom's Weekend sweatshirts—"

"That's supposed to be an incentive?" He rolled his eyes.

I laughed and ignored his disdain. I lowered my voice like we were conspirators. "I ordered Mom a size too large."

He shook his head and sat up. "You're kidding. She won't wear it."

"Not kidding." I should have walked out of the danger zone. But I didn't. I stood between his legs again and traced the broad line of his shoulders, ostensibly smoothing out any wrinkles in his shirt. "Wear this to dinner at Jason and Lyssa's tonight?"

He gave me his skeptical look. "Seriously? I'm changing the first chance I get."

I laughed. "You look so *good* in it."

He ran his hands up my bare thighs beneath my dress. "And you look so good out of this."

We arrived at the college of engineering almost late for Logan's interview. "Screw it! We'll have to park in the garage."

"I thought that's what we just did?" I grinned at him. It turned out he was right—two minutes was enough.

He grinned back. He squealed into the first available spot. We jumped out and walked hand in hand into the building until we reached the departmental offices.

Logan stopped me outside the door. "Seriously, El. I don't need you to hold my hand from here." He rubbed his thumb over mine and kissed it. "Much as I like holding your hand."

"I'm embarrassing you." I kissed his hand right back.

"I can handle this interview alone." His eyes got that sexy look again. "You'll only distract me."

"We can't have that." I kissed him lightly on the lips, trying not to transfer my pink lipgloss to him. "Come find me when you're done. I'll be in the lounge."

The student study lounge was at the end of the hall. It was mostly full of guys. I found an empty seat by the windows and checked my messages. I had one from Mom.

What kind of alcohol do you want for your jello shots?

I rolled my eyes and ignored it as my phone buzzed in my hand and another popped up.

What's the weather supposed to be like this weekend? What kind of clothes do I need to bring?

And so the sense of gloom, preceded by the sulfurous smoke of her text messages, began to settle over my happy college town. I resisted the urge to text back that the only clothes she needed were mom-type clothes—any style she wanted except skanky and cougar. I slid the phone back into my purse.

Logan found me half an hour later. He wore a huge smile.

"Looks like you survived the lion's den."

"They went easy on me. Ready to pick up sweatshirts?"

The day was partly sunny with a few nonthreatening clouds scudding across the sky and windy, like always. Logan drove us to a small old house at the edge of Greek Row and had to cruise to find a parking spot. There was a line out the door of mostly girls picking up the matchy Geed sweatshirts for Mom's Weekend. The sweatshirt enterprise was a private venture by an enterprising student, who ran the whole operation. It was a great idea. The Greeks all had their matching gear. Why not the Geeds?

Logan took one look at the line and laughed. "So this is where all the girls are." He took his phone out of his pocket.

"What are you doing?"

"Texting Collin and Zave to get their butts over here. There are some hot girls in line. I wonder if it's too late for them to buy sweatshirts?"

"I wonder why you're noticing hot girls."

"Just playing wingman for my buds."

"Nice save." I bumped him playfully in the arm. "I also wonder if it's too late to get into the matching-sweatshirt business. Judging from the length of the line, someone is making a killing."

It took nearly an hour to make our way through the line, into the beat-up house with its ratty furniture, and pick up my sweatshirts and Dex's.

When we finally got back outside, the sun was shining full on and the clouds were disappearing. I grabbed the smallest of the sweatshirts from the pile Logan was carrying, snapped a picture and texted it to Mom along with the message, *Clothing problem solved. Won't we look cute?*

"Sending her a picture of the extra small for Dex's mom is false advertising," Logan said. "You're delusional if you believe Melissa is going to wear a baggy sweatshirt."

Sometimes I forgot he knew her. I hated being reminded. I shrugged. "A girl can dream."

"That's what I love about you, El." His eyes danced. "Your naïve optimism."

"*That's* what you love about me?"

He flashed me his wolfish grin. "One thing. One of the many things."

I folded the sweatshirt and tucked it under my arm as I texted Dex. "Let's go drop Dex's off."

Dex was in his room waiting for us when we arrived. He rubbed his hands together eagerly, handed me a twenty that was part of the deal, and reached out for his gear. "Logan. Ellie. Welcome to my lair." He took his shirts from Logan and hefted them, fingering the fabric.

I laughed as I watched him and pocketed my cash. "What are you? A sweatshirt connoisseur?"

"Just checking the fabric. It's full of sizing." He frowned. "Mom will be suspicious if I wash them. She likes that fresh stiffness and the new smell." He waved us over to a chair, where he had a pile of sweatshirts. He rummaged around and pulled one from the pile. "Fortunately." He held up a finger. "I've thought of everything."

"It's nice to be friends with the great brain," I said to Logan, who tried not to snigger.

Dex wagged his finger at me. "I heard that, Ellie." He held up the plain sweatshirt. "Nothing on it, agreed? It's completely blank." He showed us both sides.

We nodded.

Logan whispered to me: "Where's he going with this?"

"You'll see."

Dex slipped the shirt on and flashed his back to us.

"So far, unimpressive," I said. "It's a new blank gray sweatshirt."

"Exactly." He hunched over and offered me his back. "Remember my puffy-paint tactile problem. Rub my back."

"I'm not giving you a back rub." I crossed my arms. Dex looked over his shoulder at me and rolled his eyes. "Hurry, Ellie. We don't have much time."

"Humor him," Logan said.

I rubbed the sweatshirt. "I don't feel a thing."

Dex glanced at his watch. "Prepare to be impressed. Now you don't see it..."

"The suspense is killing me," Logan said. "Is this an inverse magic show? Isn't it usually 'now you see it'?"

"Now you see it!" Dex said like he was parroting Logan.

"Whoa!" My eyes went wide as brightly colored words appeared on his back. "'Not my idea,'" I read aloud. "I thought it *was* your idea."

"The prank, not the matching sweatshirts. I'm going to write these words on the back of my Mom's Weekend sweatshirt and get my mother back for making me order them. And insisting we wear them everywhere." Dex looked over his shoulder, trying to see the writing that had appeared on his back. He looked a bit like a cat chasing its tail.

"Yeah, but at least you didn't have to stand in line for them. We had to wait, like, an hour to pick them up."

"Poor baby," Dex said.

"You are way too good with sarcasm," I said. "Now if you could just manage sympathy."

"Why do you think I conned you into picking them up? Waiting was part of the deal," Dex said.

"I thought being seen as a mommy's boy by half the girls on campus was why you wanted me to do it."

"Sucker," he said.

Logan shook his head. "Dex, really, you're the fool. You missed out. There were a lot of hot girls. I texted Collin and Zave to get their butts over there."

Dex nodded toward Logan. "You let him get away with eyeing other girls?"

I shrugged. "I'm not his mother."

Logan gave me a quick one-arm hug and walked over to inspect the back of Dex's shirt. "Awesome."

"Heat activated." Dex pulled the sweatshirt off over his head. "Kind of like the coffee mugs and straws that change color. This is my own formulation. I really had to work at it. Most fabric paints bead up on sizing and don't soak in. That's why you have to wash things first before applying it. It's challenging to create one that soaks through the sizing."

"How long will it take to disappear?" Logan was still staring at it after Dex laid it on the bed.

"A couple of minutes." Dex looked at me. "Where are your sweatshirts, Ellie?"

"I left them in the car."

"Get them and I'll write something on them for you."

I stared at him. "With your messy handwriting?"

"I won't embarrass you. I've been practicing my penmanship." He pointed toward the bed and the sweatshirt on it. "That's an early attempt."

"Even so, your block engineering lettering is very neat," Logan said. "And it's disappearing as we speak."

"Don't praise him," I said to Logan. "He'll just get a big head." I winked at Dex.

Dex laughed. "Too late. I've had a big head since I was born. Just ask my mom why she had to have a C-section."

I rolled my eyes.

"Seriously, Ellie." Dex went to his desk and picked up one of those fabric-pen accordion tubes. "I can write anything you want."

I pursed my lips, thinking. "'First-class bitch' has a nice ring to it?"

"'For a good time call' is always fun," Dex said. "You have her cell number, right?" Dex turned to Logan. "Logan? How about you?"

Logan shook his head and grinned. "I'm not a mama's boy. There's no way in hell I would ever wear the same thing as my mom. She knows not to ask."

Dex shrugged. "Your loss. You're missing out on an awesome prank. I'll probably apply for a patent for my ink. If you want to use it in the future, it's going to cost you. Big time."

I held my hand out to Logan. "You can't beat free. Give me your keys."

Logan shook his head. "No pranking Melissa, El. You're supposed to be trying to get along."

"Too late." Dex's grin lit up his whole face.

"What is he talking about?" Logan asked me.

"I have no idea," I said. But if Dex said he was planning something, I absolutely believed him. And hoped
it would be good.

CHAPTER FIFTEEN

We had dinner at Jason and Lyssa's. Lyssa was big now—huge in the tummy, anyway. Jason joked that the baby was reclining in there. From the back, she looked pretty normal. When she turned around, it was almost shocking to see that big basketball-like bulge. At dinner, the conversation was pretty benign. Jason asked about Logan's interview. Logan was surprisingly vague about it. Or maybe it wasn't so surprising, since he was so sure he was wasting everyone's time. I tried not to think about that. The conversation turned to IT stuff. I zoned out and enjoyed looking around the table at my happy family, wishing it would always be like this. Vowing again that I would not let my mother hurt a single person here.

After dinner, my baby sister Mia toddled around the living room, walking herself along the furniture. She was all smiles and giggles. I did the dishes for Lyssa and let her rest while I chased Mia around. At about eight, Mia's happy mood turned sour in that sudden way babies have. Lyssa picked her up and distracted her with the goodnight ritual—hugs and kisses for everyone. Mia gave big, sloppy, open-mouthed baby kisses all around.

Logan laughed as he wiped baby drool off his lips. "Your sister's a good kisser, El. You could take a lesson from her."

I rolled my eyes.

"Watch it, Walker." Jason put on the protective dad voice, but his eyes sparkled. "Those are my daughters you're talking about."

When Lyssa returned from putting Mia to bed, she focused on me. "How are you holding up, Ellie? Are you ready for this weekend?"

Lyssa was always kind and concerned, but her sympathetic tone put me on edge. She sounded too much like a counselor who was trying to fix things.

I forced a smile and deflected. "As ready as I can be. I sent you my schedule for the weekend, right?" I bit my lip. "You probably noticed I'm going to keep Mom really busy." I paused. "It's the best way to deal with her and keep her out of trouble."

"I wish you'd tell her about us," Lyssa said. "About Jason being your dad and about me and Mia and the baby."

My gaze flicked to Lyssa's big belly, puffy ankles, and tired eyes. Now was not the time for her to go up against my mom. Not with Lyssa's delicate pregnancy hormones in full effect. Mom had a tongue like a stiletto—she could slice you up and bleed you out before you realized you'd even been cut.

Jason shook his head subtly at Lyssa to warn her off. "We discussed this, Lyssa. This will be the first time Ellie's seen Melissa since...the incident. They have enough to deal with without complicating things with us."

I loved my dad so much. He was the parent I'd always dreamed of. I hated Mom even more for keeping him from me. I nodded my agreement. "Yeah, there's really no telling how Mom's going to react to that news. With the divorce and everything that's happened, she's in a fragile emotional state."

Not like I cared, but it sounded good and played well on Lyssa's sympathies.

"She kept Dad's identity from me all my life. She has to have had her own reasons." I sounded so reasonable, but really I was punting. I didn't want to tell her, ever. "If this weekend goes well, then maybe..." I shrugged.

Logan sat by quietly, but his fists were balled and it looked like he was fighting to hold back his opinions. I wondered what he knew.

"It looks like you've planned a fun weekend for her." Jason glanced at Lyssa. "We'll stay out of your way." He grinned. "I was thinking we should have a line of demarcation. Main Street or First Avenue would be good. We stay on our half of town. You stay on yours. That way we avoid any accidental meetings. But we get Walmart, in case I need to make an emergency diaper or ice cream run." He winked at me.

"Sounds fair," I said. "As long as we get all the bars. Mom wants the complete college experience."

Jason shrugged. "Hey, she's of age. She can go for it." He looked at me like *I* better not be going for it. "I'll even throw in all the restaurants with good happy hours." He laughed.

Lyssa sighed. "I really would like to meet Melissa sometime."

I wrinkled my nose and made a face. "You think you do. But trust me, once you have, you'll wish you hadn't. You'll never be her friend. She doesn't like other women."

Lyssa stared at me, not backing down.

"Some day," I said.

Logan

Logan dropped El off at class late Thursday morning and headed to the library to study for his afternoon lab.

It's your last semester. You already have three awesome job offers. Why aren't you coasting? All you have to do is pass your classes and you're out of here. Why do you give a damn anymore?

Even his profs didn't give a shit. They were as eager to graduate seniors as the seniors were to get their diplomas and blow this joint. He'd have to screw up royally and practically force them to fail him.

And yet a trifecta of specters chased him into the library when he could have been drinking with his buds—the remote possibility of grad school, which fueled the dream he could stay with El until she graduated. The trial. No way he was going to fuck up and give *Her* lawyers any ammo they didn't already have. And Mom's Weekend.

Studying kept his mind occupied and the ghosts at bay. For the most part.

He still worried about El. The stress of the upcoming weekend was making her crazy. She had activities planned down to the minute and was as obsessed with everything going perfectly as a frenetic bride. Tonight they were going shopping for last-minute stuff and then move the stuff El had at his place back to her dorm room. He'd tried to talk her out of it. They were practically living together. Why hide it from their parents? He wanted to spend every minute with her.

His mom would go ballistic, but he didn't care. It was time she realized how important El was to him. El's mom would probably throw a parade. So what was the problem?

El was the problem. And her fear of letting her mom see how in love she was with him. She'd made that mistake with Austin. What was Logan supposed to do? Act indifferent to El around her mom for the rest of their lives?

He hated that douchebag Austin for betraying El. Hated that Austin's failure tarnished him. El said she didn't trust Melissa, that her mom could seduce the most angelic guy on the planet. But unless Melissa was

willing to go as far as his old chem prof and use date-
rape drugs, Logan wasn't going to fall prey to her
charms. El was the only woman he wanted. He wanted
her. He needed her. On his arm. In his bed. On his side.

He'd rather be tested by fire with a full-on seduction attempt this weekend and prove to El he was immune to her mom than act out a charade. There was
enough bullshit he had to hide this weekend as it was.

His cell phone buzzed. He glanced at the number
and reluctantly picked up. He had to bite his tongue
not to say, *Speak of the devil.* "Melissa."

"Logan." His name slid through the phone on a
breath of seduction.

He was unmoved, almost sickened by Melissa's obvious attempts to turn him on. She was mercurial and
sneaky. Sometimes she was almost motherly. Sometimes she played cougar seductress. Knowing her past,
he understood why she was like she was and sympathized. But it was damned hard to take, especially
knowing what it did to El.

At times like these, caught in the chasm of secrets
between mother and daughter, he didn't know why he
was trying to play white knight. Getting some kind of
understanding between Melissa and El seemed impossible. Maybe not even smart. If he didn't love El so
much, he would have given up.

But he hated the power Melissa wielded over her. He
was determined to break it and give El her life back. El
held too much anger—some might call it hate—for her
mom. Bottled it up. Hate is just as powerful an emotion
as love. It has just as much power to consume. He knew.

He lived with pure hatred daily. He was going to get rid of his, too. Soon.

The opposite of love wasn't hate. It was apathy. A total lack of feeling or caring. Until El could get to the place where she could think of her mom in neutral tones and not let whether her mom loved her affect her, Melissa had too much power to destroy El. Logan worried that power would corrupt what he and El had.

He felt like a poseur. He could never present this case to El, not when he was still consumed with hate for his rapist. That was another, more selfish reason he had to testify. He hoped once he got it all out, told his story, he could let go of the rage. That was the gift he was trying to give El now. It was too bad she didn't want it.

"We have a problem, Logan." Melissa's silken voice brought him back to the moment. "Have you seen the ridiculous schedule Ellie has planned for me?"

"Is that a rhetorical question?" His laugh came out more of a snort. "She spent hours planning and agonizing over it, trying to make sure you got exactly what you asked for—the complete college experience. What's the problem?"

"Isn't that sweet of her. Friday night frat parties? She thinks her mom is a complete skank!"

"Aren't you?"

"Only when I want to be." She laughed. Insulting Melissa was practically impossible. "I didn't go to college, but I've been to enough frat parties to last a lifetime." She laughed again. "Maybe three lifetimes."

"So? What am I supposed to do about it? Call Ellie and tell her you're not up for it."

"Not up for it! You make me sound like an old lady." She sounded mockingly scandalized at the thought. "I'm not too old to party with frat boys. I just don't want to. *This* time." Her laughter would have been infectious if not for the cynical undertones in it.

"So little time. So much to do. So much to accomplish this weekend. Getting back in my baby's good graces. *Meeting her boyfriend's family.*" She let the last phrase dangle a moment before continuing. "My darling daughter's oh-so-thoughtful plans leave no time for intimately getting to know your parents and brother, Logan. A track meet? Seriously?"

"What do you have against track meets?" Logan tried to sound lighthearted and teasing, but his heart raced. Melissa had something up her sleeve. Something El wasn't going to like.

"Nothing! Are you kidding? Young, athletic men in short, tight running shorts and tank tops? What's not to love? Just the thought of all those firm, muscled legs gives me tingles. But as a place to chat, laugh, swap stories, and have a few drinks? Sadly lacking.

"I want a real social event. I'm quite happy to pass on the frat parties Friday night in exchange for dinner with your family. I'm can't tell you how much I'm looking forward to meeting them."

He bet she was. "You're asking the impossible. El won't go for that."

"Obviously. Which is why she purposely avoided it. And why I called you, miracle worker. Ellie will go for anything if you issue the invitation and beg her to come."

Melissa paused.

"Come on. Invite us, Logan. I'll crash your dinner anyway. You know I will. Do you really want me to embarrass Ellie in front of your family? And in the worst possible way. Invite me and I'll be on my best behavior." Even when issuing a threat, Melissa put a purr in her voice and spoke in silken tones. She was so damned good at seduction it was scary.

He cursed to himself for falling prey to her. He believed her. She had him beat.

"Okay," he said. "Fine, I'll see what I can do. But best behavior, remember? No upsetting my mom. No flirting."

She laughed again. "Not even with the waiter?"

He smiled. She was incorrigible. "Absolutely not."

"You'll regret it," Melissa said. "When I flirt with the waiter, I get the best service around. But if that's what it takes, I reluctantly agree."

When Logan got off the phone, he called his mom. He agreed with Melissa on one point. El was important enough to him to rate dinner with his family. His mom should have thought of it. He suddenly felt stretched and pulled between his mom and El. And it was his mother's fault. "Ma, can we add two to our dinner reservations Friday night?"

"Hello to you, too," Sue said. "You want me to add to our reservations at the last minute? Don't tell me Collin and Zave are begging to tag along now? What is it about college kids and free meals? I thought their moms were coming?"

"They are. It's not Collin and Zave. It's El and her mom. I'd like you to meet El's mom."

There was dead silence on the line. If his mom had been the kind to swear, the air would have been blue with it. Silence was her method of torture, disapproving silence to show her unhappiness with him. It had been like this since he was little.

He broke first. "Ma?"

"Yes, Logan." Frost in her voice.

Shit. He should have known this would happen. How did Dad deal with it?

"I asked you a question, Ma. I'm not coming to dinner without El. And she won't come without her mom."

"Seriously, Logan? You're going to force us to entertain that woman after all she's done to your *girlfriend.*" She ended her sentence on a snort, like "girlfriend" was a dirty word.

"This is important to me." He refused to back down.

She sighed, heavily, like she was supremely put out. "Do I have a choice? You're going to be the death of me, Logan. I'll change the reservations."

"Thanks, Ma."

"If she embarrasses us—"

"Don't ruin it, Ma. I'll be at the airport at noon to meet you. Have a safe trip." He hung up before she could harangue him and dialed El. "Ellie Elizabeth Martin."

El laughed. "Logan Walker. Are we back to being on a full-name basis again? What did I do?"

"I just love saying your name."

"Flatterer."

"Just warming you up. I have some bad news." He kept his tone light and teasing. There'd been so damned much shitty news lately that he didn't want to alarm her.

"Bad news? Like what? Don't tell me you're going to be late. I'm desperate to see you."

"Nothing that dire." He paused. "Mom has invited you and your mom to dinner with us tomorrow. Sorry, El, but she's already changed the reservations. There's nothing we can do. You know Mom, once she gets an idea in her head...El?"

"Logan." El sounded wary, like she didn't believe him, "Your mom doesn't even *like* me. She hates my mom without ever having met her. Mostly because she spawned me, the offspring that's snared her little boy. Why would she invite us to your family dinner?"

Logan sighed and went for broke. "Because I asked her to, El."

"Why?"

"Because you're important to me. She should have invited you in the first place." He waited for El to reply.

"That is so totally adorable." El's voice caught. "But you know this is completely dangerous. Our moms are going to hate each other."

"Fine. They hate each other. Not our problem. They'll have to deal with it." Logan took a deep breath, relieved. "Can I pick you up early? I miss you."

CHAPTER SIXTEEN

Ellie

I woke up next to Logan on Friday morning with my heart thumping with anxiety. Today was the first day of the weekend, followed by the week I'd been dreading for too long.

Next to me, Logan was sound asleep on his back. I sat up and stared at him like I couldn't get enough of him. And I couldn't. Not ever. I was absolutely riveted as I watched him sleep.

His hair flopped over his forehead in that bed-head way that made me happy and possessive. I was the one waking up next to him. *Me. Ellie Martin.* He was mine. I was going to fight to keep him, even if that meant going up against my mom, the cougar queen.

His jaw was firm and covered with dark stubble that made me want to run my smooth cheek up against the masculine grain of it until I got a whisker burn. He was so adorably hot. His face was relaxed and peaceful, like the Logan I first met. Lately it had been taut and stressed. My heart ached for him. I wanted this whole thing to be over. Now. Happily resolved. I kept trying to picture it, as if I could wish it into being.

He slept naked. Deliciously, tantalizingly naked, with his arms over his head and his chest exposed above the covers, his nipples poking out. They looked so totally suckable. But what was beneath the covers was even harder to resist. Logan asleep with a hard-on.

My fingers tingled as I thought of touching him. Stroking him. Watching his relaxed, even breathing grow excited and deep. His lips were moist and slightly open, practically begging to be kissed.

I slid off the T-shirt I'd been sleeping in and climbed on top of him, straddling him with my legs. Rubbing against his hard dick through my panties as I rested my head against his chest and traced the line of his biceps.

He woke with a start and a gasp and a blank expression. The kind of emptiness like he was looking faraway into a dream, or a nightmare. Before I could react, he grabbed me and shoved me off him. "Get away from me!"

I curled into a ball next to him, stunned. Hurt. Saddened. "It's me, Logan. Just me."

At the sound of my voice, he blinked like he was really waking now. He was breathing rapidly as he squinted at me. "El?"

"Yeah, it's me." My voice was tiny and tentative.

He grabbed me and pulled me to him, the whole ball of me, uncurling me until he was smashing my breasts against his chest. "Shit. Sorry about that."

I winced. My breasts were tender and sore. I had a momentary pulse of anxiety. My period was either imminent or I was pregnant. Why was nature so cruel, sending mixed signals, giving the same symptoms for totally opposite conditions?

I laid my hand on Logan's chest, trying to calm both of us. His heart hammered rapidly, like it had just had an adrenaline hit. He hung on to me as if he was afraid I was going to run away.

"It's okay," I said, hoping it really was.

"No, it's not." He took a deep breath, but it didn't mask the anger and frustration in his voice.

"I shouldn't have startled you." I cuddled into him, feeling emotional, sentimental, and on the verge of tears. This was all going wrong. "I was trying to wake you with a hug."

"You can still wake me with a hug. Or something better." He stroked my breast.

I tried not to wince. As he reached between my legs, I felt a cramp and a sudden rush of warmth. "No!" I pulled away from him and ran to the bathroom, leaving him calling after me.

I sat on the toilet, shaking, and looked between my legs. A red streak of blood curled into the water of the toilet. I put my head in my hands. My emotions were jumbled and contradictory—relief and disappointment. Not that I wanted to be pregnant, just that this was the most inconvenient time for my period to hit. Just when I had to go head to head with my mom.

Logan knocked on the door. "El? El, you okay?"

No, I wasn't okay. I was the furthest thing from okay—totally crappy. Fat and sore and emotional. And worst of all, insecure. About everything.

"El?"

"I'm fine." I wanted to cry.

There was an uncomfortable pause. "Do you need anything?"

"No. I'm fine. I'll be out in a minute."

I heard him hesitate outside the door. Finally his footsteps receded and I drew a deep breath. I got up and got a tampon from my bag. My chin itched. When I looked in the mirror, there was a giant red zit on the end of it. One of those hideous things that no amount of makeup could cover, not even with the tricks Mom had taught me.

Crap, crap, crap, crap! I leaned on the counter and hung my head, trying to breathe deeply and focus, just focus on the goal.

I didn't want Logan walking in and catching me in what I was about to do. Some beauty treatments are best left unseen. I locked the door, which rattled like it was telling on me. I heard Mom's voice in my head: *Do not squeeze. You'll scar.*

But I was so tempted. I grabbed a washcloth. Ran the water until it steamed like Mom had taught me.

Soaked the cloth, wrung it out, and covered the pimple, holding it there until the cloth cooled. Then I rubbed at the zit until it burst and I scrubbed it out.

I stared into the mirror. *Better.* But I couldn't let Logan see me yet. I jumped into the shower.

Half an hour later, I was showered and dressed, with my hair drying and my makeup on. When I opened the bathroom door, Logan was sitting on the bed, waiting for me, looking so sweetly apologetic I wanted to hold him.

"I'm sorry, El." His Adam's apple bobbed. "I wasn't awake. I was startled. I didn't mean to hurt your feelings."

"I know. You didn't. We're fine."

"We're not fine. You locked me out." He held my gaze.

What could I say? I had, but I wasn't about to explain. "I needed some time by myself."

"El, don't shut me out. I need you." He sprang to his feet. In two steps he was next to me, pulling me into him. He kissed the top of my head. "I mean it—I need you. I want you. That stupid sleepy me is just a douchebag. What does he know?" He lowered his voice into a sexy whisper. "Let's make up." He ran his hands down my arms. "This is our last chance for sex before the parents arrive."

I pulled back from him and shook my head. "I can't."

He held my arms. "El—"

I gave up and hung my head as I whispered, "My period started."

"Oh. Wow, the awake me is a douchebag, too."

I felt him staring at me and looked up at him. "You didn't know. Bad timing."

Then he grinned, looking relieved. Like this was all just female crap we could deal with.

"We'll get through it." His eyes were still begging me to forgive him.

"Yeah." I nodded. Staring at him—gorgeous, gorgeous Logan—all my insecurities surfaced. Logan was ten times the guy Austin was. Hotter, sexier, smarter, richer, funnier. How could Mom resist him?

"Promise me, Logan—absolutely swear to me that you will not let Mom trick you. Do not, absolutely do not, under any circumstance, let her get you alone."

He took a deep breath then opened his mouth like he was about to say something and thought better of it. He shut it again and paused. "There's nothing Melissa could do to take me from you. I'm yours, El. *Always* yours. *Faithfully.*"

I bit my lip and blinked back tears. Stupid hormones.

He squeezed my arms. "Do you want me to be there with you when she arrives?"

I shook my head, thinking I didn't deserve him. "Your parents are flying in at noon. Didn't you agree to meet your mom and Caleb so your dad can go directly to the College of Business meeting?"

He nodded. "I can skip meeting them. Dad can drop them off at the hotel."

I shook my head. "You'll have your hands full. And the last thing I need is to get even farther on your mom's bad side."

"You mean there's more room on her bad side?"

"Stop teasing." I smiled slightly, took a deep breath, and looked away. "I'd rather meet Mom alone." I paused. I had to meet her privately and set her straight. She was not to touch Logan. Not even a handshake. "In case things get ugly." I laughed. I couldn't help it.

Logan frowned, looking puzzled by my lunatic behavior.

"What am I saying?" I looked back at him. "This is my mom. Things will definitely get ugly. Totally hideous. Maybe worse."

Logan cupped my face in his warm, reassuring hands and smiled at me. "Nice to see you still have a sense of humor about it." He stared into my eyes. "I think you still owe me one."

I stared into his eyes and teased him. "Do I? I've lost count. Odd time to bring it up. Are you calling it in? Will I ever be out of your debt?"

"Maybe. I saved your life, El. You're the one who insisted on owing me. Now I kind of like it." He caressed my cheek with his thumb.

I wanted to melt into him. Hide out. Run.

"Trust me on this," he said. "You're tough. You've proven that again and again. This is easy compared to what you've been through with her. You can deal with Melissa."

"Thanks for the pep talk, coach."

"I'm not finished. Shut up and listen." He kept staring at me like it was important I understood what he was about to say. "You have to get to the point where you let go of the anger and admit you love her because she's your mom. And that isn't going to change. That you can't cut her off. If you go there, you deal with whatever crap having her in your life means. And as irritating and frustrating as that is, it's part of the bargain and you don't let it rule you.

"Or you get to a place where you totally don't give a shit what she does one way or the other. Like, really not care at all. She could live. She could die. She could spend her life in prison. Or move away and you never see her again. She's just a person you used to know. She has no place in your life and no control at all."

He snorted, like he was mocking himself.

"The bliss of total apathy is not an easy place to reach. Fuck, I should know. You can't fake it. And that's the bitch of it."

I ached for him. I opened my mouth to say something that would inevitably sound hollow. He cut me off with a gentle kiss, just a brush of his lips against mine that sent waves of heat through me.

Then he sighed. "I'm not saying which way you should go. Only that each path means you let go of the anger you feel toward her. As long as you hang on to it, she controls you."

I nodded.

He gave me a crooked grin and pulled me into him, cradling me like he never wanted to let go. "You're not alone this time, El. She's not all you have. You have Jason, Lyssa, Mia, another baby half-sib on the way, and me. I'm on your side whatever you decide to do. We're on your side. Use this weekend to get to the place inside yourself where you have to go to be free. Listen to what Melissa has to say—"

"She won't say anything," I said. "She never does. She just—"

He kissed me to keep me from speaking, tickling the roof of my mouth with his tongue until I tingled with need. "I love you, El. All this crap—the nightmares, the trial, our parents—they won't change that. You and me can weather anything as long as we're together."

I looked into his eyes and wanted to believe him. Wanted so much it hurt. I'd believed in another guy once. Logically, I knew Logan wasn't him. That, like I said already, Logan Walker was ten times the guy Austin was. But as the saying goes, once bitten, twice shy. My mom was my nemesis and she was completely diabolical and utterly seductive. Irene Adler to Logan's Sherlock Holmes. And that was what scared me most. Who would outwit whom?

I made Logan take me to the grocery store on the way to campus so I could stock up on necessities—candied ginger and cinnamon to fight off bloating and cramps. By the time Logan dropped me off at class, I couldn't concentrate. He pulled in front of the business building. I hugged him and hung on to him until the cars stacked up behind us, honking.

"You'll be okay, El. You will. *I* believe in you." He kissed me, leaned over me, and opened my car door. "Don't take this the wrong way, but go! You'll be late."

I stood on the sidewalk and watched him drive off, hoping his confidence wasn't misplaced. But fearing it was. I'd had more experience dealing with Mom than anyone else had, but I was still no match for her.

Class was a disaster—poorly attended. No one paying attention. The prof let us out fifteen minutes early. As I walked into the mall toward the SUB, I couldn't help noticing moms everywhere. And so it began—the squealing, the drinking, the partying, the happy reunions. Every kind of emotion. Moms ruled campus.

I had barely found a seat in the SUB and was settling down to study, when I got a text from my mom. *Just leaving, sweetie. See you in five hours! LOL*

LOL, right. More like pure terror. My hands shook as I put the cell phone back in my pocket. Five hours to prepare for battle.

All my life—at least my life since I'd developed boobs—I'd tried to be invisible next to Mom. I let her win. Let her turn heads without even trying to compete. But now I grabbed a mirror from my backpack and took a look at myself. My hastily applied makeup. My jeans and T-shirt. The hair I hadn't curled. I was tired and scared, but I wasn't going down without a fight.

It was time to show Melissa Ann Sawyer that I could compete. That her time as Evil Queen was fading and my star as Snow White was rising. When she saw me for the first time in almost a year, I wanted her to see my rebellion. I wanted her to see me as true competition.

I reached into my backpack for a couple of acetaminophen to ward off cramps and downed them with an entire bottle of water. Counterintuitive, but drinking water actually reduced bloating. I learned that from her, too. I chewed a piece of candied ginger and schemed, planning my outfit. I should have thought of all this before. Logan's pep talk had given me the confidence I needed. He was right, of course. I had to get rid of my anger. But first, I had to show Mom that I wasn't afraid of her. Even if I was.

Just before three, I made myself go back to my dorm and get dressed for my execution. Ignoring the bloaty way I felt, I put on tight, skinny jeans, heels, my peridot bellybutton ring, and a cute spring crop top that showed off my piercing and my abs. I curled my hair. Applied new makeup. And waited for her to arrive.

While I waited, I stood at my window and watched moms arrive like they'd been blown in by the wind. Watched the hugging and the laughter. The arms around each other. The introductions to friends. The pride—*this is my mom!* The embarrassment—*this is my mom.* The joy and the anxiety.

I felt that old longing again for a family. The little girl I had been wanted her mommy, the mommy of children's stories. The kind that will find and rescue her child anywhere, like in *The Runaway Bunny.* Is your mama a llama? My mama was a terror.

But I remembered her reading me those stories and the assault of my memories began. I had worked to push the happy recollections away. It wasn't that hard, because there weren't that many. Not in recent years. But when I caught a glimpse of myself in the mirror over the sink, the zit had gone flat and was practically invisible. *Mom.* She always knew what to do with imperfection. Except with me. She'd been stuck with plain old imperfect me.

A memory, just a flash, of me in sixth grade when my face started breaking out for the first time. And that awful boy in my class who called me a zit head. Running home after school and crying. And Mom telling me I was beautiful and this phase of pimples and breakouts would pass, but the key was not to let it scar me. That eventually the boys would be begging from my attention. But I had to be careful whom I gave it to.

"Don't let anything scar you, Ellie." Her eyes were fierce and protective. "Scars ruin your life." She held me tight, like she was protecting me from a dark scary world.

And then her protective mood passed. She was like that. She went all businesslike and beauty expert on me. Superficial. She bought me the best acne products. How did she know what to buy? It was impossible to imagine my flawlessly beautiful mother had ever had a zit.

She taught me the hot washcloth trick. And failing that, how to sterilize a needle to pop, but never squeeze. Looking back, remembering the ferocious look on her face, I realized she was talking about more than physical scars. Now that I thought about it, I didn't think she was talking about physical scarring at all. But I must have been wrong, because beauty was all to Mom.

I remembered other things, too. Like how she loved hair and played with and combed mine like I was her little doll. Other little girls had scraggly straight hair or common, regular braids. I had French herringbone braids. Inside-out braids. Side braids. When I was upset or hurting, Mom would sit me down and run her fingers through my hair. "I think you need a new style. Something to perk you up." And then she'd do something new and fun with ribbons and feathers and curls in my hair until I felt like a princess.

I would sit very still, enjoying the feel of her hands in my hair. Mom wasn't cuddly or maternal. This was the best touch I got.

And one more thing—the way she stared at me with an intense expression that was almost like fear. When I was little, I lived for that expression. It meant she noticed me. So much of the time I was either invisible or the competition.

But as I grew up, the scrutiny became unbearable and downright irritating.

I remembered screaming at her once. "Stop staring at me! What are you looking for?"

"The person you're becoming." Her gaze was steady, but her voice trembled. "I'm looking for your father in you."

"My dad? What about him?" I had perked up. I was going through that gawky, geeky junior high age when none of your features fit right. It was an odd time for me. Horrifying in that I felt ugly. And reassuring because I was no competition for Mom, which meant we were at semi-peace with each other more of the time than usual. "Do I look like him?"

I sounded too eager. It was a mistake.

She frowned almost immediately. "I don't know who you look like. You don't look like anybody," she'd said flatly. "Not me. Not him. You're just you. Maybe that's for the best." But she sounded disappointed.

I was always disappointing her in one way or another.

"But I have his hair color, right?" Hey, she'd opened the door. She never talked about him. I seized my opportunity. "Is he handsome? Is my dad totally hot?" I was taunting her. Why the hell had she slept with this man and then refused to talk about him or acknowledge him?

She stared directly into my eyes, but her look was faraway. "He's either hideously ugly and cruel, a real troll, or cute and kind."

"But which is he? You know. You were there when you made me. Why won't you tell me?" I was screaming at her by then.

"Shut up, Ellie." She looked tired. "Screaming makes you ugly and worries me."

I had totally forgotten that conversation until this minute. I was just as confused by it now that I knew the truth as I was then. How could anyone think Jason was ugly? It was like Mom saw things in an odd way, like two sides of a harlequin mask. There was a part of me now that wanted to tell her I knew the truth. But only a small part. The rest of me was determined to keep her from Jason.

A series of squeals in the hall pulled me from my memories. The door to our room opened. Bre walked in with her arm through her mom's. I felt a pang of jealousy. And I thought, once again, *Crap. Mom is going to eat Bre's mom for lunch.*

Bre introduced me. "Mom, this is Ellie. Ellie, this is my mom—"

Her mom smiled at me. "Call me Donna."

Donna was plain and middle aged, plump with short, graying hair in a cut that screamed *mom.* Her makeup consisted solely of a too-bright shade of lipstick that emphasized the wrinkles in her lips and made her look older than she probably was. She wore unflattering jeans that were too high in the waist and sensible tennis shoes. I had to slap the thought of making her over right out of my mind as something Mom would do, not me. I had learned too much superficiality from my mother.

"I brought you girls some homemade cookies," Donna said. "They're in the car along with some other goodies to snack on. You two are both so thin!"

"Frosted sugar cookies?" Bre's eyes lit up.

Donna shook her head. "I didn't have time. Chocolate chip."

Bre sighed. "Better than nothing. We are sick to death of dining hall food." She laughed.

"Don't tell Tay that," I said. "They've been working hard to improve the food for this weekend and the moms." I winked at Donna. "It's purely false advertising."

Donna's laugh was hearty and genuine. "Some things haven't changed. Will they be serving steak? Or is that just for Dad's Weekend?"

"I'm sure we'll have the usual selection, just a grade better," I said.

Donna was friendly and I liked her. We gave her the detailed tour of our room, our polished-to-perfection, looking-like-it-never-looked-in-real-life room. That took about two seconds. Then she and Bre went to her car to get her bags and the promised cookies.

My door was open. Bre had barely left when Nic called out to me from the hall and popped her head in. "Ellie? Are you in? Is your mom here yet? I want her to meet mine."

"I'm here. Mom isn't. Come on in and introduce yours to me."

Nic pulled a middle-aged woman into my room. Their arms were wrapped around each other like they were best friends. Even though Nic was a good three inches taller than her mother, her mom held her happily and protectively. Proudly.

"Mom, meet one of my best friends. This is Ellie Martin."

I stood to shake her hand.

She pulled me into a hug. "So you're the famous Ellie?"

I blushed.

"I'm Linda. I hear we're going to be hanging with you and keeping your mom out of trouble?" Her eyes sparkled. She smelled like a pleasant floral perfume, applied with a heavy hand.

She had a gravelly voice like she used to be a smoker, but it was filled with good humor. Dyed blond hair that was over-processed. She and Nic were dressed in jeans and matching sorority V-neck T-shirts in pale blue. She had a tiny, obviously aging tattoo on her wrist.

"Or keeping her in trouble, depending on how you look at it." I stepped out of the hug.

"Oh, I'm good at that! Bring it on." Linda's eyes danced.

"You two look very...sorority," I said.

Linda laughed. "Don't we just! Of all my girls, I didn't think this one, my sporty one, would be the one to go Greek. I haven't seen her out of sweats and yoga pants for three years. I thank the sorority for that!"

"Mom!" Nic rolled her eyes.

I laughed with Linda. She was exactly right.

"We have to go to a sorority thing tonight," Nic said. "Now that you bailed on our frat party plan, we won't see you until tomorrow?"

I nodded. "Yeah, sorry. Logan's mom invited us to dinner."

Nic laughed. "Good luck with that." She sighed and turned to her mom. "We'll have to wait until tomorrow to see if Melissa lives up to her hype. Personally, I had a few frat guys I wanted to see her shoot down. Payback."

I shook my head. "Next time."

"Okay," Nic said. "We have to be off or we'll be late to our function. Just wanted to say hi."

After they left, Bre returned with her mom, a suitcase, a bag of goodies, and two sleeping bags and matching camping pads. We set the room up. Bre and her mom left to tour the campus.

My phone sounded. A text from Mom.
I'm here.

CHAPTER SEVENTEEN

Mom's laugh was the first thing I heard as I came down the steps into the lobby. That mesmerizing, seductive laugh that oozes charm and used to make me want to please her just to hear it.

How had she gotten in? Even though it was Mom's Weekend, the doors were still locked. She'd obviously charmed her way in.

I took a deep breath and steeled myself. Mom had as many laughs as Eskimos had words for snow. She could laugh with you or at you, and that made all the difference. Sometimes she was so subtle she left you in doubt—was she making fun of you? Or were you in on her private joke?

I stood tall and forced myself to move. As I came into the lobby, Mom was holding on to a wheeled suit-

case, and her purse and a shopping bag were slung over
one shoulder. Her long blond hair fell over her shoulders in perfect, curly waves. She wore tight, skinny
jeans, heels so high no normal woman could walk in
them, and a white V-neck T-shirt right out of most
guys' wet dreams. She was thirty-eight, but looked no
more than twenty-eight, if that. Mom had dressed for
college. She looked like she belonged in the Double
Deltsie house.

She was talking—flirting with, actually—a guy
named Rusty. His girlfriend lived on the third floor. I
guessed he was here to see her and Mom had intercept-
ed him. He was carrying Mom's overnight bag for her.

I cursed men's weakness beneath my breath. They'd
do anything for a woman who knew how to smile just
right and had a figure straight off a Victoria's Secret
runway.

I hated to do it, but I had to save Rusty. "Mom."

Of course, calling out "mom" was like almost futilely
impersonal. Half a dozen heads turned toward me, including hers.

Then it was like slow motion the way she sized me
up. It must have been my imagination, because I actually thought for a moment her eyes teared up.

"Ellie, sweetie!" She ran to me and pulled me into a
gigantic hug that would have been bone-crushing if
she'd weighed more than 110 pounds. Her purse
banged against me.

She finally let me go, sort of. She held me by the
wrists at arm's length and stared at me. "You look
beautiful." She glanced at my abs and laughed. "You

got your bellybutton pierced. Finally! I like it. Nice ring."

I was being in your face with my bellybutton ring. I had rebelled against her all those years by not getting it pierced because that was what she wanted. Because she'd wanted me to be cool. And I'd wanted to not be seen. I had gotten it pierced at the first Up All Night of the school year. Because by then it was my decision, not hers.

"Thanks," I said. Was it my imagination or did she seem just the slightest bit nervous? Maybe "tentative" was a better word. "Logan gave it to me."

"Logan." She laughed. "He has good taste."

And I hope it stayed that way.

Rusty gaped at me. "She's your mom?" He sounded as stunned as he looked.

I shrugged and pulled the overnight bag off his shoulder. "Yeah."

"Wow!" He handed me the shopping bag as he practically panted over mom.

"She's older than she looks." I couldn't help digging at her.

"Not that much older." Mom couldn't resist defending herself. "I had Ellie when I was very young."

"Don't you have a girlfriend to see?" I said to Rusty. "Come on, Mom. Let's get you settled in." I led her to my room on the second floor.

Logan was right. I had to get rid of this anger toward her. It was bubbling up and twisting things inside me toward ugliness.

"Here we are." I opened the door for her and set her overnight and shopping bags on my bed. "This is my bed. Yours for the night."

Mom grabbed the shopping bag from the bed and held it out to me. "I brought you something."

"You shouldn't have." I didn't reach for it.

She rattled it. "Come on, Ellie. Let me at least play at being mom. I spent a lot of time picking out just the right thing. It's for tonight."

I sighed and grabbed the bag. I didn't want her gifts. She couldn't buy me with things. Reluctantly, I looked in the bag.

"Take it out. Hold it up. Let's see if I guessed right on the color."

I peeled back the tissue paper and hauled out the cutest, most gorgeous little pink dress. I hadn't gotten a new dress in ages and this one was the latest spring style. I must have let my lust for the dress show on my face, because Mom smiled.

"There are shoes, too. At the bottom of the bag. Take them out. Try them on."

"Mom, I don't want these." I dropped the dress back in the bag and held it out to her.

"You do, but you're too proud and stubborn." She crossed her arms and refused to take the bag. "You promised me the full experience. That was the deal we made. Every mom arriving on this campus is bringing their kid a gift. That's part of the deal.

"I promised not to touch Logan. Not to flirt with him. Not to embarrass you." She held my gaze. "If I'm going to keep my end of the bargain, you need to keep yours. Which means you graciously accept the gifts I brought."

She grinned, because she'd won. Like she always won.

I'd lost the showdown. I grabbed the bag. "Fine." I pulled the dress out. It still had the hanger. I hung it on the front of my closet and tried not to look at the gorgeous thing.

Then I sat in my desk chair and pulled out the shoebox, gasping when I saw the designer label. "No way. How can you afford these?"

"Alimony, court settlements, and sensational shopping skills." She was watching me with anticipation.

I couldn't help gasping as I pulled out a pair of pink platform sandals. They were absolute perfection. When I slipped them on, they were as comfortable as wearing air. But I would have worn them if they were the cruelest shoes on the planet. They were that cute.

"We'll look perfect tonight. We'll stun those Walkers with our class."

I looked up from staring at my dream shoes, suddenly suspicious, wondering what Mom was planning to wear and how I'd pale in comparison next to her.

I caught Mom looking around the room with a weird, wistful look on her face. "Why are we staying here? Why aren't we staying at Logan's? He has a nice big apartment, so I hear." She laughed again as I tried to measure it.

That was her show-off laugh. She was boasting that she knew Logan. I wondered if it was a threat as well.

I slid the sandals off and set them back in their box.

"Oh, come on!" she said when I didn't reply. "You two are young. He's a college kid. They're as horny as they come. I know you two are practically living together. If you aren't, there's something wrong with you. You don't have to hide it from me. I just hope you're using protection. Heavy-duty protection."

I stared at her. "Logan's family is here. You know that."

"So you're not denying it?" She studied the room and pointed. "Nice picture of you and Logan. Such a cute couple." She looked directly at me. "No family pictures?"

I shrugged, pleased that she'd noticed.

"Whose posters?"

"Bre's."

"Thank goodness. I taught you better taste."

"I'm using birth control," I said. "Does that ease your mind?"

She shrugged. "Slightly. Logan's parents are staying at a hotel."

"Collin and Zave's moms are here, too. They aren't staying at a hotel. They have a full house."

She turned her gaze on me, and for once she was serious. "And you don't want me anywhere near them."

"Do you blame me?" I said.

"I'm not interested in college boys, Ellie."

"Could have fooled me."

"That was a long time ago."

"Less than a year," I said, and stared out the window. "You have a warped sense of time."

"Are you ever going to forgive me?" She sounded truly sorry and almost vulnerable.

I sighed, caught off guard by her show of emotion. "Why *are* you here, Mom?"

She hesitated. "Because I miss you, Ellie. You're my baby. All the family I have left."

I felt sorry for her then. She may have been all alone, but I wasn't. I had a great dad and a sister, another sib on the way, a stepmom. I swallowed hard and continued to stare at the street below and all the happy moms out there. Logan was right. Having a family outside of Mom made all the difference. I didn't need her. Not like she professed to need me, anyway. I felt lighter around her than I could ever remember. Like I had choices. But I felt sorry for her, too. Compassion was killer. It would be my downfall.

"I made a mistake and I'm deeply sorry. I miscalculated with Austin."

"You really thought I'd thank you?" I turned to look at her. "Is my life a game to you?"

"Austin is a hot young man. It wasn't like you thought between Doug and me."

I turned back to the window.

"Things weren't all hearts and roses, Ellie. If you'd been around you would have seen that. The honeymoon was definitely over." She snorted. "He traveled a lot...too much. I suspected from almost the beginning he was sleeping with other women while he was on his trips. One-night stands. Code of the road. No one squealed to me." She hesitated. "Then he got cocky.

And careless. I found proof. Receipts to strip clubs. Women's phone numbers."

She paused and sighed. "What does it matter now? I could show you everything. I'm not imagining or making this up. He was a dog, Ellie. I hid it from you, but that's the truth."

I let her talk. But I refused to let her off the hook by engaging.

She came up behind me and stood. "Austin was there. Funny. Comforting. Understanding. Uncertain about you, Ellie."

"He loved me." The words just popped out.

"Not enough," Mom said. "I recognized the kind of guy he is and will always be. He's like Doug, a philanderer. That's not what you want, Ellie. You're not like me. A guy like that would break you."

"He was faithful to me until you came along."

"Was he?"

I felt my heart stop. I went stone cold. A dozen little signs and insecurities popped up. The suspicions. The things I'd ignored. "Yes."

She laughed again. "You hesitated. Because you suspected. Because you know deep down Austin is a dog, like Doug. And that he wasn't faithful with more women than me. Wasn't faithful to you before I came along. I couldn't ever take someone who didn't want to be taken. Give yourself more credit than that, Ellie."

"I loved him!" I fought my emotions, trying to tamp down the anger and the hurt and fight back tears. "You broke me." I immediately wished I could take back my words. I was too vulnerable, giving her too much credit and power over me.

"I didn't break you. You're not broken. You're stronger than that." There was that fierce, protective tone in her voice again, the one from my childhood. The one that tried to force her desire into reality. She put her hand on my shoulder.

I shook it off. "Even if you're right that Austin was unfaithful, *you* didn't have to have sex with him."

"Don't act petulant, Ellie. It doesn't help." She paused again, like she was trying to get control of herself. "You're never going to believe me, but I didn't mean for that to happen."

"You mean you didn't mean to get caught. You called him and asked him over."

She sighed. "No one wants to get caught. Whatever Austin told you, he wasn't blameless. When he came over, he knew what he wanted. He wanted to come over, that was clear. He was eager and ready.

"He came onto me the minute he stepped in the door. And I...I had just found out about another one of Doug's indiscretions. And I took revenge on him, not you. Austin was handy and you were...collateral damage.

"It was wrong. I was wrong. If I could, I would take it all back. But the point is, Ellie, it proved to you that Austin isn't who you thought he was. He's a cheater. You can blame me all you like, but you should thank me for that. You were in too deep with him.

"I was afraid you were going to do something stupid like marry him and ruin your life. You were way too young and he was way too wrong for you."

I marveled that she could suddenly sound so maternal. That if someone had walked in on the last part of this conversation, missing the part about her sleeping with Austin, she would sound completely reasonable and like a concerned mom.

"I'm going to make it up to you."

"You can't, Mom. It's not possible."

"I think it is, Ellie. That's why I'm here. To protect my baby."

CHAPTER EIGHTEEN

Logan

Logan suffered through an awkward meeting at the airport with his parents and brother. His mom kept watching him and staring at him as if he was a wounded baby bird. Logan hated that. Caleb was full of himself and shit. And his dad was his dad—brusque, arrogant, in a hurry. Harlan rushed off to his meetings with the College of Business. Logan took his mom and Caleb out to their hotel to check in and then they went to a local drive-in for lunch. After that, they went for ice cream at the university-run creamery. The university made premium ice cream and cheese.

Sue stocked up on cans of university cheese. She bought one for Logan. She swore he was looking too thin. It was all very normal, but beneath the surface, tensions simmered.

At four, he took them to his apartment. Collin, Zave, and their moms were out. Sue begged off to take a short nap on Logan's bed, leaving Logan alone with his brother. Logan grabbed two beers from the fridge and handed one to Caleb. They sat on the couch, drinking in silence.

Logan tried to make conversation. "So, this injury of yours?"

"Nothing serious. I'll be back in another week. Don't panic, bro."

"Who said I was panicking?"

Caleb sneered. "Serious?"

Logan took a deep breath. They used to be close. Since joining the major leagues, Caleb had turned into someone he didn't know anymore. "Get over yourself." He paused. "Why are you here? Did Mom drag you along?"

"Dad did."

Logan snorted. "Dad? Why? I thought the last thing he wanted was to associate any of you with me."

"You underestimate him." Caleb took a swig of beer. "He thinks my presence is good PR for you."

Logan couldn't believe what he was hearing. "You're full of shit. You?"

Caleb shrugged. "Dad knows what he's doing. Usually. You're Mom's fave. He'll do anything to protect you for her. Even sacrifice me." Caleb sounded like he really believed that crap.

"What planet are you from? Since the day you were born, you've been his favorite." Logan shook his head. "And especially since I fucked up. He wouldn't sacrifice you for me even if Mom begged him."

"Maybe he's playing us both."

"That would be like him." Logan studied his brother. The guy had everything. But Logan was surprisingly not jealous. He hesitated. When would he get another time alone with Caleb? He was only asking this because of El. He couldn't stand the thought of leaving her. "Two, I have a favor."

Caleb stared at him, suddenly interested. "That's new. What do you want?"

"Money." Logan explained the situation with Amber and the IPO.

"Shit, Logan. I understand wanting to tell Dad to shove it. You risked the money Grandpa left you? Serious, that's not like you. You're the one who plays it safe. The responsible one."

"I thought it was safe," Logan said.

Caleb nodded. "Sounds like you."

"Look, I know everyone is after your money and hitting you up. I wouldn't ask if it wasn't important. I'll pay you back as soon as we go public."

Caleb set his beer down on the coffee table. "I can't, man. I wish I could, but I can't. Dad's on my ass about how much I've been spending." Caleb looked out the window and frowned. "I blew through my signing bonus and a big chunk of my first season's pay. That put me on Dad's shit list. And now with this injury..."

For the first time since he'd arrived, Caleb let down his guard. He was the old Caleb, the irresponsible one. The good-time guy who'd part with his last dime to show his friends a good time. The one Dad was always trying to drill a sense of the value of money into. And worse, maybe Caleb wasn't worried about his injury, but Harlan was.

Caleb rolled his eyes. "Dad hooked me up with his lawyers and financial guys. He put me on a budget. I can't touch my own dough without Dad's permission. You want money, I'll have to go to him to get it. I will if you want me to. No guarantee he'll say yes. And it pretty much blows your plan."

Logan cursed beneath his breath. It always came back to his dad having the ultimate power. "No, thanks. You're right. I'll find another way."

"Another way to do what?" His mom stood in the doorway to his room.

"Logan needs money, Ma. You got any?"

Ellie

I took Mom to the dining hall to meet Tay and get something to drink. I could almost see Tay's thoughts as she sized Mom up. But Mom was on her sweetest behavior. That's the thing about Mom, she can charm when she wants to.

Tay was working the grill with one of the guys. When Mom smiled at him, he became annoyingly flustered. The guy at the checkout register fawned all over Mom, too. You know that effect Heidi Klum has on guys? They act the same way around Mom.

Back in our room, Mom insisted we get ready for dinner. "I'll do your hair and your makeup."

"I can do them myself."

She arched a brow. "Makeovers are part of the experience. Bonding."

Resisting her was pointless. If she was making me over, she'd be distracted and we wouldn't have to talk. She wouldn't bring up more suspicions and cast more doubt on people.

I was still in denial and trying to process what she'd said about Austin. Since walking in on the two of them, I had repressed all those memories and doubts I'd had about him before. I was so angry at Mom that I blamed her for everything. And Austin corroborated my beliefs. Who was telling the truth? Was anyone? Or did everyone have their own agenda?

I obediently scrubbed off my carefully applied makeup and sat in my chair while she got out the moisturizer.

She dabbed some on her fingers, ready to apply it. Mom believed in priming a face with moisturizer, even for young, oily skin.

"Are you taking care of your skin? You have a pimple." She sounded surprised, like a zit could never happen to me. "I paid for your Accutane."

She had. As it turns out, it took more than over-the-counter acne treatments to give me clear skin.

I sighed as I handed her all the ammo she needed. But what was the use? She would pry it out of me anyway. "My period just started."

"Ah." She nodded almost sympathetically and studied my chin. "I thought I detected a bit of puffiness and circles beneath your eyes. Don't worry. I can fix that. Are you drinking plenty of water?"

"Yes, Mom."

"Ginger?"

"Of course."

"This pimple looks good. Nice and flat. Not bruised. You didn't squeeze?"

"Never."

She smiled. "Good. I can fix it." As she dabbed the moisturizer on my cheek, she paused and gently touched my scar.

I thought for a moment she'd gloss over it and avoid the issue. I would have.

"This is healing well, too." She massaged it gently with her fingertips, almost tentatively. "I could kill Doug for hitting you." Her voice was fierce.

"It was an accident." I don't know why I defended him. I bit my lip. "I haven't let it scar me, Mom."

The last time she'd seen it in person, it had been a fresh wound.

"Good." Her voice broke. She smiled bravely and began her makeup artistry.

I was holding my cell phone. It rang. A text from Tay. I read it and held back a laugh.

You were not exaggerating. Your mom is way hot. Did you see the way Jake stumbled all over himself trying to get her attention, ha ha.

I rolled my eyes and typed a response.

"Stop texting and close your eyes, Ellie. I don't understand why you resist false eyelashes," she said as she applied some. "Your real ones are pitiful."

"Thanks, Mom."

"No one can claim I'm biased. I see the faults in my kid as clearly as anyone."

"Thanks again. I'm happy to be on the short end of your gene pool."

"Shut up and let me work."

She hummed as she applied my makeup, just like she used to do when I was little. She had a pleasant, mesmerizing voice. When I was young, it was one of the things I lived for. If she was humming, she was happy, and I was in a safe, good place.

I tried to fight that old feeling of calm. Mom had planned all this. She was playing me.

When she finished with my face, she plugged in a curling iron and handed me a mirror. "Take a look."

I looked in the handheld mirror and suppressed a gasp. Mom had taught me a lot of tricks. I was pretty decent with makeup. But Mom was a genius, a true artist. I'd always suspected her of holding back when she did my makeup. She hadn't today. I looked better than I ever had before.

"What do you think?" she asked.

"You've gotten even better. Have you taken a class?" I looked at my profile in the mirror. "I think you've been holding out on me all these years."

You know those department-store classes and makeup sessions at the beauty counters? From the time

I first remember, Mom had been going to those at least once every season.

"Why would I hold out?"

I shrugged, but she knew very well why.

"The MAC counter had one of their experts in recently. I picked up a few tips from him." She grabbed a strand of my hair and began curling.

She'd just finished when Bre and Donna returned. I introduced everyone.

"Wow, Ellie! You look gorgeous," Bre said.

Mom beamed.

I nodded toward her. "Mom made me up."

"I can do you, too," Mom said to Bre. "We have time."

Bre's face lit up. "Would you?"

Mom was on her best behavior. "I'd love to. What kind of a look do you want? What are your dinner plans?"

"We're going to a hot-wing place," Bre said. "Make me look hotter and spicier than the wings!"

Mom laughed. "With such fantastic material to work with? That's easy. You have a nice bone structure."

That's what they always say at the makeup counter. Sometimes I thought it was the equivalent of having "a good personality."

Donna and I watched Mom apply Bre's makeup and style her hair. I caught the worried looks Donna flashed at Bre, motherly concern because of her depression over breaking up with Dan. I also saw the grateful way she looked at Mom for perking Bre up and giving her girl confidence.

I wanted to scream that Mom was not that nice and considerate. That this was all fake. That she was only showing off. But I kept my mouth shut.

When Mom was finished, Bre looked the cover-girl model version of herself. Practically flawless, like she'd been Photoshopped in real life. She couldn't stop looking at herself in the mirror, and her eyes were round and happy. Mom had just made a fan for life.

Mom smiled at Bre. "What are you wearing tonight?"

Bre shrugged, still mesmerized by her own reflection. "I dunno."

"Mind if I pick something out for you?" Mom asked. "I'm good with clothes, aren't I, Ellie?"

Now she was dragging me in. Very devious of her. I nodded. "She has an eye for what looks good on people." I kept my tone neutral, refusing to play up to Mom and her vanity.

Bre was a true believer now. She flung open her closet doors and turned to my mom with an eager, hopeful look. Like Mom was going to pull a treasure out of the jumble of clothes. "Here you go."

Mom nodded and mulled over the possibilities, holding things up, discarding them. "Would you two like to dress alike tonight? You'd look stunning as the mother and daughter versions of a hot night out for wings."

Bre laughed, nodded, and turned to her Mom. "Mom? What do you say?"

It was impossible to miss Bre's eager, hopeful look. And clear that Donna wanted her to be happy. She laughed nervously and opened her suitcase for Mom. "You're welcome to try. I didn't bring much."

"I don't need much." Mom looked through Donna's things. After years of living under Mom's fashion tutelage, it was clear Donna wasn't being falsely humble. Mom didn't have much to choose from. I crossed my arms, leaned back, and watched the show as Mom held up various blouses and accessories.

"What do you think, Ellie?" She held up a blue blouse Donna had brought.

She was testing me and dragging me in so I'd bond with her again. I didn't want to play, but I didn't want a scene, either. And Bre was having so much fun. I pursed my lips and studied the blouse. I shook my head. "Too boxy. Try the lavender one. Bre has a complementary colored T-shirt in her closet."

Mom smiled. I'd passed the test. She pulled the very T-shirt I was thinking of out of a pile on the shelf of Bre's closet without hunting for it. "I think so, too."

Then she engaged me in the decisions about accessories and shoes. Finally, she laid out an ensemble for each—blouse, jeans, shoes, and accessories. We turned our backs while they got dressed.

When they looked in the full-length mirror that hung over my closet door, they giggled.

"We look hot, Mom!" Bre squealed and hugged Mom and looked at me like she totally doubted all those stories I'd told her about Mom all school year. "You've been holding out on me, Ellie? You never told you're so good with clothes!"

I looked at the clock and deflected. "We need to get dressed, Mom. You still need to touch up your makeup and hair. Harlan hates it when people are late."

"Does he?" A smile spread over her face. "He's one of those people who thinks others should respect his precious time, is he?" She winked at Donna and Bre. "We won't be very late, then."

We arrived at the restaurant five minutes late, both of us dressed in pink. Me in my bright pink sundress. Mom in a surprisingly sedate, but beautiful, pale pink dress. I was still trying to grasp that she'd toned down her look and picked a dress that in her opinion, if she'd admit it, looked like something a dignified mother would wear. Of course, she still looked stunning. She could wear anything and look good. Why was the Evil Queen letting Snow White shine tonight? I kept looking around for the Huntsman.

Mom wrapped her arm through mine as we approached the restaurant. She was wily. Shaking her arm off would have made me look like a bitch, and that was the last thing I needed.

"A meeting of the parents. This is a big deal, Ellie," Mom whispered in my ear. "Are you nervous?"

I stared at her. "With you for a mom? Why would I be nervous? Behave yourself."

She laughed. "Don't worry. I'll make a good impression. First impressions are so important. Now smile, Ellie. Let's make an entrance."

I was sure she'd make an impression. Just how good remained to be seen.

In a small town like this, there was no doorman. But Mom, being the siren she was, had barely wedged the door open when a man inside, a guest, stepped up and eagerly held it open for us. The Mom effect. It took me a minute to realize he was staring at me with the look men usually gave Mom.

I was so stunned, I smiled nervously at him, flustered, as we walked into the crowded foyer. What alternate universe had I just stepped into?

You know how sometimes you can have tunnel vision, even in a crowded room? My eyes went straight to Logan. My heart leaped at the sight of him. Until I saw Amber standing next to him with her hand possessively on his shoulder, laughing and whispering conspiratorially in his ear. My smile froze on my face.

"Who's the blonde next to Logan?" Mom had seen him and Amber, too.

"Amber. She's an old family friend."

"She doesn't look so old to me." Mom's eyes sparkled with the thrill of the hunt, as if she'd just spotted her rival and adversary. As if Mama Bear was going to take care of Baby Bear. "She does look friendly, though."

"I can handle her myself," I said.

"You're my daughter. I should hope so." Mom laughed.

I tamped down my jealousy and irritation just as Harlan spotted us. He was standing off by himself while Sue huddled near her sons and vied for their attention. I felt a pang of sympathy for Harlan, the outsider of his family.

"There they are." He wore his intimidating scowl. Until he saw Mom and his attitude did a 180. His face softened. His eyes darkened. And he smiled and made an expression that was almost charming. He was charmed, anyway.

He was just like any other man—infatuated with my mom on sight.

Sue and Caleb had their backs to us. When Harlan spoke, they turned to see whom he was talking about. Caleb's expression on seeing Mom was a younger version of his dad's—totally gaga. Sue had been laughing, too loudly, like she wanted attention, like she could win against Amber.

When she saw us, her face became pinched, like she was trying not to scowl. I thought at first it was because of me. It was no secret she didn't like me. Then I saw her gaze flit between Caleb and Mom and Harlan and Mom and I realized she hated Mom on sight.

For the first time in a long time, I had reaped the advantage of being with Mom. She had just upset Sue without saying a word. I was suddenly on Mom's side. She wasn't even vying for the limelight tonight. She was actually trying to be good, in her own way. The vindictive part of me would have loved to see Sue's expression if Mom had been in a mood to really sparkle.

Defending Mom? Being almost proud of her? What was I thinking? I was letting my guard down, and that was dangerous. She was bound to disappoint me sooner or later.

Logan's face lit up as he spotted me. He shook Amber's hand off and rushed through the crowd to me.

The next instant, he wrapped me in his arms and kissed me. "You look gorgeous, El," he whispered.

I smiled up at him. "It's the dress."

"It's you." He nuzzled me. "But you should have more like it.

I rolled my eyes. "Mom gave it to me."

"She has good taste."

"If you tell me I should go back to letting her pick out all my clothes again, I'm going to get violent with you."

He grinned. "That sounds naughty. I like that, too."

"Shut up." I leaned close and whispered in his ear, unable to keep my unhappiness out of my voice. "What's she doing here?"

He knew I meant Amber. "She had a dinner reservation here for one. We ran into her. It seemed rude to let her dine alone. Dad invited her to join us. I think he did it partly to get back at Mom. They're at each other's throats tonight."

"Oh, blood sport. This should be fun." I blew into his ear.

"Don't tease," he said. "I'm turned on enough just looking at you."

I smiled as I caught Amber scowling at us. "We'd better make the introductions." I put my arm around his waist. "Mom, you know Logan." I almost gagged admitting it. "This is his mom, Sue, his dad, Harlan, and his brother, Caleb. Oh, and this is Amber Ranklin." I liked adding her as if she was an afterthought. "This is my mom, Melissa Carter."

Mom laughed as she held her hand out to Harlan, who took her slender one between his two meaty hands and held it like he couldn't resist touching her.

"Sawyer, sweetie," Mom said with a charismatic sparkle in her voice. "I'm between husbands again. You know I always revert."

She was letting Harlan hold her hand, but she winked at Caleb. Very subtle, letting everyone know how single she was. I shot her a warning look while Caleb looked at her like he wanted her for dessert.

"Watch Caleb around Mom," I whispered to Logan.

"Watch your mom around Caleb. Two can take care of himself. But he's used to having groupies and getting what he wants."

The thought of Mom and Caleb together made me sick.

Harlan finally let go of Mom.

She turned her attention on Caleb. "Caleb, the famous major leaguer." Mom let Caleb take her hand and imitate his dad's gesture. "I've never dined with a professional athlete before. This *is* a pleasure."

"You're a baseball fan?" He looked like a puppy eager to please. Like her lapdog the way he fawned.

"I go to a game or two a year. But I could get more interested." She picked a piece of lint off his collar and ran her hand over his shoulder, smoothing a nonexistent wrinkle, subtly letting him know she liked touching him.

Not subtly enough for either Sue or Amber to miss. I saw their eyes harden.

Just about the time I thought Sue was going to strangle Mom, the hostess stepped between them, carrying an armful of menus. "Walker, party of seven."

I turned to Logan and rolled my eyes in relief. "And you thought this was a good idea."

"Hey, my mom's unhappy. Payback for Thanksgiving." He grinned.

"You're evil." I leaned my head against his shoulder. "But you're my hero."

He grinned.

We followed the hostess to a prime table near the windows, though there wasn't much of a view from anywhere in town. Harlan held out a chair for Sue at the end of the table, then darted to hold a chair for Mom center stage before Caleb could. He took the chair next to Mom, farthest away from Sue. Caleb took the chair next to Mom and his mom on the end. Logan and I sat across from them. Amber was forced to sit next to me and across from Caleb. I could almost feel steam rising off Sue.

We ordered a round of beverages. There was a dangerous undercurrent of tension running through Logan's family. Sue was practically glaring at Harlan playing up to Mom and Mom playing up to Caleb. Caleb was fixated on Mom. At least it took the heat off Logan and me.

"What is it you do for a living, Melissa?" Sue opened her menu and perused it without giving Mom the courtesy of looking at her.

I'm sure she thought she had Mom now, but you don't mess with the mistress of deceit and comebacks.

Mom laughed in that rich, self-deprecating way that absolutely turned men on and was known to charm the savage beast. "I marry wealthy men and divorce them for big settlements."

Startled by Mom's response, Sue dropped her menu enough to give us a view of her face. Her forehead creased and her lips curled very slightly at the corners. She was pissed.

Mom, who could read other women with the same skill she applied makeup, must have seen Sue stewing. But her expression remained sweet and cloyingly innocent. "It's a rough job, always looking for the next ex. But it's been lucrative so far." Her voice was practically a purr, full of humor and charm.

Everyone laughed but Sue. She glared at me, her gaze bouncing between Logan and me like I was the spawn of evil Aphrodite, a gold digger in the same vein as Mom.

Mom laughed like she was laughing at herself, but it was clear she was laughing at Sue. "Don't worry. Ellie doesn't take after me. She insisted on going to college and actually learning a useful skill."

Amber had been unusually silent. She jumped in now, leaning toward Harlan and capturing the stage. "Harlan, how were the business plan competition entries this year? I'm sorry I couldn't make it to judge the early rounds."

Harlan barely seemed to notice her. "Typical. Some good. Some mediocre. You'll be at finals?"

"I'll make an appearance." Amber was showing off now, too. "After I give the keynote at the Mom's Weekend breakfast."

Mom leaned over and whispered something in Harlan's ear. It was noisy in the restaurant. I couldn't hear what she said, but Harlan's eyes lit up. Mom was showing Amber who was queen at this table. Upstaging the former pres of the Double Deltsies. I was proud of her.

Not to be ignored, Caleb touched Mom's arm to get her attention. Then whispered something in her ear.

"I hope they're going to pass it on," I whispered to Logan. "I like the telephone game. When it gets to me, I'm going to make up something outrageous."

He laughed. "This is more fun than watching Collin and Zave try to pick up girls when they're drunk."

That was the way it went through ordering, appetizers, salads, and entrees. Harlan to Mom. Caleb to Mom. Amber trying to cut in. Sue fuming. Logan and me in our own world, watching the show.

Just before dessert, I pulled out my cell phone and snapped a selfie of Logan and me and texted it to Tay and Nic. Then I snapped a picture of the table and texted that, too, with the message: *Having a bloodbath. The fangs are out. Mom's winning. Great sport. Wish you were here. Ha ha.*

Amber got a phone call. She sighed with self-importance. "I have to take this."

Like anyone cared.

She excused herself and left the table to take it. Mom excused herself to run to the ladies' room.

Logan leaned in and whispered to me, "Shouldn't you go with her? Girls usually travel in packs."

I was just about to suggest it so I could corner her and tell her to tone it down with Caleb and stay away from him when she subtly shook her head and warned me off.

Caleb watched her walk away with unveiled appreciation and lust. "I'll be right back. I gotta take a leak."

"Caleb! Watch your mouth." Sue frowned her disapproval at him.

"Sorry, Ma." He grinned at her and walked off, leaving the four of us alone in tense, fuming silence. We made awkward, forced small talk for five or ten minutes and fell into stony silence again.

Harlan finally broke it. He was fuming. "Your mother tells me you need money, Logan."

I turned to stare at Logan in horror.

"Ma, I told you not to mention it." Logan glared at his mother.

She shrugged, her expression unsympathetic and angry. "I don't keep things from your father." She spat the words out.

"Sue." Harlan's tone was full of warning.

I leaned in to Logan and whispered, "Logan, you didn't."

"I asked Caleb and she overheard," he whispered back.

"Logan?" Harlan said.

Logan balled his fists in his lap. "It's none of your business, Dad."

"My son bets his inheritance from his grandfather on a shaky business deal and begs his mom and brother for money and it's none of my business? You're turning out like Caleb."

"If I was Caleb I'd be rolling in money. There's no way you could stop me from making it short of breaking my arm." Logan's voice was icy. His jaw was set.

I noticed for the first time that he and Harlan had matching expressions when they were angry.

"What are you implying?" Harlan said.

"Oh, can it, Dad. I'm not implying anything. I'm saying it outright—what kind of rumors did you get your buddies at Core Tech to spread to kill my IPO?"

"What are you talking about?" Harlan continued to glare.

Logan pushed back from the table and tossed his napkin on it. "Don't play dumb. I don't know how you found out, but you did. You couldn't stand that I was going to be successful on my own."

"That's a totally unfounded and groundless accusation. I don't know where you're getting your information. When I find out, they'll be hearing from me." Harlan's jaw ticked. "If you weren't my son, I'd sic my lawyers on you and sue you for slander."

"You sicced them on me already and tried to use them to keep me from testifying. I'm not afraid of them."

"I'm here supporting you now, aren't I?"

Harlan and Logan stared each other down.

"Harlan?" Sue's worried gaze bounced between father and son.

"Shit! I'm not going to sit here and take this." Logan pulled out my chair and grabbed my hand. "Come on, El. We're leaving."

"But what about Mom—" I grabbed my purse.

"Text her to meet us out front." Logan pulled me behind him, squeezing my hand so tightly I felt the blood pulsing in it.

I almost made a smartass remark, something like "Thank you for a lovely evening." I thought better of it at the last second. My heart hammered. I had expected my mom to be the queen troublemaker this weekend, but Logan's parents were vying for the prize.

Logan pulled me past the bar, past all the tables of moms and children laughing and drinking. Logan banged the restaurant door open as he dragged me toward the car.

We both saw them at the same time. Mom stood beneath a parking lot light in the April twilight, leaning with her back against the wall of the restaurant. Caleb stood in front of her, hands cupping her face, his head bent like he was about to kiss her.

CHAPTER NINETEEN

"Mom!"

At the sound of my voice, Mom turned toward us with a startled look on her face.

"Caleb!" Logan yelled at his brother.

Caleb jumped back and frowned. "Logan? What are you doing out here?"

I lunged for Mom and grabbed her hand, pulling her away from Caleb. "What do you think you're doing? With Logan's brother?" I snorted. "Really. And things were going so well."

"What's going on?" Mom frowned and sounded genuinely confused. "Are we leaving already? What happened in there?"

"Shit," Caleb said.

Mom turned to Caleb and shook her head very slightly, warning him off from confronting Logan.

Logan shoved his brother. "Back off, Two, and stay the hell away from Melissa."

"What the fuck?" Caleb stumbled backward. "I was helping her."

"Sure you were." Logan shoved him again.

"What the hell's the matter with you?" Caleb swore and took a swing at him.

Logan dodged the blow. "Back off, Caleb. I'm not going to ruin your pretty face. Mom will have my head for beating on my baby brother."

"Shut up, Logan. Shut the fuck up!" Caleb raised his arm, ready to swing again.

Just as I was afraid Logan was going to lose control and punch Caleb anyway, Mom stepped between them. "Enough showing off, boys." She touched Caleb's arm and smiled encouragingly to him. "Go back to your parents. I have the feeling they need you right now. I'll handle things here."

He stared at her a long minute before nodding. He shot Logan an icy look and walked back into the restaurant, pulling down his shirt and straightening his clothes as he went.

I strode ahead of Logan and Mom to her car, unable to look at her. "I can't believe you came onto Caleb. I cannot believe it!"

"That's good, because it didn't happen. We were talking, just talking."

I shook my head and glared at her. "He looked like he was about to eat your face."

She sighed. "He was helping me get a piece of dust out of my eye. You know the wind here. It kicked up some grit and I didn't blink in time." She looked from Logan to me. "Great. You two just assume the worst and blow the evening up. I don't want Logan's brother. You really think I'm stupid enough to make a mistake like that?" She sounded almost desperate for me to believe her.

I shook my head, like, *Yeah, I could definitely believe it.*

She turned to Logan. "You believe me, don't you, Logan? I promised you I wouldn't cause trouble."

I frowned, wondering what kind of wonderful promises she'd made him and just how often they'd talked. "Don't drag Logan into this."

Mom beeped the car unlocked and grabbed my arm. "Nothing happened. *Nothing. Happened.*"

I shook her off, slid into the back seat, and crossed my arms.

Mom tossed her keys to Logan. "You drive." She slid in next to me and grabbed my arm again before I could flee. "Look at my eye, sweetie. Look at it! See how red it is?"

I didn't want to look, but morbidly hopeful curiosity got the best of me. Her eye was watering and red.

I couldn't believe myself and the control she had over me, but I actually wanted to believe her story. But I knew her. I'd learned how to lie from her. Learned her mantra—every good lie starts with a grain of truth. Maybe in this case it started with a grain of sand. "What *were* you doing in the parking lot?"

Mom sighed and looked suddenly hopeful. "We were both headed back to the table at the same time and bumped into each other. We saw the angry faces and heard the raised voices from the Walkers. Caleb didn't want to be dragged into a family fight. I was trying to give them some space and save everyone a little embarrassment. Caleb and I decided to step outside and enjoy the nice April evening and sunset until things blew over.

"That's all that happened. You walked out and caught us at the most inopportune moment. But it wasn't what it looked like." She pulled a tissue and dabbed at her eye that was still watering.

I wavered, feeling almost guilty for jumping to conclusions. "But we saw—"

"What you were expecting to see." Mom crumpled the tissue in her hand. "I'm sorry for everything I've done to you in the past, Ellie. And I'm not stupid. At least not enough to ruin my only chance to fix things between us. You're all I have."

I turned from her and stared out the window. She was so convincing. But then she always was.

Logan started the car. As he put his arm over the seat and looked backward to back out of the spot, he caught my eye and shot me a look that said he was sorry, but he believed her. "I owe Caleb an apology."

"You believe her?" I shouldn't have been surprised. I had no idea why, but from the beginning Logan had always been willing to cut her slack. They had a bond that scared me. I had to find out what it was.

"Yeah, El, I do." He nodded at her. His voice was filled with sympathy. "Look at her eye."

"But, but..." I locked my jaw and turned to Mom. She stared back at me, pleading with me to be reasonable.

I was beaten. Unless I wanted to look like a bitch in front of Logan. "You were flirting with him all evening," I said.

"Sweetie, I was making conversation." She touched my arm. "Please."

I couldn't believe the turn of events. I actually felt guilty for doubting her and jumping to conclusions. That was how Mom, the mistress of deceit, could twist things. "I'm sorry." I could have pinched myself the minute the words came out. I sounded like a child being made to apologize.

Mom didn't take it that way. As she squeezed my arm, tears filled her eyes. "Thank you, Ellie."

Then I really felt crappy.

Logan smiled at me like he was proud of me and pleased, and put the car in drive. "Where to?"

"The evening is still young," Mom said. "What's there to do here in this one-horse town?"

"The official Mom's Weekend activities are shut down for the night," I said, and tried to make a joke. "But the frat parties are just getting started."

"Nice try, but you're not pushing me off on some hapless boy." Mom smiled. "Any good movies showing? Anything even remotely decent? I'll settle for palatable. My treat."

After the movie, Mom drove Logan to his apartment complex, which pounded with music just as rowdy as any regular Friday night. The moms were in a partying mood. The pool area, balconies, and clubhouse were littered with drinking, dancing, laughing moms trying to recapture their youth and keep up with their kids. And my wild mom had taken us to a movie. Life was upside down.

"Want to come in?" Logan looked reluctant to leave me. He clutched my hand tightly in his as we sat in the back seat. "Let's crash a party."

Mom looked over the front seat at us. "Thanks, Logan. Not tonight. It's been a long day and it's about to get longer. For one of us."

Mom was speaking in riddles. What was up with her? I wanted to stay with Logan. I'm sure she knew that. But I couldn't turn Mom loose on her own. She was up to something. She never got tired this early. "We'd better go. Sorry." I kissed Logan, hoping he understood.

He stroked my cheek, looking adorably disappointed. "See you tomorrow." He reached for the door handle.

"Logan?" Mom stopped him, and hesitated, kind of dramatically, like she had something important to say.

"Yeah?" He cocked his head.

"During the movie, I had time to think about something I overheard when I left the table at dinner. It doesn't make much sense to me, but I think I should tell you. Even though it exposes me as an unapologetic eavesdropper." Mom laughed self-deprecatingly. "I walked past Amber as she was taking her call. I only heard her end, and just a snatch, but I'm pretty sure she's playing you."

Logan frowned, clearly interested. "Yeah? About what?"

"You tell me. She was making a deal with someone named Cutter. She said someone, or something, named Core had better have deep pockets. Because her neck was on the line and she was pretty sure she was being watched. If they wanted more information, the price was going to double."

I was confused—how did Mom know about the deal?

Logan frowned like he was thinking. "You think Amber is behind the rumors? Not Dad? You think she's selling us out? You're sure?" He looked totally stunned.

Mom shrugged. "I heard what I heard, so yes. You have your differences with your dad, I get that. But would he really do this to you? On the other hand, greed is a powerful motivator." She laughed. "Just ask me." She paused and turned serious. "Look into it, Logan. Soon. Find out what's really going on and protect yourself."

Logan nodded. "Yeah."

"Ellie, say goodbye to your boyfriend and get in the front seat with me. I refuse to look like your chauffeur. This isn't Mom's taxi service."

Logan opened the door and tugged me out with him, pulling me to him and holding me tight.

"What was that about?" I whispered.

"Amber double-crossing us." He ran his fingers through my hair. Suddenly he looked excited and hopeful. "I have some thinking to do. And some research."

"But how did Mom know about your business with Amber?"

He shrugged, like who cares? He was clearly excited. "She may have just saved my ass and our future." He kissed me before I could reply. "Go, El. It's going to be a long night. I have a lot of work to do." He kissed the tip of my nose. "I'll see you tomorrow. Wish me luck." He kissed me once more, hard, and held the car door open for me.

"Good luck." I slid in, still confused.

He closed the door, waved, and jogged off.

Mom put the car in drive and pulled away. "You could have spent the night with him."

"Not after what you just told him." I studied her. "You totally distracted him. On purpose."

She smiled.

"How did you know about Logan's business dealings with Amber?"

Mom's laugh was rich this time. "Excuses, excuses. You could have stayed and helped with the research. You're just making sure I don't sneak Caleb into your dorm room for the night and upset Bre and Donna."

"Someone has to keep an eye on you," I said. "You're deflecting, Mom. Answer my question."

"I don't like that Amber." Mom pulled out of Logan's parking lot onto the street.

"No one likes Amber." I paused. "No one who's female, anyway, not even dogs. Guys are another story.

They fall for her crap." I shot Mom a look like she should sympathize with Amber's situation. "Turn right, here. You left the table to spy on her."

Mom put on her blinker and grinned. "Which you should have done. Haven't I taught you anything?" She shook her head. "Know your adversary. You weren't acting, so I did. She wants one of Walker boys, that's pretty obvious. She'd prefer Caleb, but she'd take Logan."

"What?" I stared at Mom. "Are you crazy?" I paused. "You saw how she was all over Logan. You aren't just making this up to make me feel better?" I looked ahead up the street. "Left at the next light."

"You know me better than that. I call them as I see them. You're blinded by your jealousy." Mom slowed to a stop at the light and hit her blinker. "Otherwise it would be clear. She was flirting with Logan for two reasons—she hates that she lost him to you and she was trying to make Caleb jealous and throw his parents off the scent. Not the best strategy, but she's an amateur. Did you notice the way she kept looking at Caleb when she thought no one was looking?"

I frowned. "I wasn't paying attention to her. I was trying *not* to look at her. She gives me hives."

Mom laughed and clucked her tongue. "What have I always told you?"

"Never trust another woman around your man," I said in unison with her.

She smiled as we drove up the hill toward campus. "Part of the art of war is knowing your enemy, Ellie. Trust me, she wants Caleb. She lost Logan. She only keeps him on her string now because of that damn business deal she sucked him into before you were in the picture."

I stared at her. "Who are you? Sherlock Holmes?"

"I have ears. How did I know about the business deal? I overheard what Logan was yelling at Harlan." She grinned. "And Caleb may have filled me in on a few details while we were waiting for a ceasefire in the parking lot."

"Shut up!" Against my better judgment, I was impressed. "So that's why you were flirting with Caleb, to show her who's the queen?"

Mom just smiled. "Nice try. I'm not admitting to any flirting. But I may have been friendly just to test my hypothesis. She's definitely hot for Caleb."

"Okay, if you say so."

"That doesn't mean you should drop your guard."

"Right at the stop sign," I said.

Mom nodded. "She'd still take Logan if she could."

"But if she's double-crossing him? How will that work out? He's going to lose a lot of money."

"She doesn't expect to get caught," Mom said. "They never do. Why do you think your second stepdad went to jail?"

I frowned. "Logan blames Harlan."

Mom shook her head. "Harlan's anger and surprise at being accused were genuine. That kind of thing is hard to fake. I should know. Logan saw what he expected to see, just like you did in the parking lot."

It was cheeky of Mom to bring that up again.

"And," she said before I could respond, "Amber set it up that way, or I miss my guess."

"You've watched one too many episodes of *Elementary.*"

She laughed. "Oh, Dr. Watson, you always miss the clues."

"There's the visitor lot." I pointed. "We should be able to find a spot there."

She got lucky and found a spot in the row closest to the dorm. "Logan needs to get out of it before it's too late."

I didn't trust her, but I played along as I got out of the car. "It's already too late."

"The show's not over until the fat lady sings." Mom got out and closed her door.

We walked to the dorm in silence. I wanted Mom to be right about Amber, but if she was, I owed her, big time. Maybe even enough to forgive her. I wondered if I really could. At the same time, I realized I was a little less angry with her.

We climbed the stairs to my room in silence. Bre and Donna were already back and snuggled into their beds, eating popcorn and talking and laughing. The room smelled like melted butter.

"We had the best night," Bre said when we walked in. "Dan was at the hot-wings place with his mom. You should have seen how his eyes bugged out when he saw me. Melissa, you're a genius. I showed him."

"Walked right past him with confidence, I hope," Mom said. "Like you didn't even see him."

"She did," Donna said, smiling like she approved.

"While we were waiting for a table, I met this great guy. It was really crowded. Tables for two were impossible to get, so the four of us decided to share a table." Bre was beaming. "He asked for my number. He's already texted."

"Oh my gosh, Bre! That's fantastic," I said.

"His mom's nice, too," Donna said. "I had a good chat with her. They're from Olympia. His dad's in state government."

Mom kicked off her shoes. "Exciting! Details! We want details. And photos. If you didn't take a selfie of all of you I'm going to have to kill you both."

Bre laughed and dragged out her phone.

CHAPTER TWENTY

I spent a restless night on the floor in my sleeping bag next to Bre. I kept thinking about Logan, hoping he found out what was really going on. Hoping he could save his investment. Dreaming of him at grad school while I finished up my senior year. Of course, there was still the trial to get through. I was optimistic that Logan would get nothing but support and that would convince him to stay. But most of all, he needed to feel like he was free from his dad, just like I needed to be free of Mom.

Mom. I couldn't figure her out. It was like she was a changed woman. But I knew better than to trust this new transformation as anything like permanent.

The four of us woke early with the sun shining through the light-filtering shades. After we showered,

Mom braided Bre's hair and styled mine. Then she did our makeup. Bre texted her new guy two dozen times, at least. Life was looking up, so it seemed.

When it was time to get dressed for breakfast, I went to my closet to get the matching Mom's Weekend sweatshirts. I had a momentary pang of guilt as I looked at the medium I'd gotten Mom. She was going to swim in it.

"Mom, I got you something, too." I pulled them out of the closet and handed her the larger one.

She looked pleasantly startled and then, crap, were those tears in her eyes? How did she make me feel bad so easily?

She shook it out and read the slogan on the back: "Home is where your Mom is." Her voice broke.

I pulled mine on over my head as she held hers up to her. I was right—it was too large. Good guess on my part. "Sorry. I had to guess on the size. You're, you know, bigger on top than I am, so I got you the larger size."

She hardly seemed to hear me. "That's nothing. I can fix it." She gave me a hug and grabbed her purse, rifling around for something. She pulled out a roll of fabric tape.

"What do you have in there?" I said, though I should have remembered she had everything in there. "Are you training for *Let's Make a Deal?*"

She laughed. "Men and their duct tape, me and my fabric tape." Within minutes, she had taped the sweatshirt in so that it was no longer boxy on her, but nicely tailored.

I should have known.

The four of us went to breakfast together. Tay was working. "What's up with Bre? She looks great and she knows it," Tay said.

"Mom and the guy Bre met last night. Mom gave her some beauty tips and did her hair and makeup. The new guy makes her glow."

"Speaking of your mom, you two look sweet in your matching sweatshirts. You must have guessed wrong on her size. I guess there's some consolation that she's bigger than you thought."

I shook my head. "No, I guessed right. Mom altered it to fit her."

"Wow, she's good." Tay handed me a cinnamon roll and coffee.

I frowned. "Yeah. If you want her to try her magic on you, just stop by. You may as well join the club of her admirers."

"I'd like that." Tay winked at me.

"Traitor."

Logan texted me while we ate, excited. He'd pulled an all-nighter, but he was on to something. Caleb was hanging with him while their parents were in College of Business meetings and events all day. Caleb wanted to tag along with us to Up All Night and see what all the hype was about. They'd pick us up at eight.

"Caleb's coming with us tonight," I said to Mom.

"I don't mind." She smiled at me. "As long as he can dance."

I shot her a warning look. After breakfast, we parted ways with Bre and Donna. Mom and I went to the mother/daughter pedis and manis appointment I had scheduled. We came out wearing special Mom's Weekend flip-flops and protecting our matching nails and toes decorated with tiny flowers.

"That was fun." Mom hugged me enthusiastically.

"Yeah, except for the part where they asked where our moms were." I rolled my eyes.

She laughed. "Look on the bright side—there's hope you inherited my young-looking genes." She studied me with that searching look again.

I brushed it off. "Or your talent with makeup."

"That just takes practice."

We headed to the coliseum to meet Dex and his mom for the craft fair. Linda and Nic unfortunately had to bail on us. It was a beautiful day. The spring trees were in bloom and the usual wind was just a gentle breeze. The campus was covered in matching moms and daughters, but very few guys wore sweatshirts to match their moms.

We got to the coliseum early.

"Dex is your genius friend?" Mom said. "What does he look like again?"

I showed her a picture of him on my phone. "But don't worry about spotting him. You'll know him when you see him. He'll be the one guy on campus wearing a Mom's Weekend sweatshirt."

"Mama's boy?"

I shook my head. "Coerced." Then I grinned, thinking of Dex's prank. "Just between you and me, he has a plan to get her back."

Mom was scanning the crowd. She pointed in the direction of a crowd of people coming to the coliseum over the footbridge from the main part of campus. "Oh, look! Is that him?"

For a second, I gave her credit for having good eyes. Then I spotted Dex, too, and broke out laughing. "Oh, no. No, no, no!"

Dex was walking next to his smiling mom with a sour scowl on his face. I swore he blushed when he spotted us. He wore the dark gray guy version of the sweatshirt. The petite woman next to him, whom I assumed was his mom, wore the light gray women's version.

Dex's had been altered. On the front, right below the university logo, it said in neat, precise lettering, *Mom's always right.*

"Shut up," he said as he came over to us.

"I haven't said anything." I shot him an innocent look.

"You've been laughing." He glared at me.

Next to him, his mom was smiling. "Oh, my little imp-a-zoid."

"Imp-a-zoid?" I said.

"What else would you call him?" She laughed. "He thinks he can out-prank his mama." She spun him around so we could read the back of his sweatshirt. She clucked her tongue. "Like I wouldn't notice heat-activated ink."

His sweatshirt said, *Not my idea.*

Next to me, Mom was trying hard not to laugh.

Dex's mom introduced herself while Dex fumed.
"Beth. Dex's mom. You must be Ellie and"—she turned
to my mom—"her mom?"

"Melissa," Mom said.

"Okay, I have to say, you do not look like a mom.
Did you have Ellie when you were three?" Beth's good
humor was infectious. She'd said just the right thing to
mom.

To my amazement, mom actually seemed to warm to
her. "Close," she said. "Kindergarten."

Beth laughed. "Thank goodness. I was insecure
there for a moment. You're putting the rest of us to
shame."

Beth was actually really cute, a quirky kind of stylish nerd girl with dark-rimmed glasses that accentuat-
ed the nice shape of her eyes and balanced her face. Her
brown hair was cut in a stylish bob. She wore fitted
jeans and bright Converse tennis shoes. And looked
much younger than she had to be. Younger in a girlish
way, like she'd never really grown up. Dex had her
nose. It was too bad he didn't look more like her, actually.

"What are you talking about?" Mom said. "You must
have been a baby yourself."

"Maybe first grade."

Mom turned her attention to Dex. "Melissa. Nice to
meet you." She held her hand out for him to shake.

Dex actually blushed. You could tell he was flustered around her. I resisted the urge to smack some
sense into him. When Mom turned back to Beth to

swap Mom stories, Dex whispered to me, "You lied. Your mom is not just hot. She's smoking."

"Not you, too," I said. "Your mom seems nice. And smart. She outsmarted you."

He frowned. "She's just got more life experience." He glanced down at his sweatshirt. "I need to get home and get out of this." He touched his mom's arm. "I'm leaving. See you later. Don't spend all Dad's money."

"Dad's money!" Beth gave him a mock-dirty look.

"Nice to meet you!" Dex grabbed my arm. "Text me when you're leaving the craft fair. I need fair warning before she comes back." He dashed off before I could reply.

"Oh, that kid," Beth said. "He thinks he's so smart. He's a showoff like his dad. Good thing I like showoffs." She made a funny face. "Stay on your guard. He'll try to get me back for that sweatshirt." She smiled. "Now, let's shop!"

Mom smiled at Beth. "I think you and I are going to be very good friends. Tell me about that fabric ink you used on Dex's shirt..."

The craft fair was crowded with booths and people. Mom's eyes went wide at the high quality and variety of goods—handmade soaps, handcrafted jewelry. Etched-glass block lamps. Hand-sewn aprons. Window butterflies. Leather purses. Fudge and candy. Carvings. Everything you could imagine that could be crafted with the university logo on it.

We dove in and spent a happy two hours browsing and buying. Mom spoiled me, buying me anything I commented that I liked. I told her to stop.

She ignored me. "You haven't let me buy you anything all year."

Beth was just as bad as Mom. I became their pack-
horse. Mom offered for us to walk Beth back to Dex's.
"There's no way you can carry all these packages yourself," she said.

I texted Dex we were on our way to his room. As we
crossed the footbridge to campus, two hot guys were
coming the opposite way. They gave me the up-and-
down, being way obvious. And completely ignoring
Mom.

As we walked past the SUB, I was whistled at, cat-
called to, given the up-and-down, and asked for my
number while Mom was almost totally ignored. The
closer we got to Dex's dorm, the more guys suddenly
noticed my hotness.

In the lobby, Todd, one of the guys from Dex's floor,
spotted me. "Ellie, you are smoking today!" He glanced
at mom. "That your old lady?" He acted totally unim-
pressed.

"Yeah." What was up with Todd today?

Dex. He was pranking me. Trying to build my confidence. Getting at Mom for me. I smiled to myself.

I cornered him when we got to his room. "How
much did you pay all those guys to catcall me?"

"What are you talking about?" He looked way too
innocent.

I knew he was guilty. "Thanks," I said, meaning it.

He blushed.

Logan

Logan had been up for over thirty-six hours when he and Caleb left his place to pick up El and Melissa. Rather than flagging, he felt energized, more optimistic than he had in months. Melissa had been right about Amber. He was convinced she was involved in corporate espionage for Core Technologies and was playing both sides, trying to maximize her profits for the venture deal she'd conned him into investing in.

He didn't give a shit about turning Amber in. He wanted the IPO to go through and turn him a nice profit. He wanted his money back, and now he thought he could get it. Thanks to Melissa.

He wished, for the millionth time, El knew what he did about Melissa. If she did, she'd forgive her mom, or at least come to terms with her. And then peace and family harmony would reign supreme. He almost snorted. Like that would ever happen.

He'd also received a letter from the university. He'd been accepted into grad school. Options were opening up.

"What are you smiling about?" Caleb punched Logan in the arm as they got into Logan's car.

He'd crashed with Logan last night and hung out all day, playing video games and drinking with Collin and Zave while their moms were out.

"Nothing. Get in the car."

"Sure. Right." Caleb got in and slammed the door. "You're thinking about getting laid as soon as you can the moms out of town. It's Saturday night. I'm not waiting. Up All Night better be full of girls as horny as I am."

"That's a physical impossibility. Most of them will be there with their moms." Logan texted El they were on their way, put the car in drive, and pulled out of the parking spot.

"There has to be one or two I can separate from their mama."

Logan rolled his eyes. "Going pro has made you way full of yourself."

Logan texted El when he found a parking spot. She and Melissa were waiting for them on the front steps of her dorm when he arrived with Caleb.

El looked way hot. His heart constricted, like it always did when he saw her. He didn't deserve her, but he sure wanted her. He ached to touch her and share his good news. All of it. But he held back the news. As he pulled her into his arms and kissed her, he couldn't resist sliding his hand up until it brushed the side of her perfect breasts. He got a hard-on instantly.

"Hello to you, too." El smiled at him. "You look happy."

"He got some good news." Caleb gave him a brotherly shove. "Tell her."

"I got into grad school. The letter came today."

El's eyes lit up. She squealed and hugged him. He wanted to tell her not to get too excited yet. He still wasn't sure he could stand another year or two here. But the thought of leaving her nearly broke him. He needed her the way he'd never needed anyone.

"Logan, that is so awesome!" El hugged.

"Congrats." Melissa flashed him a radiant smile. "That's all the good news?"

"There might be more. Later." As he put his arm around El, he caught Caleb staring at Melissa and went cold.

His brother was on the make, and from the look on his face, he wanted Melissa.

CHAPTER TWENTY-ONE

Ellie

The SUB ballroom pulsed with disco lights and eighties music and moms of all kinds—those who stood nervously on the sidelines like mother hens, those who preferred to listen to the music and remember, those who tolerated dancing with their sons like good sports, those who were pretending to be young and in college again, flirting with the college guys, writhing in ways unbecoming for people of certain ages and shapes. And Mom, who was in a class all her own—young enough to be between generations of most of the moms and coeds. Slim and sexy. Confident. Desirable. A favorite with the college guys.

She'd been on the dance floor since we arrived. Mostly with Caleb, slinking around him, gyrating her hips, shaking her bootie. When he looked at her, his eyes were dark with desire. They made me nervous.

Logan ignored them. He was as happy, glittering, as effervescent as I'd ever seen him as we danced.

As he led me deeper into the heart of the dance floor, he whispered in my ear over the music, "This is our place, our event, El. Good things are coming. Do you feel it?"

I felt *him*—his hands warm and enticing at my waist, skimming my breasts, touching my hair. He was right. This was our place. And maybe it was our time.

Bon Jovi's "Livin' on a Prayer" began to play. I felt like Logan and I were living on a prayer, too.

I caught a glimpse of Mom and Caleb. His hands were on her waist while she jumped and gyrated and swung her arms over her head, laughing.

I closed my eyes to block them out and leaned into Logan, pulling him into a kiss, opening my mouth to him and slipping my tongue in next to his. I sucked at his lip and gently nibbled as I ran my hands through his hair. This wasn't a slow song, but I didn't care. I wanted to forget all the bad stuff and just be happy in the moment.

Logan pulled me tight against him. I felt his dick go hard in his jeans. I wanted him. He knew it from the way I looked at him. He grinned wickedly and wedged his leg between mine, rubbing me.

"You'll give me a wet spot," I said.

"That's the idea."

I sighed and focused on Logan and the music. I lost count, but we danced to two or three more songs at least. I was turned on. Logan was turned on.

The latest song ended. I opened my eyes and looked around. Mom was gone.

My phone buzzed in my jeans. Who was texting me now? I pulled my phone out. "A text from Mom," I said. "She ran into an old friend. She says to text her when we're ready to meet up."

Logan's eyes sparkled with lust and promise. "Are you thinking what I'm thinking?"

"What are you thinking?" I asked, cautiously.

"That we go to my place and have some fun before we text Melissa to meet up. Collin and Zave and their moms are out until late."

"Do you really think she met an old friend? Or is she making a new one?" I frowned.

Logan tipped my face up and nibbled my lips. "I think she just gave us an opportunity to be alone." He paused. "I want you, El." His voice broke with desire.

My breath caught. I felt heat between my legs. I was already wet for him as he took my hand.

"Let's go," he said.

"I'm having my period." I hated to remind him. When I was on the pill it only lasted a few days and was light after the first day. It would be over by tomorrow.

"That doesn't bother me, as long as you're up for it."

"What about Caleb?" I looked around for him, feeling a wave of unease. Caleb and Mom were both missing.

"He's on his own and looking to get laid. Let's hope he gets lucky and is occupied on his own a while. He has a key. He knows his way back." Logan ran his hand beneath the edges of my blouse and played with my bellybutton ring.

I took his arm and pushed my worries aside as coincidence. "You're playing dirty."

"I'm playing to win."

The ride to Logan's place was one long round of foreplay. I rested my hand in his lap. He slid his hand between my legs. I sucked on his ear. He clutched my thigh. We were panting for each other by the time we reached his apartment. He pulled out his key and let us in, tugging me into the darkened living room as he slid his hands beneath my blouse and bent to kiss the tops of my breasts.

I grabbed his head and clutched at his short hair, feeling tightly wound and eager for him, reveling in the warmth of his tongue on my skin and the thrill of being with him.

He was about to slide the front door closed with his foot when we both heard the telltale thumping of sex. The walls were paper thin. The thumping could have been coming from next door, except...

The door to Logan's bedroom was closed. A sliver of light glowed beneath it.

"I am going to fuck you so hard." Caleb's voice.

Logan let go of me. "Shit. I'm going to kill him."

A woman moaned, enthusiastically, with ever-increasing intensity.

I froze. My heart, like, literally stopped beating. I broke out in a cold sweat. "Mom and Caleb disappeared at the same time."

I felt like I was going to throw up.

Before I could stop Logan, he tore open the bedroom door.

I remained glued in place, too horrified at the visions my on mind made to move. To look at what I didn't want to see. Memories of Mom and Austin came flooding back. My hand flew to my face. I swore my scar throbbed.

Doug punching Austin. Blood flying. Screams. Doug's fist slamming into me. A sob lodged in my throat.

"No!" I screamed to Logan. "Don't!" I had to stop Logan from losing control and beating the crap out of his brother. I forced myself to take a step.

Logan charged into the room. "Amber? What the fuck?"

"Amber?" My relief was so strong, my knees became jelly. I put my head in my hands.

"What are you doing, man? Get the fuck out of here," Caleb shouted at Logan.

"Get out of my bed!"

I heard footsteps. The sounds of bedsprings groaning.

"Get your hands off me!" Caleb said.

Sounds of a scuffle breaking out. A thump. Swearing.

Amber screamed. "Boys! Calm down."

Just as I moved, the living room light flipped on.

"Ellie? What's going on here?"

I spun around and thought I was hallucinating. Harlan, Sue, and Mom stood just inside the door.

"Do something!" I begged Harlan. "Stop them. Caleb's in there with Amber. Logan walked in—"

Harlan brushed past me with Sue on his heels. A second later, Sue's hysterical voice echoed, "Get away from my boys, you whore!"

The sounds of a slap reverberated off the walls.

"Get out of the way, Sue." Harlan's voice was hard. "I'll handle this." His footfalls pounded the floor so hard I swear I felt it bounce. "Boys!"

I collapsed into Mom's arms, like a little girl who just needed her mommy. She pulled me close, wrapping her arms around me while I blocked out the terrifying sounds of fighting and screaming. Blocked out the name-calling and the accusations. Hid in my mom's embrace.

"What are you doing here?" I managed to whisper to her.

"I'll explain later." She stroked my hair, soothingly, like she had when I was small as she pressed my head on her shoulder. "Oh, baby, I'm so sorry." It was clear she meant this bad scene we were in and the one it echoed. "You shouldn't have to deal with this kind of crap again. Are you okay?"

Harlan was shouting now. I pictured him pulling Logan and Caleb apart. I imagined Amber huddled in Logan's bed with the sheets pulled high.

Sue started screaming at her again, all kinds of terrible things I tried to block out.

"We should go." Mom led me toward the door.

I looked over my shoulder toward Logan's room.

"This is a family matter. Believe me, it's best to let Harlan and Sue deal with this. The less we see or say, the less they think we heard, the less embarrassment there will be later."

"But Logan—"

"You might not believe me, but he's in good hands." She put her arm around my shoulder. "My car's in the lot. You can text Logan later. Right now, I think we need at least a gallon of ice cream. Ice cream makes everything better. How about some of the university's famous concoctions?"

"The creamery's closed. Grocery Mart carries it by the gallon."

"Good," she said, leading me out of the apartment. "We'll get as much as we want, try a dozen flavors. Buy a pack of spoons and go back to your room and watch a movie." She gave me a squeeze. "Just chill until this blows over."

She walked me to the car with her arm around me. To my surprise, I didn't feel like brushing her off. We didn't speak until we were both in the car and buckled up.

I wanted to know what had happened. "How did you end up with Harlan and Sue? You texted that you met someone you knew?"

Mom nodded. "I went to the ladies' room. When I came out, I ran into Sue and Harlan coming out of a private banquet room down the hall from the ballroom. They'd been at a dinner for the College of Business that had just gotten out. I seized the opportunity and asked them for a moment to tell them what I knew. As hard-assed as Harlan is, I knew he could help Logan. We went downstairs to find someplace private to talk. I texted you so you wouldn't worry when you couldn't find me.

"After they heard what I had to say, we went to the ballroom to find you and Logan. When we couldn't find you, and neither of you responded to our texts, we decided to wait for you at Logan's. Sue has an emergency key to it. Turns out we didn't need it. You know what happened from there." She paused. "Ellie? You're still pale. In this dim light you look like a vampire."

"Thanks, Mom. You know how to pep me up."

She shook me gently. "I understand being shaken up by what just happened." She took a deep breath. "Tell me straight—you thought that was me with Caleb. At least for a second there."

I let out a breath. There was no point in lying. I nodded. "Sorry."

"No, it's okay. A natural assumption, if you were looking for it. I lost your trust. It's going to take time to earn it back." She laughed, but it was humorless. "Believe me, I know how long it can take to forgive a betrayal. I hope you're more forgiving than I am." She bit her lip. "I think you are, El. I think you're a much better person than I am."

She looked straight ahead and started the car before I could answer. Grocery Mart was just a few minutes away from Logan's. As we rode there in companionable silence, I mulled over what she'd said. I could be a better person than she was. She was trying so hard. I didn't trust her, but maybe I should give her another chance?

The parking lot was crowded. We had to wait for a spot. Inside the store was equally crowded, especially the booze section. Which was also woefully understocked. Most of the good stuff was gone.

We walked past the seasonal section, which was stocked with university T-shirts, hats, flip-flops, banners, posters, beer cozies, and key chains. As we browsed, I texted Logan, saying I'd see him tomorrow.

We finally made our way to the frozen section.

"Yum!" Mom was trying hard to be enthusiastic. She rarely splurged on desert. But it was a tradition to drown ourselves in ice cream when one of us, usually her, had a relationship end badly. "Mountain huckleberry. Chocolate chip cookie dough. Mint chip. Double chocolate whammy. S'mores. Anything strike your fancy?"

I reached into the case. "Espresso swirl. Mint chip. Huckleberry."

"Huckleberry?" She smiled her teasing smile at me.

I repeated her old mantra. "Fruit makes it all healthy so the calories don't count."

She hugged me. "That's my girl."

The aisles were crowded. People dodging this way and that. We reached the end of the aisle.

"Let's go all out and get cookies, too," Mom said. "Which way?"

"To the right." I pointed.

We turned sharply right as a man carrying a bag of diapers, with his head down as he texted, came out of the aisle next to us. He crashed into Mom. They reached out and steadied each other, each stammering apologies.

The man looked up. Time stood almost perfectly still, along with my heart, as their eyes met.

I said a prayer, but I was too late.

Mom went pale. "Jason Front?"

CHAPTER TWENTY-TWO

The round cartons of ice cream Mom had been carrying bounced out of her arms onto the floor and rolled
away. She was so stunned that she didn't stoop to stop
them.

"Melissa?" Jason's eyes were round with surprise.

Both of my parents turned to me and spoke at the
same time, "Ellie?"

"He's why you're at this school? You went looking
for your father." She spat the words out. Her eyes
flashed. Her tone was hard and angry, full of hurt, like
I'd been the one to totally betray her.

Just when things had been going so well between us.

"What are you doing here? You're not supposed to
be here." I shook my finger at Jason. "I gave you
Walmart."

"Walmart was out of Mia's diapers. Grocery Mart wasn't on your schedule. I thought I'd be in and out—"

"Ellie!" It was like Mom snapped. She looked ragged and panicked and angry. I didn't understand her. "You went looking for your father!"

"Yes. And I found him!" I snapped, too, and hurled everything I felt at her. "And I wouldn't have had to if you'd ever told me about him. Why did you keep him from me?"

She was shaking and shaking her head. "No. I can't believe this." She looked like she was on the verge of hyperventilating, she was so worked up. "Ever think there was a reason? I had a good reason, Ellie! A damn good reason." Her eyes blazed with accusation. She stabbed a finger at me. "You read my diary!" She spat the words out like they were the worst accusation she could make. Like I had violated her trust. Like she'd never read mine.

I crossed my arms and glared at her. "How else was I going to find him?"

"You think you found your dad because you read it in my private diary. The writing of a confused girl. You *think* you did. But you could be wrong, Ellie. Wrong! What then?"

Jason was standing by in stunned silence.

"Wrong? How many men did you sleep with?" I screamed at her. We were back where we started. Back to the good old bad times, like we always had.

"Shut up!" She glared at me as angry tears welled in her eyes. For the second time in my life—the first was the night of Austin—my mom actually looked ugly.

Veins even stood out on her forehead and her eyes were almost red. "You're playing with fire and you don't even realize it. I've protected you all these years!"

"From Jason? From the great guy who's my dad? You've robbed me of nineteen years with him and you're screaming that you were protecting *me*!"

People around us were staring. There's no entertainment like a good public domestic fight.

"Ladies." Jason tried to step between us.

"No, it's okay." I pushed past him and got right in Mom's face. "It's time this all came out." I pointed at Jason. "I don't know who all else you suspect fathered me. But Jason *is* my dad. We took a paternity test. He's the guy."

Mom's face crumpled. "Oh my God! Oh my God!" Her knees buckled. "Thank you. Thank you."

Jason caught her as she fell to her knees and began sobbing.

I stared at her like she was certifiably psycho. Me and half the store.

Jason kneeled beside her, trying to soothe her. "Melissa?"

She started bawling into her hands.

He looked up at me helplessly.

I shook my head and held up my palms, as clueless and helpless as he was.

She wrapped her arms around his neck and buried her wet cheek against his shirt. "Thank God it's *you*. I always wanted it to be you, Jason. Always."

Sometimes, I'm really slow. Sometimes I'm totally dense and stupid, but eventually it hits me. It struck

me now—all these years, Mom had more than one suspect in mind as my father. And one or more of them
were horrible.

The store manager appeared from the crowd.
"What's going on? Is she okay?"

"Get her some water. She's had a shock," Jason said
as Mom sobbed in his arms.

Someone handed her a tissue. The manager got a
bottle of water. Jason opened it for her and made her
take a sip. "Give her space," he said.

The crowd backed off as he helped her to her feet.

"Mom, we need to talk, the three of us," I said. "I
need to know the whole truth."

She dabbed at her eyes and nose, which was red
now, too. She was a mess. Through her tears, her gaze
bounced between Jason and me, that penetrating gaze,
like she was looking for something familiar. Looking
for my dad in me.

Suddenly, she smiled through her tears and actually
laughed like she was relieved and delighted. And even
though her mascara was running along with her nose,
and her eyes were puffy, she was as beautiful as she'd
ever been. Because she actually looked really happy.
"You have his eyes, Ellie. And mouth. You look like Jason Front. Why haven't I ever seen it?"

"Let's go someplace and talk," Jason said, shepherd-
ing us through the crowd. "The fast-food places are
open all night. Let me just text Lyssa and let her know
I'll be delayed."

There was a burger place across the street from
Grocery Mart. Ten minutes later, the three of us set-

tled into a corner booth with coffee. Suddenly, we did-
n't need ice cream.

Mom couldn't stop staring at Jason and me and back
again. Happiness and relief radiated from her. She
looked like she couldn't get over her good luck.

"What you did was reckless, Ellie," she said at last.
"But I guess you didn't know it. How could you? I
should have foreseen you'd go looking for him. But I
couldn't tell you the real reason you shouldn't. I guess
I'd always sort of hoped you'd figure it out without me
having to tell you and just stay clear." She smiled at us.
"I'm so relieved it's all worked out." She looked at Jason. "Have you told her anything about the night we
made her?"

"Everything I know." He cleared his throat like he
was suddenly embarrassed. "Not in minute detail."

Mom smiled. "You mean everything you remember."

He smiled softly. "I'll never forget a detail. I was
madly in love with you. But you never saw me that way
before or after."

It was good to hear one of my parents had been in
love with the other.

Mom bit her lip. "Yeah, I don't regret what we did.
But I do feel guilty. I just needed you so badly that
night, Jason. You were always such a good friend, the
one guy I could count on."

"Mom. Don't keep me in suspense. What happened?
Please. Tell me."

She took a deep breath. "It's not easy to talk about. I
don't like remembering it. You know what Jason told

you? That I had a fight with my longtime boyfriend Guy?"

I nodded. "At a party. You called Jason to come get you and the rest is my earliest history."

"Yeah, that's right." She nodded. "But there's more to the story. I was at a party. It was in a large, open field that belonged to one of the kids' parents. They were out of town or something. Tons of kegs and beer and music.

"Guy and I fought. I don't remember over what or why. We fought a lot. I thought that meant he loved me." She shook her head. "Yeah, misguided. He was drunk. When he was drunk, he had a mean mouth. He berated me. I stormed off.

"I don't know what I was thinking. I was just ticked, you know? I figured I could hitch a ride home with someone. I went looking for one of my friends.

"At the edge of the field, where the cars were parked, an older guy I recognized from the party came onto me. He must have been all of twenty-five. Which seemed so old at the time. He offered me a ride.

"I don't know why, but something about him felt off to me. Gut instinct. He was drunk, too, and obviously horny. I was in no mood to fight off some creep's advances. I turned him down." She swallowed hard.

"He called me a bunch of names as I walked off. I put a parked car between us and turned to go back to the party." She paused and looked far away for a minute. "The short version is he grabbed me and hauled me into his car. And raped me."

I gasped.

"He was rough. He slapped me around." She took another deep breath. "I screamed, but no one heard me over the music. The attack seemed to last forever. I thought...I really thought he was going to do worse than rape me.

"I'm a fighter. The first chance I got, I kicked him in the balls and ran. Just ran. Until I came to a nearby house. I was a mess. I made up some story, I don't even remember what, and the people let me in to make a call. I called Jason. The old woman at the house suspected something and thought I should call the police, but I insisted I was okay. She let me use the bathroom and I tried to clean up."

She wadded a paper napkin she'd been toying with. "I was so embarrassed and ashamed. I didn't want Guy to know. When Jason came, I just needed comfort. I needed him." She looked into her coffee cup and rested one hand on the table. "I let him think Guy had roughed me up."

I covered her hand with mine. "I'm sorry."

"You're not the one who should be," she said.

"Melissa—"

"It's okay. Let me finish." She looked at Jason. "When I found out I was pregnant, you were already off at college and Guy and I were back together. I convinced myself Guy had to be the father. I let everyone believe it."

She glanced at me. "After you were born, my parents insisted I get Guy to pay child support. He was suspicious and jealous. Thought I'd been unfaithful. He accused me of sleeping with Jason that night of the party. He knew Jason had picked me up. Guy insisted on a paternity test.

"When it came back negative, I was stunned. That only left two alternatives. One of them was too terrible to even think about." She stared at Jason again. "Please forgive me, but I knew you'd want a test, too. And if it wasn't you..."

"Oh, Melissa."

I was still covering Mom's hand with mine. Jason covered both of ours in his, which felt strong and confident enough for all of us.

"Fortunately, you were off at college. I moved on with other guys." She bit her lip again and shook her head, her gaze bouncing between us. "All these years, I've been watching Ellie. She doesn't look like me. She had to look like somebody. Anytime I saw anything of you in her, I wrote it off as me wanting to see it. Now the resemblance is obvious. She has your good heart, too."

I was almost too stunned to react. "The other guy, what happened to him?"

"He's in prison serving twenty-five to life for a string of violent rapes. He's a true sexual predator. I never wanted him to know about you, Ellie. Never." She sounded fierce. "I was one of his early victims. If I'd gone to the police, I might have helped stopped him.

"But I was a coward. And I live with the guilt that he hurt other women because I didn't come forward and turn him in. I'm not like Logan, Ellie. I don't have his courage."

"That's your bond with Logan?" I was incredulous as it dawned on me. "You're both rape victims?"

She nodded and pulled one hand back. Jason and I held firm over the one she had left on the table, wanting her to know we weren't abandoning her.

"I tracked Logan down because I was desperate to get you back, Ellie. When I found him, I recognized a fellow victim...I hoped helping him would help you. I was never after him. He was never Austin. You do believe me?"

"I think I do. Now."

Jason was watching me. He squeezed my hand. "Ellie's going to need time to digest this, Melissa. We all do."

She nodded, and then, just like Mom, and the survivor she was, she turned on the charm. "Enough about me. I want to hear all about you, Jason. What has my old friend and the father of my child been up to all these years?"

The three of us talked until nearly two. Jason finally went home with a pledge from Mom that she'd come back and meet Lyssa and Mia and the new baby when it was born. Mom and I went back to the dorm and talked in the lobby until dawn. She was really frank, talking to me about the effects of being a rape victim. How she used sex for power. It made me understand even more about Logan.

I shouldn't have, maybe, but she was the only person who remotely understood what Logan was going through. I told her about the nightmares. And how Logan wouldn't talk about them, but I was sure I was morphing into Dr. Rogers in his nightmares and how Logan would never let me be on top.

"Yes, loss of control." She nodded. "Don't lose him, Ellie. Whatever he needs, give it to him. You have to show him it's okay to lose control with you. That it's what you want. And that sometimes you need to be in control, too."

"That's what the counselor said. But how?" I was desperate.

"Patience. Understanding. There are no easy answers," she said.

We were too wound up to sleep. We stayed up all night. The dining hall opened at six. We had coffee and toast. Then we showered and Mom packed up to go home. We were both talked out.

I walked her to her car.

"We never got our ice cream," she said.

I shrugged. "We don't need it now. We'll get it next time." Saying there would be a next time was a huge concession for me.

She hugged me. "I may be a crappy mom, but I love you, Ellie. Always have."

I hugged her back. "I love you, too."

I watched her get in and drive off. As she pulled away, I realized I wasn't angry anymore.

I hated her for what she'd done. She was a vain, narcissistic person. She'd used sex to control her life and men for so long it was doubtful she'd be able to change.

But now that I knew the truth, I loved her for trying to protect me. What if my dad *had* turned out to be a serial rapist? What if he'd tried to get paternal visits or custody? Or just made both our lives hell? I couldn't blame Mom from sparing us both from that.

Life wasn't really black and white. It was often completely gray. Sometimes there were no easy answers.

So I loved her more because now I knew she was acting like a real mom in the way that mattered most. I understood why she had written *Ellie's dad must be Jason Front* in her diary. A scared, scarred nineteen-year-old trying to convince herself and will it into being.

And maybe I liked to believe in fairytales and that somehow she'd wished and prayed Jason into being my bio dad.

Whatever it was, I couldn't feel *nothing* toward Mom. Couldn't write her off. But it was not like I believed everything would suddenly be perfect between us. I did think, though, that we could make some kind of relationship work. And that I actually wanted one, even if we kept it pretty distant.

My cell phone rang. I broke into a smile. Logan was calling. "I was hoping you'd call. After that scene last night, I was hoping you were still alive."

He laughed, but sounded beat. "Hey, El, you don't know how good it is to hear your voice. To hear anyone who's not screaming."

"You're not mad I left?" I walked back toward my dorm, still looking over my shoulder in the direction Mom had driven off.

"Shit no. I'm grateful as hell. Mom and Dad and Caleb just left for their hotel. We were up all night hashing things out. I want to tell you both all about it."

He sounded tired, but relieved. So I hazarded the question I was almost afraid to ask. "Good news?"

"Yeah. For once. Is Melissa awake? Can I come get you and her and take you two beautiful girls to breakfast? I owe her, and you, big time."

"You're in our debt now? That's a nice change. How will I call it in? What can I extract from you?" I knew exactly what I wanted. "Stay on your toes, Walker." My heart felt so light I could actually tease. "Yes, Mom is awake. But you're too late. She just left for home. You can buy me breakfast."

"Gone?"

"Don't worry. It's all good. I have so much to tell you. You have no idea what happened after we left."

"A woman of mystery. Intriguing." He laughed. "I'll be there in ten."

CHAPTER TWENTY-THREE

Logan

El was waiting for him on the steps of her dorm, sitting, highlighted in sunshine like some kind of beautiful angel. His angel. Just the sight of her lit up his day. But the soft, happy look on her face would have brought him to his knees if he hadn't already been sitting. He needed her. After last night, he realized just how much.

She waved and bounced to her feet as he pulled up and leaned across the driver's seat to open the door for her. She slid in and their lips met. It was like fire as he slipped his tongue into her mouth. Even though he was dead tired, he wanted El.

Someone honked behind them. El pulled away, laughed, and buckled up. He put the car in drive and forced himself to look away from El and concentrate on the road.

"You look like the walking dead." She was so happy, she made it sound like a compliment as she touched his cheek and ran her fingers just over his eye. "I am so relieved that you don't have a black eye or a broken nose or a fat lip." She kissed his cheek. "I thought for sure you and Caleb were swinging at each other. You're so much hotter this way."

He loved the way she worried about him. "We did. He's slow and has crappy aim."

"I don't think he really wanted to hurt you," she said.

She didn't know his brother. Caleb had been pissed and wanted blood. He let it drop.

"How much sleep did you get last night?"

"None." He smiled at the concerned way she furrowed her brow. Everything about her was fucking cute. "I haven't slept in almost two days."

"Not at all?" She rubbed his arm.

"Nope. Keep talking or I might doze off."

She bumped him playfully. "You should have slept before you came over!" She had the cutest little worry lines.

"I couldn't wait to see you, El." Which was the absolute, desperate truth. He couldn't stand being away from her another minute. As he grinned at her, he noticed the circles beneath her eyes. "You look tired, too. How much sleep did you get?"

"None. But I've only been awake for twenty-four hours. I'm fresh as a daisy compared to you."

"You're not half as fresh as I can be." He steered with one hand and slid the other between her legs, going hard as he felt her heat through her jeans.

She rested her head on his shoulder and looped her arm through his. "Want to pick up something at the drive-thru?"

"Anything you want."

"I want cheap pancakes, sausage, eggs, and coffee in a bag to go. And a private place to talk."

"You got it. We'll go to my place. Collin and Zave are taking their moms to breakfast before they head out. Then they'll come home and crash all day after that."

Fifteen minutes later, he tossed his keys in the bowl on the console table in his entryway, set the bag of food on the table, and pulled El into his arms, right where she belonged.

She looped her arms around his neck and brushed his lips with a kiss. When he tried sliding his hand down her back and beneath her jeans to cup her butt, she pulled back and laughed. "Not until you spill everything, Logan. I want to hear your news! I'm dying here."

"So am I. I missed you."

She pulled him to the couch, kicked off her shoes, and tucked her legs beneath her. "So? What happened to the screaming Walkers last night?"

"You first. You said you had good news? Is it just that your wicked mother has flown off on her broom?"

"No, actually, it's better than that. She may not be as evil as I thought."

El told him everything—about bumping into Jason, how relieved Melissa was that he was El's father, how she'd been worried that some psycho serial rapist was, and how they'd talked a lot of things out.

"You were right, Logan. I'm not angry anymore and it feels great. I don't know what's going to happen in the future. But I kind of want Mom in it. It's hard to blame her, knowing what she went through and how she did what she could to protect me. I mean, it's not like I'm going to trust her all the way." She stroked my cheek. "Especially around you."

"I can't believe it." He was totally shocked, almost stunned speechless. "I'm thrilled for you."

"You knew about the rape." El studied him. "I know you two share that bond."

He didn't want to talk about any of that upsetting shit. "Yeah, but not the timing of it. Not that she thought it might have created you." He took El's face in his hands. "Not that it would have made one bit of difference to me who your father was, El. I'd love you no matter what. And thank the bastard for creating you."

"Well, I'm glad it's Jason." She snuggled into him and hugged him, resting her head against his chest.

"Yeah, me too." As he rested his chin on her head, a wave of sleepiness washed over him. He blinked, trying to fight it off.

"Your turn. What happened last night? Mom told me about running into your parents and telling them what she overheard Amber saying."

"Yeah, Mom and Dad were pissed at her. Mom has never liked Amber."

"She has good taste there," El said.

"Figures you agree with her." He squeezed El. "Amber's pretty much on everyone's shit list, and Caleb isn't far behind for sleeping with her."

"The favorite son has fallen."

"Yeah, I may be the favorite for a while."

"So—was Mom right? Is Amber screwing you all over in the deal? Is Harlan going to turn her in? Prison orange might be her color. I bet they'd still let her wear her Double Deltsie pin in prison."

"El, she's not going to jail." With El in his arms, Logan was relaxing. He stifled a yawn. "Dad's lawyers and connections will see to that. It's a long story. But basically, she thought the IPO was in trouble because the company we're funding was behind schedule. Amber was worried it would have to be pushed back and we'd need to put up more money to cover operating costs until they could go public.

"She's over-extended, and didn't have it. This Cutter guy from Core Technologies approached her, offering her to pay for insider information. She cut a deal, fed Core some details she thought weren't too vital, and used the money to fund our company. She claims she was always on our side."

"And you believe her?"

"Yeah."

"What does Harlan think?" El lifted her head.

Logan cupped it and pressed it back against his chest. He liked feeling her cuddled there. "That Amber's learned a lesson. And that he can salvage the IPO. We had to stay up until five, which is when this shark investor he knows gets up. We had a good talk with him. We're all going to get our money back and make a profit. It may take a while, though."

"Oh." She sounded so disappointed.

"Dad offered to fund grad school," he said. "If I decide to go."

She pulled back to look at him, and she looked so hopeful it nearly killed him. "Will you take him up on his offer? If you decide to go."

"Are you kidding? No way."

Her face fell.

"I told Dad if I opt for grad school and I still don't have my money, I'll take a loan from him. At very reasonable rates."

"That's awesome." Her face lit up again.

He nodded. "Yeah, and I don't know what alien invaded Dad's body, but he said he was proud of me for trying to stand on my own. He even suggested I contact the companies who've made me job offers and see if I can defer them a year and get them to pay for my first year of grad school before I start work for them."

"Will they do that?" El stifled a yawn. "Sorry. Didn't mean to yawn. This is great news."

"I don't know. But some companies do. It's worth a shot." He leaned down and kissed her. "I love you, El."

He scooped her into his lap and stood up with her in his arms.

"Are you carrying me to the table? 'Cause I can walk. I think. And our food's getting cold."

"Fuck our food, El. I'm so damned tired, I can't even eat. I just want to take a nap next to you, naked."

"Just sleep?" She covered her mouth as she yawned again.

She was so sexy when she was tired. She was sexy all the time. But he was so exhausted that he felt drugged. "If I weren't so damned tired, El...My head is willing, but I'm crashing. And you are, too. In another minute, I'll pass out. But when I wake up, all bets are off. I'm going to wake up horny."

"You better."

Ellie

Logan fell asleep almost the moment his head hit the pillow. I watched his breathing become calm and even and his face relax. I was so happy it was almost scary. And too tired to sleep. I wanted to. I tried to, but my mind was racing. Going over all the awesome possibilities. Like Logan staying at school with me. Like the two of us being together forever.

I closed my eyes and made my mind slow down. I slowly, almost mindlessly, traced Logan's naked chest, feeling every firm muscle and rugged contour of his body. Tired as I was, I couldn't keep my hands to myself. I loved his arms. I couldn't resist squeezing his biceps and feeling the soft skin on the inside of his arms. Such a contrast—the soft and the powerful.

His breathing, which had been deep, grew shallow and excited. I was awake now as I realized my own power. *Now is the time*, I thought.

Very gently, I pulled back the blanket he'd thrown over us and traced his nipple until it stood up.

He was so perfect. I loved looking at him. I loved touching him. I grew tight and wet. I wanted him. I wanted to be on top and chase all memories of *Her* away forever. I wanted him to know he could trust me to be in control and he could lose control with me.

I slid my hand down his body, listening to his breathing, until my hand rested on the inside of his thigh. Moving slowly so I didn't wake him, I gently stroked his dick, watching it grow long and hard beneath my touch.

Every move I made was so incredibly gentle, like I was a butterfly making love to him. Tender. Patient. I sat up slowly and the bed creaked.

Logan stirred and inhaled deeply. I stilled my hand until he quieted down, my heart pounding until his breathing became even and shallow again.

Slowly, gently, with incredible patience, freezing when the bed moved too much, I positioned myself in a kneeling position over him, one knee on either side of his waist.

He was so handsome. I couldn't stop looking at him. I took a deep breath and steeled myself, hoping this worked, hoping the risk was worth it.

I grabbed his dick. Leaned down to whisper in his ear. "It's me. El. Just me. I love you, Logan."

I slid him inside me. Naked. Without a condom. As I started rocking on him, I tipped my head back. I had never felt such pleasure. Or fear. This had to work.

# # #

Logan

El is on top of me, her prefect breasts bouncing as she rides me. Her hair falls down around me, tickling my chest and arms and driving me mad with desire. She's so fucking beautiful.

I'm so turned on, I'm afraid I'll come too early. I'm afraid I don't have enough control to hang on. I smell her perfume. I'm crazy with lust and desire. I thrust up into her and the sound of her soft moans almost throws me over the edge.

Her eyes sparkle. She smiles down and me and tosses her head back. As I stare at the creamy arc of her neck, I know she loves me and that's all that matters. She's moving back and forth on my dick, building pulses of pleasure.

Everything's beautiful, but suddenly I feel anxious. I've been here before. I'm about to lose El.

I try to open my eyes, but it's like they're glued shut. My heart races until my pulse is uneven and wild, part ecstasy, part revulsion and fear. Sweat beads on my forehead. My eyes will not open. I'm losing her.

"It's me. El. Just me. I love you, Logan." Her breath is urgent in my ear.

I actually feel her words. I want to believe her. I want to believe it's El on top of me. But I'm paralyzed with fear. Any minute now, she'll morph into the monster. I know what's coming. I have to open my eyes. I have to get her off me. This isn't El. This is a trick.

"Logan! Logan, listen to me. I'm not Her. You can control this. It's me, El. Really me. Do you feel me?" I feel the force of her words against my face.

The mirage on top of me squeezes my dick. I moan involuntarily. The pleasure is so intense. She plunges me deeper inside her.

No, I won't. Not again.

But I'm powerless to stop Her.

"It's just me, Logan." El's voice is soft, but urgent and pleading. "Trust me. Believe me, Logan. If you want me to climb off, I will. You're in control. I'll never hurt you. I'll never force you."

I want to believe her. The pleasure is building. I thrust again. Fighting, fighting, fighting. Trying to call out. Trying not to let Her appear.

Something is different. What is different?

El grows hazy. I feel sick, disgusting, like I'm a sick perv.

"There's no condom, Logan. I trust you so much, I didn't put a condom on you. Don't fight me. If you want me to stop, just open your eyes and tell me." It sounds like she's trying not to cry.

I don't want to hurt, El. Shit, I don't want to hurt her. She stops moving. I feel her squeeze me again and I realize she's right. El's voice is telling the truth. There is no condom. And that's what's different. This is really El.

Logan's eyes flew open. El was on top of him. The real El, his beautiful El, was on top of him with her hair flowing down around them.

"A guy can't get a minute of sleep around here." He grabbed her gorgeous hips and thrust up into her.

Tears stood in her eyes. Her face crumbled with relief.

"I'm back," he said. "I love you, El." He thrust again.

She gasped and rocked back into him. He let go and let her take control, matching her rhythm until she called out his name. Then he came with her with a climax so strong it took his breath away and kept coming and coming.

When it was over, she lay on top of him.

He held her against his chest. "I'm back, El. The nightmare is over." And he meant that literally. The nightmare was over. Even the thought of the trial no longer scared him.

CHAPTER TWENTY-FOUR

Ellie

I sat in the packed courtroom between my dad Jason and Caleb and his parents, watching Logan testify against Dr. Rogers. Logan had asked me, and Dad, to come. After Logan and I made love, we fell asleep in each other's arms. We slept until late in the evening and woke up starving. We ordered a pizza and he told me all the details he'd never talked about before. Admitted things he'd never told anyone else, but that I already knew. There were no secrets between us now. No reason for him to be embarrassed in front of me.

The trial was a media circus, one of the biggest stories of the week, statewide. Even reporters and news crews from Seattle were on hand. The courtroom was full of students, mostly girls. Many of them girls Logan had walked home as a security escort. Some of them wore CAPSA sweatshirts in support of Logan.

I was so proud of Logan. He looked so handsome and confident as he sat in the witness box and calmly answered questions. Nothing scared him. Not even Dr. Rogers.

She sat next to her lawyers, looking old and pinched. Ugly. She stared at Logan with obvious lust and longing, with obsession. Her lawyer kept leaning in to whisper to her. Her face would go blank for a minute and then the lust would return. Her lawyers couldn't coach her out of it.

I glanced at the jury to see if they saw what I did—Dr. Rogers and the rest of it. The way Logan looked at me when he needed reassurance. The love that shone between us. That dark, unreciprocated obsession Dr. Rogers had for Logan.

I saw the grimaces. I caught the horrified looks some of the jurors flashed *Her.* I watched their faces soften into sympathy for Logan. And I knew things were going to be okay. They believed him. The whole courtroom believed him.

When his testimony was over, the judge called a recess. Logan stepped down from the stand. His mom grabbed him and hugged him before I could, murmuring her praises. Tears in her eyes. Even Harlan looked proud, and slapped Logan on the back.

Logan finally broke free from his mom. Jason congratulated him on a job well done and stepped out of the way so Logan could get to me.

I threw my arms around him. "You were awesome up there. Nothing intimidated you." I kissed him. "I love you, star witness."

He grinned. "You were my rock." He grabbed my hand. "I am so glad that's over. Let's get out of here." We made our way through the crowd and stepped outside to the flash of cameras stuck in our faces. Reporters shouted questions at Logan. Girls screamed and shouted at him like he was a rock star.

"My son has no comment," Harlan said to the reporters as he ran interference. "He's done his duty. Please, leave us alone now."

We made our way through the crowds to the parking garage, losing the reporters at last. We were supposed to go to lunch with Logan's family and my dad.

"We'll meet you at the restaurant," Logan said as he opened his car door for me.

I slid in. He went around to his side. He took the long way to the restaurant, stopping at a park about a block away.

"Why are we stopping?" I asked.

"I just need to breathe for a minute." He grinned at me and got out.

I joined him. He took my hand and led me into the park. It was a beautiful day. We stopped in front of a small pond.

"It feels good to breathe," I said.

"I'm glad that's over." He took my hands in his.

"You made a lot of fans." I stared down at our hands and ran my fingers over the backs of his hands.

He nodded. "Yeah. It might not be a bad thing to have a fan club. For a year or so."

My gaze flew to meet his. "Does that mean?"

"Yeah. I've decided on grad school."

I went up on my toes to kiss him.

He dropped my hands and cupped my face, stopping me before my lips met his. "There's more good news."

"More?" My heart was so full. How could it hold any more?

He nodded. "Dad thinks I'll be getting my money soon."

"Logan! That's fantastic."

He kept nodding. "Yeah, and as soon as I get it, I know one thing I'm going to buy for sure."

"Spending your money already?" I laughed and clucked my tongue, teasing him.

He didn't even crack a smile. He looked completely serious. "I'm going to get you a big-ass ring."

My eyes went wide. "Ring? Like..." I pointed to my left ring finger.

He nodded.

I was totally confused. We hadn't even talked about it. I cupped his hands cupping my face and took a deep breath. "Are you proposing?"

He laughed and leaned his forehead against mine. "Nope. No way. When I propose, you'll know it. I'll do it the proper way—with flowers and romance and all that shit. So there's no way you can refuse."

He took a deep breath. "This is just me bringing up the subject. You know, just talking about it. Like, in the future some time, would you be totally opposed to marrying me?"

I was so happy that I couldn't stop smiling. I blinked back tears of happiness. He was so darn adorable looking at me with his heart in his eyes. "Not totally, no."

"Good, glad there's hope. Because I can't live without you, El. I love you."

And then he kissed me.

ABOUT THE AUTHOR

Gina Robinson is the award-winning author of the contemporary new adult romances *Reckless Longing, Reckless Secrets,* and *Reckless Together* and the Agent Ex series of humorous romantic suspense novels. She's currently working on a new contemporary romance/new adult series called Switched in Love, all about the perils of falling in love with someone who isn't who you think they are. What happens when you find the love you're looking for in the most unusual circumstances with the last person you ever thought you'd be attracted to? Look for the first Switched in Love romance in early summer 2014.

Connect with Gina Online:

My Website: http://www.ginarobinson.com/

Twitter: @ginamrobinson

Facebook: www.facebook.com/GinaRobinsonAuthor